RHONDA PARRISH ANTHOLOGIES

Available Now

A IS FOR APOCALYPSE
B IS FOR BROKEN
C IS FOR CHIMERA
D IS FOR DINOSAUR
E IS FOR EVIL
F IS FOR FAIRY

FAE
CORVIDAE
SCARECROW
SIRENS
EQUUS

MRS. CLAUS: NOT THE FAIRY TALE THEY SAY
TESSERACTS TWENTY-ONE: NEVERTHELESS
METASTASIS
NITEBLADE MAGAZINE

FIRE: DEMONS, DRAGONS AND DJINNS
EARTH: GIANTS, GOLEMS AND GARGOYLES

GRIMM, GRIT AND GASOLINE

Coming Soon

HEAR ME ROAR
SWASHBUCKLING CATS: NINE LIVES ON THE SEVEN SEAS

C is for Chimera

Book 3 of the Alphabet Anthologies

Edited by Rhonda Parrish

Poise and Pen Publishing

EDMONTON, ALBERTA

www.poiseandpen.com

Publisher's Note: This is a work of fiction. Names, characters, places, and incidents are a product of the author's imagination. Locales and public names are sometimes used for atmospheric purposes. Any resemblance to actual people, living or dead, or to businesses, companies, events, institutions, or locales is completely coincidental.

Book Layout © 2014 BookDesignTemplates.com

C is for Chimera / Rhonda Parrish. — 1st ed.
ISBN 13: 978-1-9882330-0-0
ISBN 10: 1988233003

CONTENTS

A — ALEXANDRA SEIDEL   1

B — KV TAYLOR   7

C — MARGE SIMON   15

D — PETE ALDIN   19

E — MICHAEL M. JONES   29

F — SIMON KEWIN   39

G — BD WILSON   53

H — GABRIELLE HARBOWY   65

I — SARA CLETO   67

J — MEGAN ENGELHARDT   83

K — MICHAEL FOSBURG   91

L — MEGAN ARKENBERG   103

M — LILAH WILD   107

N — LAURA VANARENDONK BAUGH   119

O — MILO JAMES FOWLER   143

P — BRITTANY WARMAN   147

Q — MICHAEL B. TAGER   157

R — L.S. JOHNSON   171

S — BETH CATO   191

T — C.S. MACCATH   197

U — SAMANTHA KYMMELL-HARVEY   201

V — STEVE BORNSTEIN   223

W — SUZANNE VAN ROOYEN   235

X — MICHAEL KELLAR   243

Y — JONATHAN C. PARRISH   251

Z — AMANDA C. DAVIS   253

BIOGRAPHIES   257

Alexandra Seidel

I

Blood, all day blood. This is how I learned to write. This is how the story begins, the first words. She told me to use the carving knife on my own skin, reach through and feel what lies beneath.

I love you, sister, and you will do this for me, she said.

Before the study of secret runes and sacred ratios, I wanted to be a musician. I might have bled myself on the strings to birth the song, but my sister would hear nothing of it.

You will be an alchemist with me, she said, and so it was.

II

The girls were born on the solstice—one into the longest night, and one just after. For three years they grew together, played together, became mirrors to one another.

Every year after, their mother cried.

III

We used to love the stories of chimaerae, me and Etia. All those wild tales of fire. When she made me work so hard through the first few months of our apprenticeship, I thought I might grow to hate her or become bitter. But at night, when she had bandaged the skin where my knife had broken it, she would tell me chimaerae tales. I always fell asleep cradled in my older sister's arms.

It took me less blood than I had feared to learn the scripting. It was a year to master it, really much less than was average, and I saw pride in Etia's eyes when the master told us this.

What made her reach for the stories again even though my skin was healing, I do not know.

Have you ever thought about what it would be like, having two heads like a chimaera does?

I stopped brushing out my hair. *What it would be like to breathe fire?* I said.

No, no, not that, Etia said, weaving my hair into a thick braid for the night. *Having two heads. What would that be like, what sorts of thoughts would you think with two heads?*

She was done with the braid, fixed her work with a ribbon of crimson. Then she ran her hands along my shoulders and arms. I flinched as my skin was still raw and deeply scarred from the scripting, and she saw it at once.

Etia looked at me through the mirror. *You are hurting still*, she said.

It's nothing, it will heal.

Perhaps I should have never suggested that you learn it on your own skin.

Didn't you hear? It takes everyone else longer. I think it's because they just do it on paper.

Etia smiled at me, but her smile turned sour. *I would never want you to hurt. I have an idea.*

And with her idea, it all began, so very slowly at first.

"You want to buy a live bullsnake?" the trader at the market asked me. Her eyes were wide, but the idea had taken seed in my head. I would not be swayed.

"Master, will you teach me how to make strengthened gold thread today?" I asked as the idea budded, ready to bloom.

The night it flowered fully was a solstice night. The entire city was out celebrating—no one would ever know what we did in the abandoned workshop.

You will only ever be able to wear long sleeved robes after this, my sister said.

I don't care about that, I replied and looked at the bullsnake in her cage, tasting the air with her tongue; perhaps she knew better what was coming than I did.

Oh, but you are afraid to kill the snake? my sister said, a candle flame twinkling in her right eye.

Etia, I know we both wanted this but...

Etia's hands are stronger than my own. I have not ever mastered the art of breaking free of her grip. *Yes, we both do. Have you forgotten that we promised we would never leave each other alone?*

And then she reached for a knife, my carving knife, and went to the bullsnake's cage. She cut the snake's head clean off, and we worked all through the night to get the carving done, get the skin to fit just right.

When I woke the next morning, I could feel every movement in our master's house through my new skin.

IV

When her daughter left to become an alchemist, the mother did not understand. Had her youngest child not always loved the harp, played songs as if the ghosts of muses lived inside her hands?

But the girl said she wanted nothing more to do with string, and ever since that moment, her harp would not speak another sound.

V

It was all my fault. I was clumsy and spilled acid over my sleeve. Ordinarily, I wouldn't have given it any thought at all, but the master was there.

"Oh dear, clean it with water, quick," our master said and was pouring water from a jar on my arm before I could so much as protest. With a deft gesture, he pulled my sleeve up. "Oh, what have you done!" he said.

He became rather much louder than usual, and his tirade ended in dismissal, of course. Any alchemist knows how valuable a reputation is, and not one among the lot would ever tolerate an apprentice that might ruin theirs.

You must not cry, my sister said, carrying one of only two bags with our entire belongings in them. *We can still get you what you are missing.*

I believed her. There was not a time in my life that I did not believe my sister.

"You have a caramel colored goat?" My sister had suggested it, said it would go best with the other skins. The farmer looked at me like I was slow, but I had the coin to make her doubts disappear.

The lioness was more difficult, but Etia knew to find things and people in the lower parts of the city in a way that I could only ever dream of.

I think she bought the feline from a sailor, but I cannot be sure. I never saw a face, could not even say if it was a man or a woman taking our money. In the cage, the animal was sedated, and it would not wake again, not really.

This place is too small for us, Etia said, her arm including all of the small shed we called home in a swiping gesture. *And you will soon be able to take bigger.*

No one will bother us here, you said that was all important.

So I did. Oh, little sister, the skin on your face, it will hurt so much even after the pain is dampened. Let me pull it off for you, she said.

Her hands moved quick, the quickest hands to ever learn the scripting. It was the familiar feeling of my carving knife, just like back when I learned to write. I was reminded of how she would always braid my hair, each and every night before we climbed into bed together.

The face of the lioness had to be adjusted to my bones, but my flesh had to be adjusted to the beast's flesh. To finish all of it, get all of it just right, was work of three days. The drugs lost some of their effect by the second day, but by then, Etia had begun work on my vocal chords, and if I cried, if I screamed, only she knew of it.

On my tongue she scripted the words for fire. *You must be careful when you speak now*, she said with a smile. Her smile looked different than I remembered from before, but that could just be because my eyes were different now, cat eyes, slit in the middle to eat light like sugared candies.

The goat will be a perfect fit, Etia said on the evening of the third day. I was sitting in a corner, lying down would have hurt too much.

When my sister said it though, I had to look up, and my new eyes saw the goat. I did not know how to handle the skin of a lioness, and so I felt the sting of her instincts through my entire body, felt the vibrations echo in my bullsnake skin.

I tried to speak, but my voice was changed, and all the words I had were fire, hot and bright.

Nothing was set aflame, but Etia's eyes caught the brightness. I took the knife from her hand, and with one quick stroke, the goat's head was ready for the scripting.

Then we shall finish this tonight, my sister said, and the lioness inside me nodded.

After the lioness, the goat's heat was a simple matter. I used my hands to draw the proper words over my flesh, over the bullsnake skin that was already my own, and over the lioness skin, so that all three would be well bound.

I pulled the golden thread through my skin, tight as love.

On the morning of the fourth day, I walked to the mirror.

There, Etia said, but for the first time since forever, I could not see my sister's face.

Where are you? I wanted to ask, but I had no more human voice, my voice was that of a chimaera now, and I had no idea how to use it. The only sound I made was a groan, and a soft bleating from my other head.

But I am here, I heard Etia, her voice so faint, so very faint.

I looked deep into the mirror. I saw pieces of her, the fire in her eyes was the fire in my lioness eyes, the way she moved, was the movement in my bullsnakeskin, and the horns of my goat head reminded me of the tilt of her neck...*looked like a broken neck of a three year old child...*

This is the last thing I will ever write. I will send you this notebook, Mother. See in it all me and Etia have accomplished! We are together now, she and I, in this body that was forged in pain. I know what it is to be a creature of two heads, and so I can carry these two, just like you carried us inside you. Mother, can you stop crying now?

A is for Alchemy

KV Taylor

Dr. Addario was an anomaly in town: a real doctor with a real medical degree from the University of Pennsylvania. Not one of those quacks with their snake oil, but the genuine article. My own physician, in fact. His practice was the bottom level of his house on High Street, and I liked to go in early and admire the prints he kept framed on walls. Da Vincis and Michelangelos—more of the former, I suppose, seeing as Da Vinci had the flying machines, didn't he? I never went upstairs, into the home, like I did on the evening in question. Now, I can't say whether I wish I had or am glad I hadn't.

"I live alone, Jackson," he always said, "because I'm married to science. Someday, science will let us fly. Let us touch the clouds. Isn't that worth being married to?"

I figured that was just as well as them as married the Church, so I never thought anything much of it. Some said he was an invert; I didn't care, so long as he set the bones and staunched the wounds. He did have that pretty assistant, Matt Tabler, come in from his folks' farm on the outskirts some weekends to help, but there wasn't any harm in it. Even if Matty did look like the boys in those Renaissance paintings. I don't believe in judging a book by its cover, but if I did, wouldn't that just make him angelic?

The doc only had to go missing for a few days for folks to get nervous. They sent me, the new policeman, to check up. When no one answered the door, I jimmied open a window like we used to do when we'd stay out too late and our father would lock the doors on us. People don't usually lock the second story ones, not properly, so it wasn't hard.

It happened to be the door to the room full of wings. Taxidermied, spread wide, pinned to the walls like strange larger-than-life wall paper. Imagine it: spilling out a window into a dark, dusty room full of wings separated from their avian companions, just covering the place. Eagle wings, had to be, they were so big and beautiful, hawks, crows, down and down to tiny, glittering bits of feather like the hummingbirds at the orchard in summer. Brown and black and white and jewel-colored, like the fabric of a fine lady's dress, colors fit for a queen, illuminated by a ray of sun slicing through the gloom like a bright, white razor.

Wasn't any rhyme or reason to the arrangement as far as I could tell. Probably there were matching pairs, but maybe not, maybe just one from each. Where the hell the rest of the birds' bodies went, I couldn't have said.

I still have nightmares, sometimes, thinking of a lot of wingless birds, half-rotted and mad as fire, coming up out of the ground for me.

What I mean to say is, the place gave me the chills. One of them full-body shudders, almost right away, soon as I got to my feet and took the full measure of the room. But then, being married to Science was as serious as keeping any lover, probably, so what did I know?

I left that room quick as you like, nearly stumbling into the hall. That was a relief, let me tell you, because it wasn't coated in feathers.

Dusty, but being a bachelor, I never let that bother me. But the curtains were drawn over the windows at either end, so I yanked the first set open as soon as I could. The dust danced in the slice of light, but everything was quiet.

My voice never sounded so loud as it did when I asked, "Dr. Addario? It's Jackson. People's getting worried about you, doc." The echo of it in my head, down the stairs, up to the ceiling, made me shiver again, tied my stomach up in knots.

Probably I was going to find him dead. Wasn't a pleasant business, and that was why they'd sent the new kid to do it; fair enough. Any policeman who enjoys finding people he grew up knowing and liking dead—well, you don't want to know that policeman, obviously.

The nearest room to the window was open, empty except for furniture, some kind of guest room. Except there was a picture in a frame, a real nice photograph of a dark man with a magnificent mustache, smiling real smart-like. Handsome, you know, like the kind you expect on stage. I popped it out of the frame, just out of curiosity, and on the back in the doc's scrawl, read:

Class of '29

See you in the sky!

Yours,

Gage

Some kind of doctor's joke, I guessed, and put it back where it belonged.

The next door creaked in a way that made my hair stand on end, like an old woman crying. The windows were shut up, and there wasn't any gas laid on in town back then, so I had to stop and light up the lamps to see what was inside. I lit two and carried one with me, over to the wall where the window should've been. Looked like it was covered over in bookshelves.

Looks were wrong. Oh, they were shelves, but there sure as hell weren't books. Glass jars of all kinds, smelling like sickness. I nudged at one with my free hand and the liquid inside sloshed. A free-floating eyeball inside turned like it was staring at me, and I nearly dropped the Goddamned lamp. I tripped backwards, but there was no escaping that wall of horrors: arms, legs, feet, fingers, all manner of pieces and parts that shouldn't never have been separated from the rest of the human that once owned them. Six, seven feet high, twice as wide. I tried to stumble out, but tripped on a pile of books. Notebooks, as it happened, full of scribbles like the doc's, and one other hand. I just managed to land on my backside safe with the lamp, then sat there staring at those books for a long time, feeling like if I moved the things in the jars behind me would come after me. That eyeball—I knew it hadn't moved on its own, not really, but then I never seen an eyeball removed from a person's head before. There's all kinds of scraggly bits attached. Nothing pretty about eyes for me after that, I don't mind telling you.

By accident, I read one of the pages I'd knocked a notebook open to, as I sat there staring. You know how it is, you just absorb writing sometimes, like that. It looked familiar, but not like the doc's scrawl, which I'd seen often enough. It was a drawing of a finger being, well, reattached is the word, I suppose.

I remembered, then, that this was Dr. Addario's—as in a medical man of science's home. Of course he had some scientific items that struck me as ghoulish. Why, that was probably a cow eyeball, and the rest might've just been donations—there was a big stink in some of the cities back east about times being so dire that medical students had taken to robbing graves for materials to practice on. Maybe the doc just kept what he could find, and all that, for his sciencing.

I shook off the shivers and made my way out of the room, but didn't look back at the wall of jars. Just in case.

Was only two more rooms in the upstairs, and one of 'em was obviously the doc's. The other—well, I tried not to let it bother me none, but it was more wings. This time they were moths, though, full ones, some big as my own head. Butterflies too, in every color of the rainbow and some I wasn't even convinced could be natural, papering the wall. I threw back the curtains to let the dust dance in sunshine, and the walls flickered like the infernal bugs were still alive, twitching and flickering bright sapphire, emerald, and ruby.

Just a collection, I told myself, like all these strange educated types liked. But as I settled my hand on a door—I thought it'd be a closet—I couldn't set my heart at ease. I gripped the lamp hard enough I was worried I'd crush it, and pulled the door open.

Stairs. I'd found the attic. Almost done with that uneasy house, and I still hadn't seen hide nor hair of the doc. When my footstep creaked on the first stair, a whispering sound drifted down, soft and gentle. "Doc?" I called up. "Dr. Addario? You up there?"

Floorboards creaked over my head, and I knew he must be. I forgot everything, all my fears and misgivings, imagining the poor doc alone upstairs for two days after some terrible accident, and ran up to the attic full tilt.

The first thing I saw was—well, it looked like some thick, elaborate spider-web in the near corner. The window was old and gray and thick with grime, but the midday sun filtered through and landed directly on the mess of webbing, lighting it up with white sparkles like tiny diamonds. I stepped nearer and reached out to touch it. Reminded me of caterpillars in spring, but the size of a man.

Reminded me of that room downstairs, with all the butterflies.

Something creaked in the far corner, and the knot in my stomach tightened. On unsteady feet, I got myself turned around and lifted the lamp, so the shadows seemed to squat.

A low, fat shadow shifted in the corner. I stepped around the stairs and toward it, swallowing a lump to say, "Doc? Dr. Addario? You okay, sir?"

There was a gurgling sound, followed by that whisper. This time, so close, I knew it for the sound of wings. Not feathered ones, but more delicate, fragile.

I stepped nearer, lamp still held high. Two more steps, and the light sent the shadow running.

Dr. Addario was there, prone on the ground, clothes ripped to shreds, pale as a corpse—which he was. The creature that crouched over him, though, was something else. Black eyes like an insect in its human head, a fine mustache, and long, fine limbs.

That, I suppose people believe just fine.

It's the wings they don't believe. The wings, far too large for a butterfly, but far too small for a man, like the biggest of all monarchs, thrashing gently behind the creature. I didn't need to get close to know they burst from between his shoulderblades—who would want to anyhow? I do remember that, thought he colors were monarch, like, they were softer—and the underside of the wings was a sickening iridescent purple.

Beneath the mustache was the real horror, though—or maybe it was above. The creature had one of them long things, a proboscis, sticking out, like some kind of long tube. And it was inserted just into Dr. Addario's pale chest. Right where his heart should've been.

The creature's wings fluttered, causing the room to buzz, and I lost myself. I must've thrown the lamp, for fire exploded in the corner and I raced down the stairs on tripping feet, desperate and howling.

They put out the fire soon enough it didn't destroy all the notebooks, but Dr. Addario and his cohort—Dr. Gage, some guessed, were pretty well burned to a crisp. For a while, seemed like I'd be hung for murder, but with all the ghoulish surgeries, reattaching limbs and bits and pieces, plus the testimony of Matt Tabler that the doc had him bring live game most every week—birds and insects, mostly, supposed to be undamaged...

Well, I came out looking less sinister for disposing of the doc than he looked for the kind of things he got up to. Anyone who argued just had to look in that room of jars to think otherwise. And if they could stomach that, the notebooks would turn them right around.

You want to know my personal theory, I'll tell you: Man wasn't meant to fly. Da Vinci tried it with his machines and failed. Dr. Addario tried it by making some kind of flying Sphinx, and I damn near had my juices sucked out by it. Nobody talks about it nowadays, and that's why I don't, either—but there's no fear in me anymore, not since that day.

Except, I don't much care for butterflies, anymore.

B is for Butterfly

Marge Simon

He is dreaming …

A beautiful woman stands at a window overlooking the ocean. She is wearing a gossamer fabric that ripples along her contours like ascending smoke. She is eating a peach. Her skin is flawless. Her golden curls are swept off her neck in a pearly net.

Once I was young like you, Robert._ She takes a bite. _My body got the best of me. My loss. You can't fill the empty spirit with food, Robert.

You're very quiet, Robert. Why?

His eyes follow the tip of her tongue as she licks the fruit.

Three times she asks her question. Three times he can't answer. She finishes the peach.

Flings the pit at him. Disappears.

He is dreaming...

He stands before a rolling mansion. A beautiful woman in a red cape much darker than her hair walks toward him. She says something he can't understand, and motions for him to come through the courtyard gates.

The woman seems happy to see him. She wants him to play with her pets, one is gray and one white. They are Great Danes, but he has never seen one before, and thinks they are ponies. The gray one comes up to lick his hand. He tries to feed it some grass, but it runs off.

She brings him tea and sugared apricots. They make a picnic by an indigo stream. She says it is immortal, this stream. He doesn't know what to say. He smiles, touches her hand. It is a soft hand, but strong. Her nails are immaculate. He likes this. He likes to look at her.

Once I was young like you, Robert. She takes an apricot, holds it between thumb and forefinger.

Once before, my body got the best of me. My loss. You can't fill the empty spirit with food, Robert. You're very quiet, Robert. Why?

He watches her tongue flick juice from the fruit.

Three times she asks her question. Three times he can't answer. She finishes the apricot. Flings the pit at him. Disappears.

He is dreaming....

Sunlight flickers in and out of the dense foliage as he runs through a forest. A clearing forms ahead. As he draws closer, he sees a beautiful woman bathing in a pond. There is an aura over the pond and the air is alive with pebbled light.

The woman nods his way and ,smiling, rises from the water *At last you've found me,* she says. *I've been waiting so very long.* Before he can speak, she is in his arms. Her hair smells like golden apples.

Once I was young like you, Robert. It is a whisper. She plucks an apple from the air, nestles it under her chin. *Once before, my body got the best of me—*

Her lips tease the apple. Her teeth are so white, so sharp.

You're very quiet, Robert. Why?

He watches her teeth dig into the apple and tells himself this is a wondrous thing, this woman, this apple.

Three times she asks the question. Three times he cannot answer.

She frowns. *I'm sad for you, Robert* She opens her mouth. It is a very large mouth that becomes wider as he stares.

In this forest, he could see no horizon until now. It is lined with razor teeth. In his nostrils, the smell of decaying fruit.

Once again, my body gets the best of me, Robert...

C is for Captive

Pete Aldin

Alec broke the surface of troubled dreams with a snort, jerking upright in bed as sleep's soft threads fell away like torn gossamer.

To his right, Jen snored on, her rumpled hair discernible in the light of the streetlamp outside their apartment. To his left...

The Intruder was huge, head bowed beneath the ceiling, features hidden within what looked like a long hoodie, shoulders wide enough to belong to a running back. Strangely, Alec felt no shock at the sight of this hulking home invader, only whispered, "Well, shit."

The blur's massive shoulders rose and fell in a sigh. "I so hate it when they wake up," it said, its voice distorted, like three throats speaking at once: one hissing; one grating like a low-budget BBC monster; one a cultured, professorial murmur. "I don't suppose there's any chance of you going back to sleep like a good boy, before... "

"Before what?"

"Well, I'm not going to say it out loud. That would be indecorous."

The Intruder raised a hand to toy with his hood. In the low light, Alec caught a glimpse of rail-thin arm and pencil-thin fingers. He rubbed at his eyes, gritty with sleep.

"I'm still dreaming."

"Ah!" The Intruder coiled his fist in a thumbs-up gesture. "Yes! Precisely. Go with that. So lie down, dear boy, and let the dream, er, take you."

The arm lowered slowly, forefinger tracking toward Alec. As it neared his forehead, he felt a chill: cold radiated from that hand the way heat might radiate from a grill.

Finally alarmed—and thinking it was about frickin' time he was—Alec scooted sideways from the refrigerated digit and bumped against Jen who snored on. He shook her quickly without taking his eyes from the home invader but she did not respond. He'd always said she'd sleep through anything.

The Intruder bent at the middle and the finger closed the distance. Tangling in blankets, Alec made an undignified exit down the center of the bed and struck his toe on the wheel of Jen's chair on his way to the doorway.

Gargling curses, he limp-ran into the kitchen and wrapped his fingers around the biggest handle poking from the knife-block. Intending to return to the bedroom before Coldfinger—he barked a hysterical laugh at the wisecrack—could molest Jen, he whirled around.

He pulled up just short of crashing into the giant. The hunched freak towered over the fridge and reeked like wet earth.

He pressed back against the bench, knife up, robbed of the ability to speak. There was more light in the kitchen, what with Jen's laptop still on and the blue LED microwave clock but the light was making things worse, not better. The Intruder's hoodie was, in fact, a cloak. And the cloak was rippling—a crawling mass of earthworms, roaches, earwigs and some specks too tiny to identify in the gloom. Worse even than this horror was the face revealed within the cowl—a melted mask, a lump of potter's clay—shimmering and flickering as if revealed by capricious candlelight, the human features of eyes and nose and mouth a suggestion, as if someone had referenced humanity and with irony.

Alec managed a kind of strangled squeak. "What are you?"

The shoulders rose and fell again, sending bugs scuttling and writhing. "This is the problem with them waking—they always want conversation. You'll be bargaining next."

Alec slid sideways along the bench, sweeping a cereal packet to the floor as he went. The Intruder kept pace, silent on the linoleum floor. Alec glanced down. The creature's feet were as odd as its face. One was a human foot but skeletal and gaunt with nails that appeared to have faces and tiny mouths opening and closing without sound. The other was shaped like a bird's with three talons. One talon—a snake—writhed and wriggled. The middle one was gnarled and cracked, a tree branch or root. And the last resembled the head of an eel—it snapped at him and he slipped in the Sugar-O's on the floor, had to catch himself on the bench.

"What are you?" he repeated, righting himself. He slashed the air with what he hoped was gangsta gravitas.

"Alec," the creature chided gently. "You know me."

"I...?"

He saw it then in a flash of insight—or was memory? The one never far below the surface—all he had to do at any given time was scratch the veneer of Now and the images and sounds and smells and emotions would come screaming into center-camera as if it was happening all over again. The wreck. The flames. The blood. The screaming.

Nineteen years old and just having fun, out driving with Mike. Stupid drunk Mike who never should have been behind the wheel even when sober. Mike driving without lights while Alec cranked up the stereo and hollered in testosterone-inspired glossolalia. The little Toyota appearing from nowhere at the intersection, the pickup hammering into it and sending it spinning spinning spinning until the telephone pole arrested its dance. Mike bleeding from the forehead and nose, slumped back in his seat, groaning...

Alec sobbing *no no no* as he stumbled on bruised legs toward the other car. Fire leaping from under the hood. Inside the driver enmeshed in metal, his brains leaking from his head and his clothes dyed red; the front passenger crying and jiggling her door which wouldn't budge even when Alec reached it and used all his strength against it; and the girl in the backseat–a girl named Jen–unconscious, slumped against her seatbelt. Her door worked, so–

He growled, blinked it away and put his head in his hands. "Stop it! You're making my life flash before my eyes, you goddamn cliché!"

"I'm not, I assure you." The Intruder had been begun sliding closer, but it stopped and put a finger to its approximation of a mouth. "Although when I say *I*, I really should say *we*. But it's just so complex speaking in multiple composite identities. The pronoun *we* doesn't really do it justice. Another problem with conversation. Another reason to avoid it."

"Multiple..."

"My boy, as the story goes, we *are* many." Coldfinger's fingers scraped the chest, parting the cloak, revealing a second swirling mass beneath the creepy crawlies. Across this pale phantasm, faces boiled and swam, climbing over each other as if surfacing for air. Alec saw the tiny heads of lizards and Neanderthals, lions and lambs, marsupials and mammoths, a Native American in battle headdress, a bearded Mongol, a woman peppered with pustules, a serene face in a nun's habit, a raven.

He reached deep inside him for every swearword he'd ever heard and found them all, spewing them out in what must have been a full minute of invective.

"Inventive," said the Intruder. "I hadn't heard some of those combined that way."

Alec leaned on the bench, panting—all that swearing had winded him.

"Of course, vulgarity does nothing to prevent the inevitable."

With one foot coated in Sugar-O's and the other throbbing like a bastard where he'd cracked it on the wheelchair, he replied, "If you have to kill me, can you at least stop talking like that?"

"You mean like an aged theatrical actor?"

"…Exactly."

"Actually, I prefer it. Helps the gravitas, you see."

The roach-and-worm cloak fell back into place, covering the ribcage of heads. That cold-radiating finger stretched toward him.

"Wait, I have more questions."

The Intruder dropped the hand and sagged against the bench. "Here we go."

"What's actually wrong with me? What am I, you know, suffering from?"

"Does it matter?"

"Yeah, it matters!"

"The result's the same."

"I have a right to know."

It shrugged. "Aneurism. You worry too much, eat too many saturated fats. Is that your only question?"

"No. I have more. So you're… you. Okay. Freaking me out, but…you came here, specifically for me. What's so special about me?"

"Nothing. Why would there be?"

"It's just that I didn't expect, well, you."

"I visit everyone."

"What, like Santa Claus or something?"

"If you're asking whether or not I'm omnipresent, then the answer is yes. Certainly. Name me a place where things don't die. Where I'm not required."

Alec shifted and cereal crunched.

"You're evil."

The Intruder regarded him with forced patience. "I'm evil. I'm good. I'm value-neutral. I'm mediocre. I'm everything and everyone that ever was. You think I'm here out of cruelty? Perhaps I am. We certainly have enough of that wriggling around under here." He tapped his cloak.

"Well, if there's good in you, then let me go."

"Bargaining. I knew it."

"I'm not bargaining, I'm asking you to be compassionate and let me go."

"Go where?"

"Back to bed?"

"And live another thirty, forty, fifty years? I'll still come for you. What's the point?"

"I'll have had another thirty, forty, fifty years."

"And what will you do with it? Start a charity? Write a world-changing self-help book, *My Brush with the Other Side*?" The visitor looked him over, the approximated mouth turned down. "You're not one of the memorable ones, Alec. Nothing special about you, I'm afraid."

There had to be more. There had to be something. His last moments and he was standing in crappy cereal in his t-shirt and undies, arguing for his life by the light of a laptop. And he couldn't think of a single reason why his life should go on. But there must be something. What else could he do with it? What had he left unfinished, except a good night's sleep, except—

He was back in the memory then, yelling, "I'll be back for you" at the front passenger, trying to raise his voice above the ringing in his ears and the cries of the woman whose legs he'd found out later were trapped beneath the dashboard and who was watching the flames with increasing panic. "I'll get her safe and then I'll get you out!"

Manhandling Jen as best he could from the wreck, carry-dragging her ten feet, then twenty, then forty–was this safe enough?–sliding her onto the grass, turning to run back, the flames reaching gas tank, the Toyota erupting, the screams of the trapped woman…

The years of self-punishment, wondering how he could have done it different. If he'd told Mike they should just get pizzas and DVDs. If he'd been driving and with the headlights on. If he'd been faster out of the pickup. Then none of the last twenty years would have happened.

Jen's hero worship that he'd never deserved. Her unreserved love for the man who'd risked his own life to get her out of that burning car–as if he could've stood by and done nothing. The months of operations she'd endured, always smiling, always positive. The way she'd decorated her first wheelchair with decals. Her gratitude that he would visit her ward so often…

Her proposal. His acceptance, painting a smile on his face he didn't feel deeper than his skin, accepting the jokes about it not even being a leap year.

The chain of days since. His forced happiness at anniversaries. Saying *I love you* and every time meaning *I'd leave you if I could*…

And that was his life since that night. Always helping her. Always sparing her pain.

Always sparing her—

"This is my purpose?" He asked it as a question, but he knew the answer. The purpose of his life was up to him. It always had been. Coldfinger's shrug seemed to agree with him.

I'd leave you if I could. He'd wanted to say it a thousand times. Ten thousand. Well, now he could. And he didn't want to. He didn't want to because he didn't want to die. And he didn't want to die because…

"Let me," he began and had to clear his throat to continue, "let me leave a note for my wife at least."

The putty-mask within the cowl pinched. Perhaps it squinted at him. "A note for your wife? This is your last wish? Not that I grant last wishes, of course."

Alec tossed the knife aside. It was redundant. He folded his arms across his t-shirt. "This is my last wish. Let me tell her all the things… all the things I should have told her every day. How brave she is. How pretty the curve of her neck is when she has her hair up. How she still makes me laugh unexpectedly. How amazing she is to find a way to exercise everyday despite the chair. How I respect the way she fights me on important things, the way she fought to have me to herself. How committed she is to a dope like me. How–" His voice snagged in his throat. "How much I love her."

He did. He *loved* her. Sheesh! It must have happened sometime when he wasn't looking.

Coldfinger peered closer and gave a low whistle. "You're a good man."

Alec huffed a laugh, wiped at his eyes. "You sound surprised."

"I am. We are. Thought you were one of the selfish ones."

He sucked in air, tasting hope. "So you'll let me live."

"No. But it's nice to know we'll have someone else in here to redress the balance."

"Balance!"

"Balance, Alec. If the world were kinder–if the creatures who currently rule it were kinder–I would be too. You're a kind man. You're needed in here."

Alec kicked Sugar-O's across the floor and thought of diving through the window. But a four-storey plunge to the pavement would only result in his new pal—

"—scraping your soul off the concrete anyway," the Intruder finished for him. It added, voices soft, "Alec, these things happen. They must. But we can make this one kind for you. And for Jen."

He sucked air again and this time it tasted of powdered cereal and stale coffee grinds in the trash.

And of wet earth.

It tasted like inevitability.

He wiped at his eyes again, cleared his throat. "Kind, how?"

The Intruder shifted to peer past him. "You could sit in your armchair over there. The green one you love and Jen hates. You like sitting there, don't you? She could find you there. It would be quite peaceful. And less traumatic than waking to find a cadaver in the bed with her."

"This is the best I can hope for?"

The Intruder nodded slowly. "It will be kind for her," it repeated.

"Dead man walking," Alec muttered as he trudged into the living room and stopped by his favorite chair.

He ran his palms along the rough, frayed fabric. He put his feet up on the coffee table. The living room air was thick with the ozone tang of electricity creeping from a dozen appliances and with the sweetness of wet earth, freshly turned earth. Jen's recent birthday card stared back at him from the TV shelf. Thirty-four. She was still young.

He lowered himself into it. "Dead man sitting."

She might find him in the morning and think about the shortness of life and how much she could still pack into it for herself. She might realize she didn't need him to make her feel safe, that she was brave enough and strong enough to have whatever life she chose from here on out.

And young enough perhaps find another man, a man who didn't take so long to realize all of this.

If he'd had a prayer, that would have been it.

When the hand reached for him this time, it did not seem so cold. And Alec took it.

D is for Death

Michael M. Jones

I am a shadow who once was a girl.

I flit through the hallways, darting from one dark place to another, leaping from person to person as they talk and laugh in the brief moments between classes. Every now and again, someone detects my presence, shivering despite the late spring heat and ineffectual air conditioning. Even rarer, one of them stops and turns, trying to figure out what they've seen out of the corner of an eye.

A bubbly gaggle of girls comes out of the bathroom, giggling over some shared joke. I linger on the nearby lockers and borrow one brunette's laugh, trying it on for size. My attempt to join in comes just as the group quiets; they look around, baffled and just a little uncomfortable.

The laugh doesn't feel right to me and I leave it behind as I continue my journey. The girls' group disbands as they move along to their various classes, their shadows following obediently, nothing more than patches of darkness.

I duck through a door just as its closing, and for the next while enjoy a class on poetry while resting in the shadow of a young man who spends the period making obscene doodles in his notebook. It takes energy for me to move about on my own but I am rejuvenated by the lifeless shadows of other people. Sometimes I think about what it would be like to stay with a person, to live their life as they do, to be their shadow, instead of on my own. I often find myself "shopping" for people as one would a dress.

Robert Frost doesn't move the boy in the least so when the class is over, I abandon him without a second thought.

And so the day goes, with me picking and choosing from everything the school offers its hundreds of students. I learn about the Great Depression in American History, listen to verbs being conjugated in French, and look over shoulders as students conduct weird experiments in Physics. The lectures echo inside me with odd familiarity, though today they feel new and interesting.

When classes let out for the day, I go to play in the shadows of the auditorium, where they assemble sets and rehearse for the spring musical. The auditorium is perhaps my favorite place in the entire school because its backdrops and catwalks, its curtains and dangling roles, create a playground of light and shadow, and who'd notice if something flickers and darts in a way it shouldn't? The lighting designer keeps yelling for adjustments, causing students to scramble up ladders to reposition equipment. I probably shouldn't tease him so.

But eventually, everyone leaves for the night. Lights are turned off, doors shut firmly, and I am all alone, save for the single light left on stage as part of theatre tradition. It creates the best shadows, and I dance through them until reality sinks in.

With the school empty, I can no longer distract myself.

I am a shadow that once was a girl. I play at fitting in by attending classes and listening to conversations, but I am alone.

I had a body once.

I remember it like a much-faded dream.

Something happened and the body and I parted ways. Was it dead or simply lost?

When I think of the body—of my former self—I conjure an image of a young woman who'd be right at home in these halls. Blonde and blue-eyed, with fair skin and soft features but when I focus on the details, they slip away like mist in the sunlight.

I think something *bad* happened. I think—*NO!*

When I return to my senses I'm far from the auditorium, pressed into the corner of a classroom with morning light streaming in through the windows.

This happens whenever I dwell on the unknown past too often. It's taught me to avoid the hard questions as much as possible. And yet…the curiosity nibbles at my resolve, leading to moments of weakness. Perhaps if I try too hard, I'll remember everything, or lose it all for good.

The next day is Friday and as soon as that final bell rings students stream for the exits, chattering about dates and parties and all the other details that make up their weekend lives. But when I try to leave the school, I'm stopped at the doors by an invisible barrier. I am tied to this building. I can stand at the door like a child with its nose pressed against the window of a toy store but I can go no further. I don't even bother trying to push at the boundaries. They never budge. Instead, I aim, as always, for the auditorium where I know I'll find people in rehearsals.

The sound of crying catches my attention. This is not an unusual sound in itself; school has a way of bringing out emotions one prefers to leave hidden. But this sounds different from the "I failed a test" sob of frustration or the "we broke up" expression of heartbreak. This is despair and hurt, and it sparks some instinct I can't quite explain. I follow it into the girls' restroom, ducking under the door and along the floor. I find the source of the crying huddled in the corner of the handicapped stall, a girl who has tucked her knees against her chest, arms wrapped tight around them as if to present the smallest possible target. A backpack is nearby, its contents strewn on the floor, papers torn and wet, books much-abused.

I know her, if only by sight. A freshman, a loner, not part of any pack or clique. She always keeps her head down, gaze fixed on her feet. She rarely speaks up, and sits alone at lunchtime. Sometimes, she seems miserable. Today, she's wrapped up in utter despondence.

With an entire school at my disposal, I'd never given this girl much notice. I'd followed the bright, shiny ones, the noisy ones, the ones who I most wanted to be like. She had been in the background, part of the faceless crowd, easy to ignore.

Much like myself. I felt a sudden pang of empathy as I realized we'd both been invisible, though for different reasons.

I flit closer, as if I can comfort her somehow. Her shadow lashes out at me, and I retreat quickly, startled by its vehemence. It's like an angry guard dog, fangs bared, and I can't come any closer. There's a puddle of shadows by the door, and I take up a wary position there. I've never encountered a shadow like hers before, active and aware and aggressive. It's not like me. I don't sense an awareness, merely a raw, seething mass of pain and anger.

The crying eventually stops, and the girl gathers her belongings and leaves. I follow her to the main door, where I can't go any further, watching until she's out of sight. Then, it's off to the auditorium, but even there, I can't get her out of my thoughts. Her shadow intrigues and bothers me. I must learn more.

Over the course of the next week, I make a point of studying the girl, though always at a safe distance. I attend classes with her. I'm under the table at lunch. I'm always watching but I never get close enough to risk her own shadow's wrath. Its volatility fascinates and frightens me. Shadows are supposed to behave themselves. I was the exception.

As I pay attention to the girl, I learn several things. Her name is Madeline, and she always has the right answer when called upon in class, but never volunteers otherwise. She loves poetry. She has no friends. Sometimes she stands close to the theatre or art crowds, radiating silent longing, but she doesn't seem to know how to get involved. She was homeschooled until this year, when her family moved to Puxhill and she still hasn't adjusted. This last I learned by chance when she was called in to talk with the guidance counselor. I pay closer attention, not just to Madeline, but to those around her. I get as close as I can without her shadow snapping at me, even when it means I'm wrapped around a chair leg or squeezed into a corner. Then I see it, the way she stares at another girl, a mean-spirited queen bee whose soft beauty conceals a poisonous soul. Madeline watches her with a mix of desire and dread, and the gaze lasts just a little too long for it to be casual. It's a little too frequent to be accidental.

Oh, Madeline, *no*.

It strikes me right to my core, the certainty brought by realization.

I know that forbidden feeling. These bullies know Madeline is different even if she doesn't know herself.

I once shadowed the queen bee, attracted by her popularity and beauty like a moth to the flame. Unlike the moth, I recognized a danger and fled when I realized she thrived on tearing down others.

The queen bee and her swarm catch Madeline after school, crowding her into the restroom where they taunt and tease her. Words like dyke, lezzie, fag and freak stab into her, vile and poisonous. They accuse her of staring in the locker room, getting too close in the showers after gym. They tell her she's ugly and no guy or girl will ever want her. As their words take on an awful droning, I shrink back into the shadows, reeling as though I am under attack, something dark and vicious stirring deep within me. Madeline wilts under the onslaught knees buckling under the unfair weight of the slurs and accusations. Her back finds the wall, and she crumples to the ground in a forlorn heap, head buried in her arms to block out the taunts. One girl draws back to kick her, the queen bee purses her lips as if to spit. I reach into the hallway where I find some passing jocks. I borrow one's deep voice and enthusiasm, and cry out in protest. The queen bee and her friends are startled enough to stop, to leave before they've had their fill of abuse.

Madeline weeps. Her shadow snarls and lashes out at me when I approach. I wish I could say something to make it all better, but my attempt to help has exhausted me. Who listens to disembodied voices anyway?

Long after she leaves I remain in the restroom, lost in thought. My memories stir and swirl, bringing me dangerously close to the awful truth behind my origins. I smell aftershave and sweat, experience phantom fingers on my body and a soreness between my legs. Pleasure and pain. Satisfaction and guilt. Desire and shame.

I'm torn between pushing for enlightenment and retreating to safety. Before I can make up my mind, things settle back into place and the sensation is lost. If I could cry with frustration and relief, I would.

The next day, Madeline seems different. She walks in despair, her shadow fierce and angry. Her eyes are haunted and empty. Something has broken within her, and now she's brittle, ready to shatter at any moment. I'm there when everything falls apart. It's in English after lunch, and she's already in her seat when the queen bee enters. They lock gazes, and the queen bee's lip curls. "Just wait until I tell everyone," she hisses so only Madeline (and I) can hear. She holds up her phone and taps it meaningfully.

Madeline flees, tears already forming. I follow as quickly as possible, ever mindful of her shadow, which lunges at everything in its path like a rabid dog on a chain. I hear the confusion of classmates and teacher in her wake, but I don't leave her. Though what can I do?

Madeline ends up backstage in the empty auditorium, a wounded animal seeking a safe place to heal...or die. But as she climbs up into the catwalks, I finally see what I'd missed all along.

Her shadow isn't protecting her.

It's feeding on her. Her despair and pain has infected it, turning it toxic, capturing her in an ever-stronger trap. The harder she struggles, the tighter it becomes. It's killing her spirit, destroying her will to live.

I throw myself at Madeline, diving right into her shadow. It tears at me with frenzied viciousness, ripping at my essence. Desperately, I reach out and draw from the shadows all around us, taking them into myself to replenish my form and gather strength. It steals from Madeline, and she gasps with a heartsick pain. I try to rip it away from her even as I struggle to keep it from doing too much damage to me.

As I wrestle with her shadow, we become one and the memories rise to the surface. First hers and then mine.

Madeline, at home. She gets a text from the queen bee, who claims to be sorry, apologizing for everything. Asking for forgiveness. Suggesting that she's attracted to Madeline. Asking for… more. A cruel seduction. A terrible trap. All the right words to override Madeline's wariness, preying on her weakness. Madeline makes a very bad decision. Regrets it immediately. Too late.

Me, once upon a time. Falling in love with the wrong person. Used. Discarded. Disgraced. Disowned. Heartbroken and so very foolish. I feel the sharp pain in my wrists, smell the growing pools of blood, embrace the coming darkness. Even so, part of me refuses to move on. I cling to life, even as it abandons me.

Madeline's shadow takes on the shape of a frenzied wolf, jaws wide, razor-sharp fangs eager to rip into me. It goes on the offensive even as I batter at it with my recovered memories, pouncing at me, knocking me down, going for my throat. I thrust upwards with both hands, fending it off desperately. My shame and pain act as my armor; the fangs dig into my haunted past and tear away shadowy chunks. There's a sharpness in my chest, but I feel better almost immediately, as though I'd lost something weighing me down and poisoning me. I gather up that dark part of me and feed it to the wolf, forcing it down its throat even as it recoils, weakening from the unexpected meal. As it devours my self-loathing and regret, my desperation and pain, all those things which broke me when I was alive and kept me tied to this place, I grow stronger. I gain clarity. I understand things I'd lost long ago.

As the wolf loses its strength, I see how it's connected to Madeline, how it's anchored within her. I see where it's vulnerable. And I know what has to be done. I give it the last of my inner darkness, and it shudders, falling away from me. Between Madeline's pain and my own, it's simply eaten too much. It's dying. It snaps at me as I wrap around it, but it's half-hearted, ineffective. I stroke its head and whisper reassurances. I tell it that everything will be okay. Madeline's shadow shivers, and as it fades, I'm able to sever its connection with her and draw it into myself. I'm strong enough to do this, now that I've been healed. It's a dull ache deep within me, but nothing I can't handle. And then I reach out to where the connection used to be, where a shadow should be, and I give myself to Madeline. I sink into place as though coming home.

I feel her heart beating, her chest rising and falling as her breathing steadies. I feel the immense weight of despair lift, and the flash of hope that comes with the passing of darkness. I tell her I'll always protect her, that she'll be fine. No, she'll be magnificent. Together, we'll overcome the things which destroyed us as individuals. I tell her I care. That she matters. That things will get better. "I love you," I whisper, and I mean it. I tell her my name, a secret just between the two of us that she may or may not remember in her dreams.

When she walks out of the auditorium, she does so with newfound strength and confidence. Class is just letting out. How did all of this happen so quickly? It felt like forever while I was fighting her shadow. When Madeline sees the queen bee, looks her tormentor right in the eye, then sweeps past her to reclaim her backpack. She's been through the crucible and is so much stronger for it. The bullies, thrown off-guard, do nothing.

That afternoon, Madeline heads back to the auditorium, to see if there's anything she can do to help with the production. Yes, I might have influenced this decision, but she'll need friends if she's to survive this period of transition. I don't know what will come of our new partnership, or of her battles with the queen bee. I don't know what it will be like, to be Madeline's shadow, whether we will remain separate or blend together or if I'll gradually grow quieter until I can finally sleep. I suppose we'll find out.

I was a shadow that once was a girl. Madeline was a girl consumed by her shadow. We're both doing much better now.

E is for Eidolon

Simon Kewin

Eventually he grew weary of the long winter he'd escaped to.

It wasn't the cold; he could withstand that well enough. His body was strong. There were fish to catch in the icy waters, and sometimes he could creep up on a seal and wrestle it to its death. The flesh and blubber could feed him for a month. He hated to butcher the creatures but it was a matter of survival. His house was built from their furs lashed over whale bones. He'd extended and reinforced it again and again over the decades. When sickness came, as it did even to him, he could lie on his seal-hide bed and shiver through until it subsided.

Water was always plentiful.

In the early days he'd had fights with the arctic bears, those roaring monsters with cruel teeth and butcher's hook claws. Some were taller even than he when they reared up on their hind legs, but he was nearly as strong and made up for the lack in cunning. Now the bears walked a wide path around him, watching from the distance and sniffing at the air but daring no nearer. They had to be the descendants many times over of the originals but still they kept away, wariness passed down from mothers to cubs. The arrangement suited them all.

No, it wasn't the cold, or the four-months of utter darkness in the winter, or the bears. It was loneliness, finally, that spurred him back into life, that made him gather his few supplies onto his sled and set off. He knew he would never have the companion, the mate, he craved. The possibility of another like him had died with his creator. It was a loss that, even now, cut through him more sharply than any wind from the north. He was a monster, forever an outcast.

But, loneliness. Loneliness had grown within him, gestating over the decades and centuries into something that couldn't be denied. It appeared he wasn't going to age and die as he'd assumed. His creator had done his work well.

There were things he needed to understand, too. Questions that needed answers. Whose fingers did he slip into the fish's mouth to break its spine and end its suffering? Whose muscles sawed at the ice to open up access to the water? Whose eyes did he see the world through? Whose brain, even, thought these thoughts, asked these questions? Who were they, all the poor, broken wretches that were *him*? Young or old? Male or female? He could tell from his external appearance that young, strong men made up a large part of his anatomy. But his organs? His inner workings? He didn't know.

He didn't know who he was.

But he'd seen signs in the sky. Miracles. Wonders. For many years he'd been utterly alone, and everyone else on the Earth might have been dead for all he knew or cared. He'd wanted no more to do with any of them. But then one day he'd seen a light in the east. A shooting-star. Except not a shooting-star. It didn't blaze and fade but was constant, moving across the night sky with slow precision, as if a star had worked itself loose and set off on a journey. He'd watched in wonder as it arced across the darkness. The following night it was there again. All the yearnings, all the questions he'd tried to suppress blazed into life as he sat and stared upwards.

And so he set off. Finding his way was easy. Even in summer the sun was low in the southern sky. All he had to do was head towards it. If there were still people in the world, the thought of being among them again gave him little pleasure. He remembered their revulsion all-too well. But if there were answers to be found they lay among humanity. He had no choice but to face them, just as he'd once faced the white bears.

He spied the ship in the distance after two weeks of hauling his sled across the ice. The black speck against the endless white slowly took on shape as he approached. It was trapped, far from open water. Summer was coming and the floes were breaking up, but the ship must have been marooned there all winter. It was large, too. Large and strange. His maker had endowed him with good eyes, and he could pick out fine detail from a safe distance. It appeared to be made from metal rather than wood. At night lights blazed out from it, brighter than any lantern he'd ever seen. Icicles festooned its rigging, but there were no sails in sight. There were definitely people on board. He could see them clearly: stick-figures milling around on the decks, or even venturing onto the ice to engage in activities he couldn't begin to understand. One or two of them always carried long-snouted rifles. Guns for the bears, most likely, but they'd work on him just as well. Even he couldn't withstand the sort of damage they'd inflict.

He counted nine people in the end, assuming there was no one who stayed below decks. He couldn't fight nine of them, especially not when they carried those guns. But perhaps he could pick the people off, one by one. Break their necks before retreating into the icy wastes. The thought gave him little pleasure but it was his only hope. They'd come hunting him, as he'd been hunted in the old days. But the ice was his domain. Once it was done, the ship could transport him far away, to the cities where he might find the answers he sought.

He watched for three days, crouched behind his upturned sled for camouflage, while he waited for the right moment to act.

Helen Magnusson crouched to study the GPS marker they'd left embedded in the ice. She popped the rubber cover on the USB socket and plugged in to download the latest readings to her device. All in all it had been a good winter. Lots of good data. They needed to do more analysis back in Copenhagen, but it was already clear they'd learned significant amounts about the movements of the ice floes. Repeat readings taken over successive years would give them invaluable insights into climate change.

As a biologist the floes weren't her main area of interest, she was much more intrigued by the alterations they were seeing in the microfauna populations. Larger creatures were being affected too. The migration patterns of fish, whales and polar bears were all altering. There could be no doubt. The world was changing.

While the data downloaded she glanced up at Kurt, standing guard nearby with his rifle at the ready. Kurt the pacifist vegetarian who'd never intentionally harmed any creature in his whole life. He really wasn't going to be much use if a bear did attack, was he?

"Hey, Kurt. It's gone ten. Why don't you go make your Skype call to the lovely Margarita?"

Kurt's voice was muffled behind the frost-rimed scarf covering half his face. "I'll stay."

She knew how much he looked forward to these daily calls with his young wife. The winter away had been hard on him. "It's okay. Go. I only have five more probes to do. I'll be back on board in fifteen minutes."

Kurt gazed around the ice, looking for any threat. The white silence stretched away in all directions, utterly unblemished.

"Go," she said again. "I'll be fine. Leave the rifle. If I see a bear I'll shoot the damn thing myself."

With a grunt of gratitude, Kurt laid down the rifle and strode back to the *Kraken*, adding another line of boot-prints to the well-trampled ice around the frozen research ship.

She was on the last probe but one when the attack came. She was thrown to the ice, a cruel blow to her side knocking the wind out of her before she could even scream. A moment later she felt the pain of it. *Ribs cracked*, a detached part of her mind observed. It was agony as she scrabbled about for the rifle but it was too far away, over by the probe. She half-rose, trying to call out. Her attacker filled her vision: a huge shape against the bright sky, rearing over her for the final blow.

He woke in a laboratory. Another laboratory. Different from the one his creator had used, of course. This one was cleaner, shinier, red and green lights twinkling away on incomprehensible contraptions all around him. But he knew the smells, knew what places like this meant. He keenly remembered the agonies he'd suffered. Raw pain thrummed away in his side, his leg, across his shoulders. Memories came back to him. Memories of the fight. He'd thought to show them his true self. Despite everything. He'd thought to reveal the person he was beneath. What was he thinking? They'd seen none of it. He cursed himself for his own stupidity. Mankind hadn't changed. They saw something monstrous and assumed it was a monster. He should have stayed in the high ice where he was safe.

When he tried to rise and found he was restrained, bound to the bed by shiny straps, he knew the worst of it. The straps cut into his limbs as he struggled. Furious with himself, at his own weakness, he tore himself from the metal slab they'd laid him on. He ripped aside, also, the tubes and wires they'd attached to him.

He had to get away, out onto the snow. There were no portholes in the laboratory; it was impossible to know how many decks he had to climb. He padded down a metal corridor lit by harsh white lights, no flames in sight.

He made it half-way up the first flight of steps when they came for him. They stood at the top, three of them, looking down upon him. Roaring, he charged. If he could throw them aside, fight his way above decks, he could jump from the ship, get away. He was conscious he was playing the part of the monster they saw when they looked at him perfectly, but he had little choice.

One of his captors raised a gun. It was only a pistol. He ignored it. When the shot struck him it was little more than a wasp-sting. He'd nearly reached them when his head began to swim. Clouds descended, filling his brain. What had they done to him? He tried to shake the fog free, but there was too much of it, the weight of it too great.

Dizziness overwhelmed him. His last sensation was of falling backwards, the people who'd captured him receding into the darkness above.

When he awoke again it was to the gentle rocking of the ship. It took a few moments to grasp what that meant. How long had he been asleep? What had they done to him?

As before, he tried to rise. As before he was bound. He was naked too, now. A single white sheet covered his body instead of the furs he'd been dressed in. To what end? Had they been examining him? Preparing their fresh torments?

One again he struggled, trying to tear himself free from their bonds.

"Hey, it's okay. I'll undo the straps for you." A woman's voice, speaking accented German, as if it wasn't her native tongue. "You do understand me, right? You speak German and French?"

He stopped struggling. "Why am I bound?"

She set about working at his wrists and ankles. She was young, her blonde hair long and soft. He marvelled at how smooth her skin was. Cream compared to his own scarred and pitted hide.

"We went through some rough seas yesterday," she said. "Didn't want you to fall out of bed."

"But before. When you first captured me. I was bound then, too."

"You kept fighting us in your sleep, even when we were trying to treat you."

"You are a doctor? A woman?"

She smiled a little smile to herself. "As it happens I am a doctor. But a biologist not a medic. We had you in the sick bay for a while but then we needed the room so we wheeled you in here."

"So you could study me?"

"So you could sleep."

She finished untying him. Warily, expecting some cruel joke, he swung his legs round to sit upright. The room lurched for a few moments before settling back into place.

More memories returned to him. "You shot me."

"Darted you. You were delusional, a danger to yourself and others. It was all we could do."

He didn't understand all her words. He towered over her but she didn't appear to have any fear of him. He wondered, briefly, if she was blind, like the old man. But no. She could see him well enough. She held out a bottle of water for him, constructed from some strange, flexible material and not the glass he'd expected.

"How long have I been asleep?" he asked after he'd drunk. The water trickled cold inside him.

"Ten days. An ice-breaker came for us a week ago. The captain wanted to air-lift you off. I thought you might want to decide things for yourself. Given your past."

"You know what I am?"

"Who doesn't?"

"And that doesn't alarm you? The fact that we're here alone in this little room?"

The woman shifted in her chair. But she wasn't uneasy. Getting comfortable if anything. "You saved me. Out there on the ice, when the bear attacked. Never seen anything like it. A man fighting a polar bear and winning. Incredible."

"I killed it?"

"You did. Not before it gave you some terrible injuries. It took all of us to carry you on board while staunching your wounds."

"Were you harmed?"

"I'm healing. The painkillers help."

He looked around, uncomfortable at this intimacy between them. With his bed and her desk and the shelves full of her books there was little room left. She'd clearly been studying insects as part of her researches. On her desk, next to a microscope, beetles crawled around in a series of glass tanks. Beside them, butterflies fanned their wings upon a purple-flowering plant. They appeared to be free to fly wherever they wished.

"Why are there insects?"

"I'm studying the effects shifting magnetic fields have on their life-cycles."

He nodded, although her words still made little sense. "You said I was a *man*. If you know who I am you know what I am. A monster. A concoction of broken parts. A chimera."

She shook her head. "Those are bad words. Is that how you see yourself?"

"It's how the world sees me. And … I have done terrible things. I've taken the lives of others."

"Terrible things were done to you. Seems to me you had plenty of reason for doing what you did."

"You may think like that. The world won't."

She didn't reply for a moment, looking at him, considering him.

"Why did you come south after all this time?"

"I … I wanted to find out who I was. What I was."

She nodded, as if this was a perfectly normal thing to say. "You know, the world has changed a lot since you last walked it. Now you would be a marvel. A wonder."

"These are simply other terms for *mongrel* and *monster*."

"No. People would love you. Scientists, obviously. I mean, how is it you've even survived this long? But everyone else too. You'd be famous. Trust me. You'd be a huge deal. We'd help you find your answers. Everyone would want a piece of you."

"A piece of me?"

"Sorry. Bad choice of words. I mean everyone would want to find out about you. You'd be huge."

He tried to make sense of her words. Clearly the way in which people spoke had changed over so much time. Was this all some trap? Some way of luring him back into the clutches of what was laughably called civilisation? Sometimes, back in the north, he polished a slab of ice so he could see his own reflection. Thinking that, maybe, he wasn't as lumpen and scarred as his memory said. He was always disappointed. "I'm still a monster. I'm still this assemblage of stolen body-parts."

"And, what, you think we're all pure, all perfect? I've been thinking about you while you slept. Let me tell you, we're all mongrels. We're all a mishmash of human ancestries. Neanderthal ancestries, too, come to that. Amphibian, reptile, you name it, it's all in there. Maybe 10% of our DNA is from viruses, absorbed into our own millions of years ago. You think you're a mongrel? Welcome to the human race."

"I don't know what any of that means."

"Look. You want to know whose hands those are? Whose face, whose limbs? Is that it?"

"I do."

"Well I can tell you. They're yours."

"Once they weren't. They were stolen for me."

She studied him for a moment. Then, unexpectedly, she began to unbutton her shirt. Confused, mouth dry, he could do nothing but watch as she revealed her breast. An old thrill of delight through him, like torches being lit in rooms long left dark.

Beneath the fabric of her undergarment, running the length of her sternum, crawled a long centipede scar. She traced its line with her blood-red fingernail.

"You see this? I was born with a congenital cardiac condition. My heart didn't work properly. So they gave me a new one. Some unfortunate died, I don't know who, but I got to live. Their heart beats in my chest. There are lots of people like you. Like, I have a cousin lives in Stockholm. *He* was born a *she*. Surgery can fix many things that nature got wrong."

Such marvels, such wonders. This was a place of magic. Terrible magic. Except, not, of course. It was all natural science. He of all people should understand that.

"No," he said. "You're still *you*. I'm only an assortment, a collection. There is no *me*."

She shrugged. "Bodies are just things. Collections of organs and limbs that allow us to live. Even our minds. Our ideas, our thoughts, our desires. Our way of seeing the world. Everything's inherited, stolen, borrowed. Or else it's something new and unique, something we came up with for ourselves. How are you any different?"

He didn't speak for a moment, trying to understand what she was saying. He looked away, conscious he was staring at the glorious swell of her bosom. He was suddenly aware of how flimsy the white sheet covering his body was. His loins, for so long mere functional plumbing, were stirring into life.

"You … you should button your garment back up now."

"Forgive me," she said. "Things get pretty relaxed onboard as the winter wears on." He thought she was going to take offence. Scream or swoon. Instead, seeing the movement of his body beneath the sheet, she laughed. "You see? You're *definitely* human. No doubt about that." One of her eyebrows arched in something like amusement. "You didn't come south again just to find answers about your origins did you?"

"I don't know why I came. I felt compelled."

"Oh, come on. You've been alone for a long time. You're looking for love, right? Or, failing that, you're looking to fuck. Who wouldn't after all this time?"

He winced at her rough choice of words. "That possibility died with my creator a long time ago."

"Bullshit."

"I'm sorry?"

"That's bullshit. What, you think you have to find someone just like you? That's not how it works these days. I guess that's not how it ever worked. Love comes in endless shapes and sizes and combinations. These days, we're all about our variety, our individuality."

"That wouldn't extend to me."

She shook her head. "Don't kid yourself. You're strong and thoughtful. Kind, too, I think. You're going to be famous. You also have – her gaze flicked briefly over his body beneath the sheet – some impressive physical characteristics. Trust me. You'll have no trouble finding love."

"I planned to kill you all," he said. "Take you ship."

She looked amused. "Really? That was your plan? You're good with modern navigation systems are you?"

He didn't reply for a moment, considering her thoughts. He could maybe still escape. Dash her to the ground, make a bolt for the sea and swim for the ice. Escape to the safety of the far north. Except, where would that get him apart from back where he started?

"You are sure of this?"

"Look, it's up to you. Say the word and we'll lower you a lifeboat, let you paddle away into the darkness. We won't tell a soul. Or you can stay with us and rejoin the human race."

He watched her for a moment, half-expecting some joke, some elaborate cruelty to be revealed. Instead she sat quietly, awaiting his reply.

"You will help me?" he asked.

"Least I can damn-well do."

"And what should I call you?"

"Sorry. Should have said. I'm Helen. Helen Magnusson. And your name I know, of course."

"No. I have no name."

"Of course you do. It's Fra…"

His expression must have stopped her mid-word. A wave of revulsion had washed through him. Revulsion and anger. "Don't say it. Why would you call me by that foul name?"

"But … but that's what you are. Everyone knows that."

"No."

"What do you mean, *no*?"

"That was *him*. The monster who created me. The butcher with the knives and the saws. Who hacked up the bodies of the dead, who picked and sorted out parts to stitch together into the shape of a man. Into *me*."

"I didn't think. Forgive me." She considered for a moment. "You aren't grateful to him at all?"

Was he? It was hard to know. It was complicated. "I am glad to be alive," he said finally.

"So he didn't name you at all?"

His rage subsided a little, to be replaced by an old emptiness. "No. *Things* don't have names."

"Then you're going to need one." She considered for a moment. "How about, I don't know … Neumann."

"Neumann?"

"Sure. That is what you are. *New Man.*"

Neumann. He turned the word over in his mind. He liked it. Liked the shape of it. In some unexpected way this strange woman with her gift of water had anointed him. Baptized him.

"Neumann," he said out loud.

One of her butterflies flittered through the air to settle, unexpectedly, on his scarred hand. He reached out to touch it. The creature's iridescent wings were like paper. It flew off, but not before some of the tiny, colourful scales had rubbed off onto him.

He studied his fingers. The rainbow stayed when he tried to scrape it away. His skin shimmered. As if he had become part-butterfly, his fingers taking on the dazzling colours. Taking on, also, their beauty.

Marvelling, Neumann held out his hand to the young woman who'd befriended him, showing her what he'd become.

F is for Frankenstein's Monster

BD Wilson

Bairn knelt beside the door in the Gardens, listening to the sounds of the match and the crowd, faint and tinny through the backstage projection. He pressed his hand to the ground, but could not feel the chill of the stone. They covered the ground here with sindon mats, protecting both the surface and any who fell—or were thrown—onto it. He tapped it, and tried to make sense of it.

Cement was cheap. People were cheaper. Sindon cost.

He couldn't make it work in his head, not beside pieces pulled from the Dogfights, like the stagehands armed to prevent escape. It sat inside him, an uncomfortable itch reminding him something was different and different was dangerous.

Bairn frowned, and felt his face paint tug. Everything about the wait and the preparation was as familiar as breathing. Everything right, but also wrong, because the armed stagehands greeted performers by name, and no one was dragged to their places swearing, motivated by shock-sticks and iron knuckles.

This is the way it should be, a deep and buried part of himself whispered, even as everything else that he was told him it was wrong. It was wrong and he should leave, and he could leave because they weren't guarding the doors the way they should, not really.

He made a fist and punched the ground, but the buffered surface just increased the conflict within himself. He closed his eyes, and took a steadying breath. This wasn't what he'd planned when he left Queens, wasn't what he'd planned when he made that foolish promise in the first place. It had seemed so straight-forward before. Survive the Dogfights, get free, come home, reunite with his family. But Finley had been right about one thing: it was nothing more than an illusion.

Reality offered no such comfort.

The acid rain had carved away his skin, eating rivers through flesh and welcoming infection. Bairn spent his first week in the city fighting fever dreams where Samuel LeVarne sold him again and again and Anton chased him back to the Pits with a train, until he reached his family only to have them shatter into spinning shards melted by the rain. By the time he could think clearly again, he found himself off the streets and in a hospital.

He felt as if he'd just finished an entire tournament fight and his arm was as weak as if he'd broken it. As he went through the motions needed to return his strength, he thought about Finley doing the same in his off hours, and wondered if anyone had told his old mentor he was gone. One promise kept, one promise left.

...I'll come back...

No one stopped him on his way out of the hospital. There was no Dogfights cart waiting to take him back to the barracks or the training pit. He had earned his freedom, and for a few days he let that exhilaration fill him as he walked the streets without restriction, searching the city for a way to contact his family.

None existed. Conscript fighters were kept isolated, no matter who was asking or how many credits were offered. There was no way to let them know he had kept his promise, but at least his fragmented memory had retained his parents ring names, enough to track their history, and their decline.

They'd never recovered from the sale of their son, and their fall from the main event was rapid and irreversible. His brother and sister hadn't stood a chance. They were talented, he could see it in the records of their matches, but by the time they debuted their family name no longer drew an audience. They had never even been given a main card match. At the rate they were going, it would be ten more generations before the family was able to work off that crippling old debt.

He was too late.

In the arena, his family's music hit. There were so many things Bain couldn't remember, things he'd been forced to forget, but this was held in his very soul. He ground his teeth, forcing back the twenty years of lonely hope it stirred, and watched the projection for his first sight of his family.

A young man and woman came out first, dressed in matching green and yellow ring gear. The crowd's response was muted, but the two still grinned, and in their expressions he recognized his brother and sister. They'd grown up strong and athletic, carrying the tradition of joy into the ring, but the audience no longer cared.

The older couple that followed them wrenched Bairn's heart. His parents had aged far more than twenty years, and though they smiled and waved at the crowd, there was unconcealed exhaustion behind every move. He couldn't see even a trace of the determination and showmanship they'd drilled into him. But at least for them the crowd still seemed to carry some affection. There were cheers now, carrying them to the center of the ring where their opponents, and Exhibition Chairman Shanae, waited.

Shanae took center ring and looked out at the restless crowd. "Tonight has been a celebration of everything the Exhibition believes in," she began. "Of wonder, of spectacle, of friends and enemies, and of course, of family." She directed the last bit at Bairn's family. All four returned her smile with wary looks.

It was impossible to tell which way things would go in moments like these. The Exhibition was a twisted creature bound to drama, without concern for the fighters. That piece had long since been pulled off and replaced with disregard and sacrifice, with ownership instead of patronage. Bairn knew how this speech would end, but didn't know how much pain his family was going to experience before it was over.

"Like Malosi and Eseta, I grew up in the Exhibition," Shanae continued, "We've lived our entire lives devoted to the glamour, the magic, of the show. When you're a child, that magic is easy to believe. You know, without a doubt, that your parents will succeed, that good triumphs over evil, and that promises are always kept."

The projection in the stadium changed, Bain's last moments in the Exhibition appeared. He, they all, watched his father get pinned, and Shanae's father sign Bairn over to Samuel LeVarne. In the present Bairn's parents held each other, lines of pain etched on their faces even as they struggled to hide it.

Bairn ground his teeth. There was too much posturing here. This should have been quick, like breaking a limb, not a long drawn out suffocation.

"But as we grow up," Shanae said, "we learn that isn't always the case."

"I'll come back!" Bairn's childhood voice shouted at the crowd, at his family, at himself.

"Sometimes, we fail, we lose, we break our word."

The next scene was one he didn't know. His family backstage, brother and sister gangly teenagers, parents worn but still proud, as a stagehand called them over to a waiting woman in a suit.

"Wildfire, Monsoon, I regret to inform you that your eldest son was pronounced dead in the Dogfights training pits this afternoon."

He saw his father crumble, the weight of the loss and its consequences destroying what strength he had left. His family tried to hold him together, but his will slipped through their arms until they were left holding only a shell.

Bairn was so close. Close enough he could scale the walls of the Gardens, fight the guards inside, and storm through long-forgotten halls to find his family, earning a personal debt to add to the family one. It had taken him too long to come back to add to their burden without searching for an alternative. He turned from the walls, instead walking through the displays outside. Halls of history, the nature of the Exhibition lain out for anyone with the eyes to see.

The Exhibition was all about the story and show. It was at the heart of its origins, from back before the shelters, when the fighting was nothing more than that, a show, an act. It clung to that part of its tradition even as everything around it changed. Bairn understood, had always understood it, and kept that philosophy at his core even as pieces of his spirit were torn out and other unfamiliar ones tacked on in their places.

Everything could change in the ring, now, the show had given way to fights that needed the reality of the Dogfights to keep the audience's attention. A win was never guaranteed, a loss never certain, and the show shifted and twisted itself to handle the success or failure of the fighters.

A bet could have the Chairman crowing victory over his friendly competitor, or giving up the child from a family with roots as old as the Exhibition itself. Either way the show carried on and took the crowd with it. The mashup of history and necessity created something that worked, something that sustained, something that would be around much longer than the people it consumed along the way.

Bairn had fought his way out of the Dogfights by adopting the pieces he needed in the same way. He earned his freedom with the showmanship he'd learned as a child, but lost the care for a good fight and replaced honor with ruthlessness. The Dogfights meant broken bones, broken enemies, and broken soul. When he left for good, he was someone patched together from fragments of that child, the fighter who would do anything to win, and the death mask persona who drew in the audience.

But he'd pulled himself forward, all the way from the shithole arena in Queens to the Gardens, reveling in the freedom he'd earned, until he realized it was just a different kind of trap. He was made for the Dogfights, for the goal of returning home. Without either, he didn't fit anywhere, not in either city, not even within himself.

The arena was silent in the face of the painful memories, no cheers or jeers as the crowd remembered Monsoon and Wildfire had once been heroes, and their fall had happened outside the ring.

Shanae paused just long enough, letting the clip fade before she continued. "But today, we're here to believe again in the magic of our childhood."

"At your mark," a stagehand said, and Bairn stood behind the door, cold and calm falling over him out of habit.

"Because there truly are some promises that must be kept, and some people that even death cannot stop."

His music hit.

The door opened.

Bairn entered the arena.

This, at least, was exactly the same. The crowd reaction, cheers that felt like a pressure against his chest and settled around his shoulders like a well-worn cloak. He knew his part, the role he'd made, and the sounds helped to ground him in the persona that had brought him here, holding back the piece of himself that wanted to throw it all aside run to his parents.

They were inside the ring now, standing between his brother and sister, holding tight to one another. Projections around the arena showed close ups of their faces, shock and the first signs of tentative hope.

Bairn kept his focus on their faces, on the eyes he had held in his memory long after he had forgotten his own name. The path to the ring stretched out before him like the Dead Lands, and he felt as if the ground was once again melting beneath his feet, every step taking three times longer than it should. By the time he reached the ring, he'd begun to worry this was another nightmare, that he'd reach his family only to have them shatter into pieces and melt away at his touch.

Instead, his father grasped his outstretched hand, warm and solid and real. He felt callouses from a lifetime of ring-work, and then he was pulled forward. His father's arms closed around him as the crowd renewed their cheers. He broke character and returned the embrace.

"Aleki," his father said. "You're alive. You're home."

Bairn tried to find some connection to the name they gave him, but there was nothing. That part of him was gone, one of the many replaced in the Pits.

The Exhibition Chairman agreed to a meeting within minutes of the request.

"Bonne Nuit, it's a pleasure to meet you."

Bairn shook her hand, but didn't say anything. She motioned him to a seat and then took hers behind the desk again. The chair was delicate, made to look like wood and padded with soft colors. He felt larger than his size as he settled into it, afraid it would break and almost wishing it would. He didn't fit in the tidy office, with no scuff marks on the furniture, a room with no signs of fights or brawls.

"When I heard you were in the city, I'd hoped you would come visit. I don't get to Queens as often as I did when I travelled with my father. I'm afraid Anton and I aren't exactly friends."

He didn't know how to respond to that. Negotiations with Anton, such as they were, had always been easy. They hated each other and each knew it. This required more finesse than he was used to. "Anton doesn't seem to know how to cultivate friendships."

"No he doesn't. I don't know whether that's a blind spot for him, or just fortunate for us." She smiled, and Bairn almost found himself returning it. "All the same, I've managed to keep up with the fights as much as any fan outside of Queens can. Your championship run was unprecedented. It's a shame it ended so suddenly."

"All championship runs end suddenly. Mine just ended outside the cage."

"They're telling people you used performance enhancing drugs."

"I'd expect fans to believe that, but not the Exhibition Chairman."

She grinned again. "I didn't say I believed it. So, what did happen?"

"I earned out. I left."

She laughed. "I bet Anton loved that. No wonder he's not admitting to it. So what brings you here?"

Bairn breathed deep, savoring his last fragment of illusory freedom, and then gave it away. "I'm here to help my family do the same."

Bairn stepped between the ropes, waiting beside his brother as their sister started the match. A main event, the first demand for which he had traded his hard won freedom.

"Hold the tag rope," his brother whispered.

Bairn looked over, and Malosi raised the small rope tied to the turnbuckle. It took him a moment to remember what it meant, and then he took hold of his and tested the distance it gave him. Not much. They were, after all, supposed to be tethered to the corner, a goal for their partner to reach. It was one of the old things, like tapping and the three count, a holdover from the origins of the Exhibition. It was poor tactics, but part of the show, and his chest tightened as he felt the rope against his palm.

Bairn tightened his grip on the rope, grinning as he watched his sister drop kick her opponent and heard the audience cheer. She followed it up with a leg drop, and then climbed up the to the top turn buckle for a moonsault. Her opponent rolled out of the way at the last minute, and she hit the mat hard. But the crowd was on their side already, shouting her name as she struggled to get to her feet.

The ring was a square, there was no cage, death was not an option. It had all the trappings of the Dogfights, but the risk was lower. Bairn settled in to the oddly disjointed pieces of past tradition and present need, and the knowledge that every so often the tug of the future could change the beast yet again.

The Dogfights knew what it was. It was a slaughter house, something you survived if you were lucky, but nothing more. The Exhibition wasn't so focused, but it was life, and for the first time in years, Bairn could feel it in his bones.

He evaluated their opponents as his siblings traded off. They were talented and well deserving of their place on the roster. Bairn kept to the sidelines as his brother and sister showed the audience—and the Chairman—they had always belonged here, too.

Malosi was tossed into the ropes, bouncing back and into a clothesline. Eseta was calling his name, reaching out, even though their brother was all the way across the ring. Bairn's attention was on Malosi, when he caught a flash of movement from the side.

He called out, but he was too late. Eseta was yanked off the apron, her chin hitting the edge of the ring. Bairn dropped down beside her, but their opponent ran back to her corner before he'd even taken a step.

Inside the ring, Malosi had briefly stunned his opponent, giving him time to drag himself to their corner of the ring. Bairn swore, but left Eseta on the ground and jumped up to make the tag.

The audience screamed as he stepped between the ropes, past his brother, and over to where the opposing fighter scrambled back. Bairn tilted his head, sharing the audience's amusement as a new fighter tagged in, one far less eager to enter the ring than his partner had been to leave it. When he made no move to step into the center, Bairn shook his head, and went to get him.

He charged forward, and drove his palm into his opponent's chin. The man's head snapped back and he stumbled into his corner. His partners raised their free hands to prevent an accidental tag, even leaning back. They looked like they were one step away from jumping off the apron and leaving him to finish the match alone.

It was a gratifying response, good for a few moments amusement, but not what the fans were here to see. Bairn stalked to the corner, grabbed the legal fighter, and yanked him back toward the center of the ring.

He flew farther than he should have.

Bairn followed, maintaining a neutral expression while he tried to figure out what had happened. The crowd clearly loved it, and that make it click. The other team wasn't going to win this one, they all knew that, but a dramatic loss went over best.

Fine, he could play along. Bairn followed his opponent, yanked him forward and threw him toward the ropes. The man added his own momentum, bounced off and back toward Bairn. He'd intended to clothesline him, payback for his brother, but the man ducked, running under his arms to launch himself off the ropes on the opposite side of the ring.

Bairn spun, but he his timing was off and the man's fists slammed into his face, knocking him over. His back hit the mat, and his opponent dropped an elbow down on his chest. He clenched his teeth against the groan, waiting for the next blow to fall, exhilaration tensing his muscles at the unexpected turn in the fight. He fought against the grin that wanted to crack through his persona as he pushed away the pain. When the next blow fell, he rolled out of the way, and the slam of the impact echoed through the arena, enhanced by the mics. Too much show not enough fight. The difference was grating, but the challenge sent his blood pumping and still had to grind his teeth to keep the smile from his face.

Before his opponent recovered, Bairn grabbed his arm and swung it into a lock. The move was practiced, instinctual. He applied pressure, felt it reach the straining point, and then felt rapid slapping at his leg that was not the normal response. It wasn't an effective blow after all. His confusion lasted until he heard the bell.

Tap. He's tapping.

...You incapacitate them, you break them, or you kill them...

"Let him go," the ref yelled at Bairn, waving her hands in an emphatic gesture that could have meant anything, but the command broke the conflict between the pieces of his training and his past. He let his opponent go, and stood in the center of the ring, trying to find his equilibrium. His brother and sister joined him as the ref raised their arms.

The roar of the crowd crashed over him. His siblings grinned, jumping on the ropes to stir them up more. Bairn stayed in the center of the ring, settling back into himself, truly calm for the first time since leaving Anton's office. He'd given up his freedom, but he couldn't feel the loss as he stood here, at the end of a match well-fought and won. Ring or cage, past or present, slave or free, the fight was all he knew, what he had been built for.

Within it he was where he belonged. Within it was home.

G is for Gladiator

Gabrielle Harbowy

The lab is chilly. It feels sterile and heartless. Most of the cages/...are empty, which gives me the creeps, but the one that's not vacant is worse./ It huddles, frightened or maybe just shy, at the back of its kennel./ Feathers, claws, and scales, a sleek swath of brindle fur. And always, the eyes./

Big and brown and smart, those eyes might be from a doe, or from a puppy/—a much-kicked one, too, perpetually on the verge of full-blown tears./ It uses those eyes to get what it wants from us: food, lights on, blankets. A hand through the bars? Nice try, creature. No chance in hell. Not with that beak./

My dorm room number is five seventy-five, and so is the lab, too./ Coincidence, right? At least I won't forget, not that I'm forgetful much./ Anyway, my point: even in my room I feel the reach of those eyes./ Big, wet and pleading, without being able to tell me what it wants./

Five-seven-five. Funny how our brains do that; a number, or a phrase,/ once we notice it, we see it everywhere. (Bleh—I hated psych class.)

But it's like the thing / is all up in my thoughts and / maybe my dreams, too. // I'm not forgetful / but I know I locked my door / last thing before bed.

Like I always do.
Like I always lock the cage.
Always. That sharp beak.

But those pleading eyes,
It always looks so lonely.
One touch couldn't hurt...

H is for Haiku

Sara Cleto

At night, Leah dreams of pomegranates. She plucks a single fruit from the branch overhead and holds the heavy weight in her cupped hands before cracking it open like a jewelry box. Red, and not the dull shade of the foxes that haunt the garden or autumn leaves before they fall, but brilliant and strange enough to make her eyes water. Carefully, reverently, she pulls a seed from its nest and places it on her tongue. When it bursts between her teeth, the juice is sharp and bright, and for a moment, she hears her mother's voice.

When she wakes, she can never remember the words.

Her father's house is cold and dark, even in the summer—or what passes for summer in the far north. Always, she wears thick wool socks. They keep her feet warm against the unyielding marble floor, but they muffle her footsteps so that she feels like a ghost drifting through the halls.

The house slides inexorably into grey with each passing year. Even the weak sunlight that slants through the clouded windows leaches color from the drapes and paintings, and dust clings to every surface like a lover. Leah ties a kerchief around her mass of black, tightly coiling hair and wields her feather duster with the exactness of a rapier, slicing through grime until color glows anew—though she is streaked in shades of ash. Late at night, when she washes away the dense layer of powder, she holds her breath until her bronze skin appears, shining under the water.

In her room, she lights candles—a small act of resistance, since her father has forbidden open flame inside the house. The candlesticks were retrieved quietly, one at a time, from her mother's room, until her father noticed the room's attrition of objects and locked the door. The writhing shapes are heavy with years of wax, their original designs long buried. Sometimes, Leah tries to guess what they have become, but the silhouettes change too quickly in the flickering candlelight for her to decide.

Sometimes, she lets the melting wax drip onto her hands, obscuring the fine tracery of scales that shimmers just beneath her skin.

The garden feels alive, though quiet, so quiet, next to the dead house. Nothing blooms. Buds remain pursed as lips over a secret before wilting, but the vines are green and thrum with life under Leah's fingers. Most of the trees are pines, tall and fragrant, and their needles whisper under her bare feet.

In the center of the garden, there is a tree that is different. The trunk, barely taller than she, is a faded grey, but the leaves are dark and glossy and flat. The branches are haunted by fruit that once grew there.

When Leah is seventeen, her father rouses himself from his study and returns with a bride.

Annabel's long golden hair falls past her knees, or it would if she did not braid it tightly and wrap it in a crown around her head. Her eyes are cornflowers in a face of ivory, set off by the yards of bright fabric that tumble from her shoulders to the floor. Her waist is cinched with a long leather strap, bifurcating her body with a narrow precision that mimics a winged insect, and Leah wonders how she bears it. Still, with her colorful silks and bee-waist, she looks like a garden, the kind that breathes and blooms in picture books and behind other people's gates.

Leah stands before her quietly, hands clasping and unclasping. She knows her hair is escaping from its scarf in wild curls and tufts, and her skin is mottled with dust.

"Kiss your stepmother hello, Leah," her father tells her. These are the first words he has spoken to her in a week.

"I'm dirty from the garden," she says, and her voice rasps faintly with disuse. "I'll hurt her gown."

Annabel holds out a hand, dainty in its white glove. "A little dirt never hurt anything." Carefully, Leah edges forward, lays her fingertips in Annabel's palm, and leaves brown smudges all along the lace. Closing her hand before her husband can see the damage, she says, "Do you have roses here?"

"No," Leah replies quietly, "nothing flowers here."

Annabel nods once before her husband takes her other hand and pulls her down the hall and behind his bedroom door.

Weeds have sprung up between the paving stones, and vines scale the stone walls that circle her tree. She pulls the weeds but lets the vines crawl where they will. When she turns back to the house, she sees Annabel's pale face in the window for a moment before her father's hand appears and pulls the curtains closed.

Leah's shoulder blades itch, and so do the backs of her hands. When the sun slants through the leaves overhead, her skin gleams greener than the filtered light and angular scrollwork unfurls down her fingers. She rolls her shoulders hard and sinks her hands wrist-deep into the soil, tiny roots curling round her fingers like rings.

Little changes in the house after Annabel's arrival. Leah carries on her losing battle with dust inside the house and her stalemate with weeds in the garden. But the air feels heavier, fuller, and she can feel the breath of a third person pull the tides in the air with the inevitability of a moon.

Sometimes, her father will bring her a garment—a thin nightdress or swishing petticoat—and tell her to mend it. The hems are tidy, even, and the pleats fall neatly, but they have long rents in the material around the waist. Leah mends them with even stiches in threads of marigold and rose, bright against the white fabric, and leaves them by the bedroom door. Twice, she knocks, but the room within is quiet.

One afternoon, her father hands her a delicate slip. When she unrolls it, the pale silk is mottled with dark brown smears and splotches. She sniffs it cautiously, inhales the metallic tang of copper. That evening, when she hears her father's tread in the study, she creeps to the bedroom door and tries the doorknob, but it is locked.

"Annabel?" she whispers through the keyhole.

A rustle, a light step, and cornflower blue blinks back through the crevice in the wood. "Go back to your room before he sees you," she whispers back.

"There was blood on your slip. You're locked in your room. How can I get you out?"

A dry laugh. "There is no 'out' for me."

"What do you mean? Why did you agree to come to this place and marry him?"

The silence within the room is heavier than the third night of a wake.

"Father, I need your keys. There are locked rooms that haven't been cleaned in years. And I thought perhaps Annabel might like some things from Mother's room."

Her father almost looks at her over the top of his paper, but his eyes skitter away from her face and back to the curtailed grids and numbers in black and white that march across the page.

"What's locked should remain locked. Remember that, Leah."

"I'm out of thread for mending. I know where Mother's sewing box is, and I could use it to fix Annabel's slip."

A measured pause, while Leah fights not to itch her arms, clasping her hands behind her back. Her nails lengthen, bite into her palms for a moment before receding. Then her father pulls the massive ring of keys from his pocket and drops it on his desk. "Bring it back to me this evening. And, Leah, I will know if any keys are missing."

She nods and hooks the ring onto her belt. The ring, thick with keys, bites into her waist so that for a moment she, too, feels bifurcated, insect-like, under her father's gaze as his eyes finally rise to look at her. She takes slow, measured steps across the room and into the hall, then breaks and dashes for the garden, keys slamming into her thigh and ringing discordantly with each step.

She bursts through the door, gasping in the cold air, and quiets the keys under her palm. She has to decide what to do, and quickly. There are locksmiths, she knows—she has read about them in books—but she does not know how to find one, and she has no way to pay. She could go upstairs now, unlock the door, and hope that they could run fast enough. Turning to look at the window, she sees her stepmother's face for an instant before her father appears beside her, his fingers curling on her shoulder.

Leah shudders and looks away, pushing deeper into the garden. When she reaches her tree, she kneels in the dirt near its base and presses her forehead against the bark. With her eyes closed, she can pretend that it is her mother's knees she is leaning against, her fingers moving through her hair instead of the wind. The flat, glossy leaves above her head rustle, and one falls, brushing against her cheek before landing on the back of her hand.

"*Bury it.*" The words caress the back of her neck.

Leah's head jerks, her eyes open and wild. "What?" The garden is empty and utterly silent, the wind stilled. After a long moment, the leaves rustle again in the dead air.

"*Bury it.*" The voice is a low, sibilant hush, lingering in her ear. Her skin prickles furiously, and she sinks her nails in her arms until blood wells in tiny crescents.

"Bury what?" she whispers.

"*The key.*"

Leah looks down at the ring on her belt, and one key flashes gold in the low afternoon light. When she grasps it between her fingers, it feels warm, as if it has been lying in the sun, absorbing heat for hours. She pulls it off the ring, and digs into the soil. The roots part under her fingers, drawing delicately away and reforming into a shallow, textured basin. Leah drops the key into the little hollow and smooths dirt over it before rushing back into the house.

As she goes about her chores—unlocking, polishing, collecting, relocking—she listens for the leaf-voice, even though she instinctively knows that it can only be heard in the garden. Still, she lingers in her mother's room after she has shaken the dust from the curtains and wiped down the wooden surfaces and the floor. When she picks up the bag she has filled with throws and dresses for Annabel, she turns for one last look at the room and sees a small box on the vanity—a box that hadn't been there when she had polished the other trinkets on the counter.

She walks to the vanity and examines the case, which is made from a smooth dull wood that retains a familiar fragrance. When she opens the box, she finds a nest of velvet ribbon with something small and brilliant gleaming underneath. The ribbon unwinds to reveal a round, faceted garnet the size of her thumbnail. Tiny golden leaves sprout from the top. She wants to put it in her mouth and let it burst on her tongue, but instead she drops the ribbon over head and tucks the jewel beneath the front of her dress. When she crosses to the door, she stops for a moment, tracing the splintered grooves gouged into the wood. Her fingers fit into the marks, too deep for human nails to carve.

She returns to the tree at dusk, just before her father returns to his study, and begins to dig. In the little root hollow, she finds the golden key that she buried hours before. When she lifts it from the root-basin, she sees a second key beneath. Instead of gold metal, it is the smooth, grey wood of the tree, of the jewelry box.

When she returns the key ring to her father, he lets the bits of metal trickle through his fingers like water before pausing on the key to his bedroom door. He taps it gently against his desk and watches packed earth fall from the grooves and notches in the gold.

"The key is dirty," he observes mildly.

"The house is dirty. The garden is dirty." She raises her chin slightly, gestures at her grime-streaked cheeks and blackened fingernails. "And I'm always dirty from trying to keep things in order."

Her father leans back in her chair, still tapping the key on the desk. Leah's blood pounds in time with the sound.

"Perhaps it's time we had help around the house. I will never find a man who will agree to marry you in this state."

Leah hides her balled fists in the folds of her skirt and thinks of the school she had briefly attended as a child, the pictures of taverns and other people's gardens she sees in the books she took from her mother's room. She is not afraid of work, but inertia and habit have made her wary of the world beyond the garden. Still, she is more afraid of the locked doors, and for Annabel behind them.

"If I could go out again, meet people, perhaps I would meet someone," she ventured.

"It would not be appropriate without a chaperone."

"Would not my stepmother be a suitable chaperone?" she says, her eyes wide and guileless.

"Your stepmother is much occupied at present."

Leah presses her tongue against the roof of her mouth and waits.

"The prince is hosting a ball in a few days. Perhaps, if I hired..." he trails off, still tapping. "No. Too big, too much spectacle. It would be overwhelming for a recluse like you."

"I would like to see a ball."

He shakes his head and, finally, drops the keys. They land with a splintered chime on the desk. "You don't know how to waltz or hold of flute of champagne. You don't know how to talk to strangers or how to pin your hair. It would be a disaster."

"Annabel could help me."

Her father sweeps the keys into his pocket. "No. She cannot."

Three days later, her father puts on his finest suit, emeralds at his wrists and silk at his throat. He saddles their only horse and rides in the direction of the castle, keys jangling in his pocket. Leah watches him depart through her bedroom window, and when he vanishes around the bend in the road, she races through the halls, woolen socks sliding recklessly on marble, and slips her wooden key into the lock.

Annabel is in a chair by the window, the stub of a pencil in her hand. The corner of a piece of paper is just visible beneath a heap of fabric. She is thinner, and there are blue marks around her wrists and at her throat, dull lapis to her husband's shining emeralds, but her hair is neatly braided, and her back is straight. When she sees Leah in the doorway, she releases a breath and leans back in her chair.

"It's you. I was afraid I was going to lose my paper again. Richard says too much stimulation *unsettles a woman's mind*." She shoves the bundle of fabric away, revealing a graceful sketch of the garden. Leah's tree is in the center, rendered in careful detail, but there are round shapes hanging from the branches, shapes that echo her dreams and the charm around her neck.

"What are those?" she asks, forgetting the ball, her father, everything else.

Annabel blinks at her. "Pomegranates, of course. I thought you knew—it seems to be your favorite tree."

"I told you—nothing blooms here. There have not been flowers or fruits in the trees since my mother died."

"You look nothing like Richard," she says lightly. "You must take after her."

Leah thinks of her filthy hands and feet, her unwashed hair in a coil under her scarf. "No. My mother was beautiful."

"As are you." She watches Leah brush at the dust and ashes on her arms. "Remember, I said a little dirt hurts nothing. It helps things grow."

"There is a ball tonight," Leah blurts. "I don't know how the world works, but I know how balls are supposed to end. We could go, maybe find help." Her hands stilled. "At the very least, we could see something alive, something that blooms."

Annabel shook her head. "Balls are beautiful, but they can be dangerous. Where do you think I met your father? Well, where my father met your father. It was love at first sight—matching cufflinks, matching ideas about my future."

"Please come with me. I don't know how to do this alone."

Annabel tries to stand, but her leg buckles. She sighs and lifts her skirt, revealing a tattered piece of fabric wrapped round and round her calf and knee. "I cannot, but you can. And I'll show you how. Bring me your sewing kit."

"I thought you couldn't sew—that's why Father brought me your things to mend."

"No," she says gently. "I am very deft with a needle. Which is why Richard took mine away after I stabbed him with it."

Leah retrieves her kit and retreats into Annabel's bathroom, where a hot bath is waiting for her.

"Use the soap in the red bottle," Annabel says through the door. "I'll have a dress ready for you when you are done."

As Leah scrubs her skin and hair with the soap that smells of roses and citrus, Annabel tells her the names and titles she will hear and how deeply to bob her head or curtsey for each one. She tells her what sounds to listen for—the bright, brassy sound of trumpets and the chime of spoons on glasses. In case of dancing, she says to follow her partner and to move her feet in a square and, in case of drinking, to hold the flute between her thumb and first three fingers.

When Leah steps from the tub, Annabel hands her a dress around the door. Leah recognizes it, a bright, crimson silk of her mother's that she had brought Annabel a few days before. But now threads of burnt orange, fuchsia, and persimmon shimmer at the waist, cinching tight before bursting across the skirt in a kaleidoscope of scrolling scales and feathers.

"How?" Leah breathes, stroking the tiny stitches.

A silence behind the door. "It's a…talent. One that earned my family's fortune before my father tired of my small rebellions and sold me to the highest bidder. Your father planned to use it, I think, before he saw me and decided I had other uses."

Leah slips the fabric over her head and went back into the bedroom. "My mother had talents, too. She made things grow. And change."

"Many of us do."

"But she couldn't live here. I think this place and my father...she was from the South, and the cold inside this house killed her."

"Which is why we are getting you out. Sit." Annabel gestures to the chair and carefully works a comb through the snarled curls before twisting them into braids and weaving them round her head in a crown. "I wish I had shoes to give you, but I'm afraid mine are too big." Her fingers move to the ribbon around Leah's neck, knotting it deftly so the pomegranate hangs in the hollow of her throat.

Leah rises and takes her hand. "I think I know what to do."

They take the stairs slowly, Annabel hanging on Leah's arm, her gait uneven. Out the back door and through the garden and to the pomegranate tree they walk, the girl in crimson and the girl in white. At the base of the tree is a pair of shoes—crimson leather with wooden heels that twist daringly, like the tail of a snake. Beside them is a compress that smells faintly of roses and the bark of the tree. Leah slides her feet into the shoes, and Annabel slips the compress under the bandage around her knee.

"Leah," her stepmother says, "if you get the chance, if you find help, a stray horse, anything...run. Don't come back here."

Leah shakes her head, her braids trembling. "I am not leaving you here. I'll come back for you." She presses the wooden key into her hand. "I'll be back soon. Use this to lock yourself back in. Or out."

The strange heels add a spring to her gait that eats at the distance to the palace. She arrives at the gate in a matter of a few moments, a few steps.

Torches line the path and spark along the tops of the walls. Surreptitiously, she dips her fingers into the first flame as she walks past—they feel warm for the first time in months. Through the main doors, up a long corridor, and down the stairs—she dodges the man with the starched shirt and long list of names, as Annabel told her to do—but she can not stop the trumpets sounding and the drums beating as she descends the stairs. She tucks her head low so that her father will not recognize her if his is one of the faces turning towards her in the crowd.

When she reaches the bottom, a man is waiting for her. He has dark eyes, like her mother's, and Annabel's fair hair, but his hands are long and graceful and entirely his own, with scars on his fingers and a trace of dirt under his nails. He is beautiful. He doesn't offer his name, so she dips a low curtsey, grateful her skirts cover her feet.

He bows with the lithe elegance of a fencer. "Dance with me?" he asks, holding out a hand.

She does. She trips a few times, but he shows her how to loop the hem of her skirt in her palm, how to follow his feet in a square, and then other more elaborate patterns. She finds herself laughing as she turns and turns in his arms. After a time, they pause, and he brings her a small flute of champagne, which she holds carefully between thumb and fingers. It sparkles in her throat, unlike anything she has tasted before. When they return to the dance floor, she stops thinking about her feet, stops thinking about the cold house and locked doors. Faster and faster they dance, until she is not sure if she is touching the floor or dancing above it.

When the music pauses, he asks, "Can I show you something? In the garden?" His hand on hers is gentle and tentative, ready to let go should she pull back.

She tightens her fingers around his. "Yes."

He leads her through the crowded room and down another long hall before slipping through a side door. The garden is alive with a thousand different scents, a thousand open blooms waiting in the still night air. "What's your name?" he asks as they walk into the garden.

"Leah. Leah Glass. What is yours?"

"Henry, I'm afraid. There was no getting round it."

"Why not?" she asks, pausing briefly to caress the petals of a massive white and pink blossom.

"Seeing as the last eleven kings have had it, I suppose my parents felt compelled to make it an even dozen."

"So *you* are the prince," she says. "In that case, I need to ask for your help."

The path swerves, and they enter a small orchard. "What can I..." he trails off, smiling, when Leah drops his hand and runs to the nearest tree.

"Pomegranates!"

"I thought you might like them, judging by your necklace."

"I've never seen a real one before." She thinks of her mother, of Annabel standing still beneath her tiny tree, and she swallows hard.

Henry pulls a pomegranate, red, ripe, heavy, from a branch overhead and opens it like a jewelry box between his long fingers. He offers her the two halves, gleaming garnet-bright. She pulls a seed from its cluster and places it on her tongue. The taste is everything she remembers from her dreams, made sweeter still by the smile in Henry's eyes.

"Thank you," she says. "I—"

"*Leah.*"

Her voice dies in her throat as she sees her father appear over Henry's shoulder. He looms huge in the moonlight, and his booted feet crush flowers with each slow step.

No. He has taken too much from her already. He will not take this, too. Her arms do not itch—they *burn*—as scales slide through her skin and fur rolls up her neck and cheeks,

"Leah!" It is Henry now, his hands on her arms, slipping, losing traction on the dark scales, but he does not back away even as she feels her teeth lengthen past her lips.

"*Leah.*" Her father is close now, close enough for her to see the disgust twisting his lips. "Just like your mother," he says, and she sees something sharp and bright in his hand. He turns his wrist, and light slides along the blade. She looks at Henry, kicks off her shoes, and throws one, heel first, at her father. She hears a hiss and a howl of pain as serpentine teeth slid home in his flesh. Then she turns and runs as the clock in the great hall begins to chime.

Leah runs on legs that bunch and then lengthen. When her gait becomes unsteady, she drops to all fours. The ribbon tightens as her neck expands and thickens with muscle, but Annabel's knots come loose, and the garnet swings easily against her fur. Her vision sharpens until her eyes cut through the night with perfect clarity, and her center of gravity lowers as she feels her tailbone extend and hit the ground. She picks up speed, feeling once more the grace and speed that was hers on the dance floor, but without the assurance of Henry's arm or the delicious blankness of thought. Instead, her mind churns— Did Henry have a way to defend himself from the knife in her father's hand? Did he get away? Was her father behind her? What would happen to Annabel, with her swollen knee and bruises, when her father arrived home?—and she demands more speed from her hybrid body, more power from her twisting tail and cloven hooves.

The journey is longer without the crimson shoes. When she reaches the garden wall, she leaps over it and canters towards her mother's tree. Annabel is asleep among the roots, her hair freed from its braid and tangling with leaves.

Leah pounds the ground with her hooves and roars.

Annabel is moving before her eyes open, scrambling back against the trunk of the tree, her mouth opening to scream. Then her gaze fixes on the pomegranate glistening on Leah's fur, and her mouth closes, reshapes around her name.

"Leah?"

Leah steps closer and nudges her stepmother's shoulder with her head. Annabel closes a hand in her fur.

"Lock up something long enough, and it doesn't know how to leave," says a voice behind them. Leah whirls, tripping over her serpentine tail, but her hooves bite into the earth and keep her standing. "Your mother never left this house after I found out. Once I realized what she was, a monster, a *chimera*, how could I let her?" He appears from behind the tree, the knife still in his fist. "Your magic seemed small enough," he spits at Annabel, before returning his gaze to Leah, "but *you*. I had hoped you had not inherited her sickness, or that I could at least pass you off before it became apparent." He takes a step closer, and Leah herds Annabel behind her. "But now there is nothing to be done. It is time for you to join your mother."

Another step, and he lunges.

"*Breathe*," says the leaf-voice, branches shivering in the still air.

This time, Leah does not hesitate. Her breath rushes from her chest with all the heat she has been denied, all the rage of enclosure, all the joy of her small rebellions with her stepmother and her dances with the prince. She breathes with her mother, and flame pours from her throat and envelops her father like a luxurious coat. For a moment, he is lit, incandescent, and then he is nothing but ashes beneath a tree heavy with fruit.

When Henry arrives at the front door an hour later, crimson shoe in hand, he finds two women, cinder-shod and smiling, lighting fires in every hearth in the house.

I is for Ignite

Megan Engelhardt

Back in the days when grass was tall and plentiful and the stars shone clean and piercing among the white-black swirling skunk hide sky, things were different. There were giants in those days, trees and men and animals that towered over their peers, casting long, long shadows over the world. Eyota was taller and wiser than all other villagers, was mother to man and animal alike, and held the respect of every creature. Hoddmimi groves reached higher toward the sky than any other tree, sheltering and shadowing other plants under its branches. And there was the sasquatch, not quite man and not quite beast and taller than all around. The sasquatch was between worlds, and it was large, and it was a danger for the other animals to find themselves defenseless in the face of the sasquatch's easily roused anger.

Now Jackrabbit was not a giant, for all that he was larger than the other rabbits. His ears were long and his hind feet were long and he cast a long shadow in the afternoon sun, but speed was his gift and prescience his blessing. Those who set out to harm him all too often found themselves just where he was not.

But sasquatch could move silently through the woods, so silently that long ears could not hear it, and it possessed a quickness belied by its size. Jackrabbit knew it would be hard going for him if sasquatch ever turned its anger on him so one day he began to look for ways to defend himself.

Jackrabbit sat in the mouth of his burrow and considered Turtle. Turtle carried armor, hard shell grown all around her, easy to move in and good for hiding. When danger threatened, Turtle just waited until it went away. That seemed good to Jackrabbit, and so he began to make himself some armor. He worked in secret, so no one would know what he was doing. He kept so secret and solitary as he worked that the only witness was a tumbleweed.

Now in those days the tumbleweeds were everywhere. They rolled from place to place, picking up dust and branches and secrets. Prickly things, the tumbleweeds took what they wanted and deposited what they were done with, dust and branches and secrets left scattered behind.

This tumbleweed, full of thorns and red clay dirt and things that were better left untold, let the wind blow it past the river, across the hills and into the shade of the hoddmimi grove. There the sasquatch gathered to hunt and mate and call to each other in long, haunting whoops and yelps that echoed for miles.

One sasquatch, gray-backed and long-toothed, picked up the tumbleweed and shook it—tossed and tickled and twisted it, until it dropped all it had been hiding. Among the shower of dust and branches Jackrabbit's secret came tumbling out.

Now, this sasquatch had never hunted Jackrabbit. He had never been outwitted by Jackrabbit's long ears and wily ways, he had never been outraced by Jackrabbit's long legs, but Jackrabbit's secret made him angry. The gray-back sasquatch thought he was very clever, and if Jackrabbit thought he could trick the sasquatch by pretending to be another creature, he would soon prove him wrong.

Jackrabbit worked night and day on his armor, weaving together twigs, spreading pebble-specked mud and drying everything in the sun until the armor was baked hard. Jackrabbit slipped into the armor and hopped down to the river to see how he looked in his new shell.

And my, didn't he look fine in the mud brown rock-daubed shell all around his middle. Even Frog took note.

"What are you wearing, Jackrabbit?" Frog asked, plopping out of the water for a closer look.

"I am not Jackrabbit," Jackrabbit crowed. "I am Jackturtle, and this is my shell."

"What is it for?" Frog asked.

"It will protect me from the sasquatch if that old beast ever comes looking for me," said Jackturtle.

"I hope you are right," Frog said, and plopped back into the water as a huge shadow fell over the two animals. Jackturtle looked up—and up—and saw the gray-backed sasquatch reaching for him. Jackturtle tried to run but his shell got in the way, and that sasquatch grabbed him by the mud shell and hauled him into the air.

"I have you, little Jackrabbit," growled the sasquatch.

"He is not Jackrabbit. He is Jackturtle," said Frog from the safety of the river.

"This is not a turtle," said the sasquatch, reaching to pull Jackrabbit out of the shell by his long ears. But Jackrabbit had slipped right out of his Jackturtle shell and ran as fast as his long legs could, leaving the sasquatch behind with just an empty mud shell.

Jackrabbit ran and ran, far away from the river, into the rolling hills where the grass grew tall and danced in the wisping, whirling wind under the bright firefly stars. He rested in a hollow, a little valley between hills, and watched the dancing grass tickle across the sky while he considered. The shell worked for Turtle, but clearly it would not work for Jackrabbit. He would have to think of something else.

Jackrabbit slept in the hollow, long ears perked to hear any enemies, long legs tight against the ground ready to run. In the honey warm early morning sun, Jackrabbit nibbled on green plants hid among the grass and considered Porcupine. Porcupine had quills all along his body, sharp prickles that warned enemies away. If they didn't listen, if they came closer, Porcupine could throw the quills and stab his enemies with the sharp points. That seemed good to Jackrabbit, and so he began to make himself some quills. He worked in secret, so no one would know what he was doing. He kept so secret and solitary as he worked that the only witness was a tumbleweed.

Now in those days the tumbleweeds liked to cause trouble. Talk was everywhere about the gray-backed long-toothed sasquatch who was hunting for Jackrabbit. This tumbleweed, carrying fallen seeds and broken grasses and Jackrabbit's secret, rolled across the hills and down to the river where the sasquatch gabbled and grunted and growled in his rage. The sasquatch was angry that Jackrabbit had escaped, and was determined to catch him this time, quills or no. Jackrabbit had slipped away once, but he would not do it again.

Jackrabbit worked night and day on his quills, sharpening twigs and sticking them into his fur with sticky burs. He swayed back and forth and was pleased to hear the same clattering clack-clack that followed Porcupine everywhere. And my, didn't he feel fine in his sharp new coat of sharp stick quills. Even Crow took note.

"What are you wearing, Jackrabbit?" Crow asked, fluttering down to the dust for a closer look.

"I am not Jackrabbit," Jackrabbit said, "I am Jackupine, and these are my quills."

"Are they to protect you from the sasquatch?" Crow asked.

"They are," said Jackupine, and clattered his stick quills proudly.

"Do you think they will work?" Crow asked.

"Of course they will," said Jackupine.

A tumbleweed rolled past and Crow fluttered back to the sky.

"Good luck," he cawed, "and watch out for the tumbleweeds!"

"Tumbleweeds will not hurt me," Jackupine called back, and went on his way, stick quills clattering loudly with every hop-lope. Jackupine was very proud of his stick quills, and loved to hear them clatter as he went. But Jackupine had forgotten that the sasquatch can be quiet, so he was very surprised when a large, hairy hand grabbed him by his long ears and pulled him up, face to face with the long-toothed sasquatch.

"I have you, little Jackrabbit," said the sasquatch.

"Watch out! I am a Jackupine and I will stick you with my quills if you do not let me down," said Jackupine, but when he shivered and shook his body he did not hear the clatter clack. He looked around and saw that all the sticky burr stick quills had been shaken from his fur.

"You are not a porcupine," said the sasquatch, pulling Jackrabbit closer for a better look, just to be sure. Jackrabbit kicked with his powerful long legs and hit the sasquatch in his broad face. The sasquatch let go of Jackrabbit's ears to clutch at his bleeding nose and Jackrabbit took off, gone away down the hills and into the woods.

Jackrabbit ran and ran, deep into the woods, close to where the villagers lived, knowing that the sasquatch would be right behind. It grew dark, and through the trees Jackrabbit saw a red orange flicker among the tall trunks and spreading branches—fire. He knew that the sasquatch did not like fire, for fire often meant men. Jackrabbit did not much like fire (or men) either, but he liked them better than he liked the sasquatch, so he hopped closer to the fire until he saw that there was no one around. Someone may return later, but for now Jackrabbbit decided he would sit by the fire and rest, for he was truly so tired he could not run any longer.

Jackrabbit nibbled on some grass beside the fire and considered other animals. A shell like Turtle's had not worked. Sharp quills like Porcupine's had not worked. Maybe he could try wings, like Crow, or learn to sink into mud like Frog. Or maybe, he thought, watching a tumbleweed roll past the fire, he would just curl up and roll away forever and become a tumbleweed himself.

Suddenly Jackrabbit remembered what Crow had said about the tumbleweeds. He realized that the tumbleweeds, gossips and troublemakers, were telling the old sasquatch where he was and what he was doing.

"This will not do," he said, and kicked out with his long, powerful legs and thrust that tumbleweed right into the fire. He did the same with the next, and the next, and by the time the tumbleweeds learned their lesson and started keeping away from Jackrabbit, the fire in the clearing blazed bright and sent dancing shadows out among the trees.

But the sasquatch had already spotted Jackrabbit's trail and followed him into the deep woods. That sasquatch was quiet as the wind, and no man and few creatures would have heard the faint breaking of twigs under foot or rustling of branches brushed aside. Jackrabbit, though, had long ears and a good reason to be alert. He heard the sasquatch coming.

Jackrabbit sat frozen and considered his predicament. His shell hadn't worked, and his quills hadn't worked. His long legs were too tired to run, and all his long ears were good for were so he could hear his doom approaching.

Jackrabbit thought and thought as the footsteps of the sasquatch grew closer and closer. Then he saw some sticks, and a hollow log, and he had an idea.

When the gray-backed sasquatch approached the clearing, he saw a huge fire, cracking and snapping with dust and branches and secrets. He saw shadows, dancing among the trees, some small, some large, and one very large. The very large shadow was as tall as the sasquatch or taller, had long ears and large many-pointed antlers. And it spoke.

"Beware the Jackalope," it said.

"I know of no Jackalope," the sasquatch said. "I see no Jackalope. All I see is a shadow."

"You do not see my long legs that can kick so hard they break bones?" bellowed the shadow. And sure enough, there was the shadow of a long leg cast black and menacing among the trees.

"You do not see my large antlers that stab and pierce the toughest hide?" And sure enough, there were large antlers, points sharply menacing even in shadow.

"You do not see my long ears that will hear you wherever you go so I may hunt you down and stab you and kick you, so I may break your bones and pierce your hide until you are no more?" And sure enough, there were long ears, nearly as sharp and menacing as the antlers, rising up from a long shadow that grew longer and larger as the flames crackled and popped.

Now the sasquatch thought it was clever, but it was not. It was, however, smart enough to know when to be brave and when to retreat. That is how it had grown to be old and gray-backed and long-toothed. There is strength in courage but there is also strength in knowing which battles to fight and the sasquatch, seeing the sharp shadow, hearing the booming voice, feeling the warmth of the hated fire on its hide, knew it was time to return home. It turned and left, determined to find the Jackrabbit another day, when strange fierce beasts were not wandering the woods.

Jackrabbit heard the sasquatch go and put down the hollow log he had been speaking into. He moved his head and saw the shadows reflect the sharp sticks he had bundled into the shape of antlers. He laughed, because he was proud.

"That was clever, little Jackrabbit."

Eyota, taller and wiser than all other villagers, mother to man and animal alike, stepped out of the woods and stood beside the fire. The flickering flames made her smile strange.

"Thank you, Eyota," said Jackrabbit.

"But why were you not content with your long ears and your long legs?"

"I was afraid," Jackrabbit admitted, for none could speak falsehood to Eyota. "And I was jealous of the other animals who had more protection."

"Silly little Jackrabbit," said Eyota, "you had all the protection you needed in your speed and prescience. It was when you became discontent that your troubles began."

Jackrabbit was shamed, knowing that what Eyota said was right. The sasquatch had not bothered him until he began making his shell, and when his long ears and long legs would have saved him, his mud shell and stick quills had gotten in the way.

"Still," said Eyota, "those antlers do suit you. Here then, little Jackrabbit, is my judgment. As a punishment for your discontent, the sasquatch will always hunt you, wherever you go. As a gift for your cleverness, you may keep your antlers."

Eyota bent down and touched Jackrabbit on the head. His stick antlers burrowed between his ears, grew heavy and strong, and stood sharp and proud, real antlers with which to defend himself.

"Are you rested, little Jackalope?" Eyota asked. Her smile, no longer strange, was amused and pleased as she looked down at her newest creation.

"Oh, yes, Eyota, thank you," said Jackalope, and it was true. His long legs felt strong and powerful, ready to run for miles and miles. His long ears twitched, catching every sound from the whine of a mosquito to the distant stars chiming in the sky.

"Then run, little Jackalope," said Eyota.

And Jackalope ran, out of the forest, over the hills, bounding over the river. He ran and ran, and his antlered shadow in the moonlight was strong and proud and just right.

J is for Jackalope

Michael Fosburg

The Maw

Jacob took the rain-slick stairs down into Kadal Station. Lighting snaked across the sky, illuminating ragged clouds and distant curtains of storm. Magelight cast a watery glow across the nearly-empty terminal, giving the scene a fathoms-beneath-the-sea feeling. The man in the booth who sold Jacob his ticket could've been a waterlogged corpse in a sunken gibbet for all the life he showed. His eyes were craters filled in with night, his skin clammy white.

Behind Jacob, the steam engine known throughout the land as the Beast pulled into the station in an earsplitting haze. Its whistle, sharper than a trapped animal's howl, cut through the thumping of pistons and venting steam. Porters clad in liver-colored robes disembarked from carriages to stand before the doors, staves held out before them.

He looked from the ticket in his hand to the restlessly idling engine.

What if... he thought, his mind leading him to drink from a poisoned trough for the thousandth time. *What if I go back to Khara, one last time? Beg on my knees for her forgiveness, for her love—perhaps if we spent some time in the country, mended fences...*

But the country was already curling at the edges with the Blight, and Khara was done with him. Had been done with him since Jonboy died. If Jacob's mind was slow to catch on, his heart was ahead of the curve. There was nothing of his old life left—not even the gardens that were his life's great joy and work. Those too had been caressed by the inexorable gray that crept across the land. And as a dying man's limbs will grow cold and gray before the heart finally seizes, the Kingdom carried blithely on, ignoring its dying hinterlands with decadent unconcern.

He travelled light: two changes of clothes, a few vials of fungicide, and his last specimens of Blight. These he stored in wax-sealed glass jars swaddled in silk. There was little else to bring.

His hand tightened on the ticket.

Waiting to board, Jacob found his eyes drawn to the curves of the Beast's chassis, which shone verdantly beneath the magelight. It had an almost chitinous flair, reminiscent of the carapaces of the beetles he'd see about his now-Blighted gardens. The frame stood a monstrous ten span high from wheels to roof. Once, while idling away a holiday at his family's cottage on the Shellstrewn Shore, he and Jonboy had come upon a beached whale dying under the summer sun. The creature's rubbery skin was cracked and oozing, its great eyes clouded over, and yet the sheer immensity of the thing had still radiated awful, primal power. Jacob felt that now, standing before the rumbling steam engine. It was foolish to feel so awed by a machine. But he eyed the Beast uneasily all the same.

A lad who looked about Jonboy's age was hopping and jumping impatiently in the next line over. Perhaps sensing his stare, he glanced at Jacob and grinned widely. It was a look that promised adventure and trouble and an endless sunny summer far and away from heartache. It was Jonboy's grin. A lump rose in Jacob's throat. He swallowed it down and tried to return a smile despite the sadness and guilt that whipped at his exposed soul like cat o' nine tails. A tall man who seemed to be the boy's chaperone stared at Jacob. He could've been the brother of the ticket seller, wrapped as he was in pale skin which just barely covered his bones. He smiled with lips that had too much flesh relative to the rest of his body, and then the Beast's piercing whistle called its scant passengers to board.

Jacob spared one last glance at the lad as the tall man—his father or uncle, surely—led him away through the swirling curtain of steam and smoke.

The Belly

He boarded, melancholy smothering him like a damp shroud. Porters slammed shut the doors and disappeared into compartments at the head of each carriage, and then the Beast leapt forward, nearly knocking Jacob over as it caught its speed without the gradual building of momentum he'd been expecting. The whistle shrieked and the Beast surged again, and this time Jacob *did* fall, his feet tangling beneath him, arms pinwheeling for balance. His head struck a seat on the way down, and the world flared red then fizzled to black.

When he came to he was seated by a window, the Croagh River flashing by, its inky skin filmed sporadically with lightning. Kadal Station had dwindled to a vague smudge of magelight to the south. Across the aisle from Jacob sat a bespectacled young man with thinning red hair and a scholar's gray frock, who was looking at him nervously. Jacob groaned and rubbed his head, and the young man let out a relived breath.

"Thank gods," he said. "I really didn't want to sit next to a corpse until New Razen."

Jacob winced as the fingers exploring the back of his head came away red. He would have a knot there soon enough.

"Varish," the scholar said, retracting his outstretched hand when he saw the blood and pivoting the gesture into a halfhearted wave. "I picked you up when you knocked your head. People aren't prepared for the acceleration. A wondrous fast thing, this," he said, gesturing expansively to the Beast.

"That it is," Jacob said, and introduced himself. He looked around. The carriage was nearly empty.

"Is the Blight truly as bad as they say?" Varish asked, peering at him owlishly from behind his spectacles. "We hear rumors that it can't be stopped."

"It's cancer in the land," Jacob said, and reached into his bag to reassure himself the seals of the jars had not been broken. The young scholar shifted in his seat uncomfortably.

The moment was smoothed over by the arrival of a young woman wearing a dark brocaded coat cut in a fashion that Jacob hadn't seen about the Kingdom. She took a seat across from the scholar, resting her knee-high black boots on the empty seat beside him.

"You both look as though someone killed your dogs," she said, biting into an apple.

The scholar offered the laugh of a man overeager to please. Jacob's smile was polite and thin. His head throbbed and he closed his eyes as a dizzy spell dropped his skull into his feet.

"This is Carmine. Carmine, meet Jacob." Varish straightened his shoulders and puffed out his chest, looking from the woman to Jacob, who could tell this sort of introduction was a novelty for the lad. Beautiful women didn't make a habit of courting Mice, as gray-clad scholars were often called.

And she *was* beautiful, in an indirect sort of way. She had skin pale as cream but marred in places by dark, chevron-shaped birthmarks. Ebon hair fell in artless curls past her shoulders. Her eyes were the verdant green of spring's first rain-fed shoots.

"We met at DuCorte Station," she said. Her smile was wide and just a bit wicked. "I bumped into poor Varish and made him drop his books."

"It was really quite a scene," Varish said.

"Most academics treat their dusty old tomes like children. It was so refreshing to meet a man who didn't come apart at the sight of a dropped treatise on Skivaldric funeral dirges, or whatever it is you study."

"Cryptodemonology," Varish said.

A crooked finger of lightning jabbed the earth. The windows blazed with purple-white light and thunder split the night like a titanic axe. The scholar jumped in his seat, and the woman laughed.

"So you're a summoner of ancient spirits, then?" She asked playfully.

"Invocation is *strictly* forbidden," Varish said, grinning boyishly and waggling a stubby finger. "I dabble. It's all very *hush hush* at the Academy, you know."

Carmine smiled and turned to Jacob. "And what is it that *you* do? And where are you bound on so strange a mount as this?"

"Stragnos—end of the line." And remembering her first question: "I was...I *am*, rather, a botanist. I've been working on a counter to the Blight, but my efforts...well. They haven't been met with success."

Carmine made an impressed noise that might have been artfully masked boredom.

"And you?" Jacob asked.

Carmine tipped her head toward the scholar. "As I told Varish here, I'm a traveler. I study the world, and my lectern is the road beneath my feet." She clicked the worn-down heels of her boots together. "I've seen all I cared to of the Kingdom, so I figured I'd shoot north and see where I land."

Jacob nodded. Those were the bones of his plan as well. Perhaps there were answers there that he had overlooked in the Kingdom—

different species of toadstool to study, possible weaknesses to exploit...

The dry whisper of flesh made other as Blight filled every pore, spores exploding from Jonboy's transformed flesh in wheezing bursts—

The memory cleaved Jacob like a bolt of lightning through a dead tree, demarking life as it had been—a happy, humdrum existence with wife and child and teeming green gardens—and as it was now. And what did he have now, truly? A seat on a monstrous steam engine, a bag filled with death, and a heart much the same.

Carmine's hand rested lightly on the scholar's robed knee, but her eyes were for Jacob, regarding him with something that resembled concern but felt like something else entirely. Varish seemed aware only of the small, pale hand inching up the gray slope of his leg.

Jacob looked away. The land sped by in a dark blur.

The Heart

He dozed. And dreamed.

He stumbled through a forest overtaken by Blight where unspeakable things grew tall and glowed faintly in the spore-obscured twilight. From somewhere close by came sounds of choking and thrashing. Sounds—to Jacob's ears—like the Blight at the terminal phase of its fruiting. Sounds that forced thoughts of Jonboy into his mind.

Jacob shut his eyes and willed it away, and eventually the sound faded, and the thick, swampy air was still again.

The ground was soft with rot. He sank up to his knees in foulness with each step.

He labored to reach the tree at the end of the path, driven by the obscure motivations of the dream, and when he looked down he saw gray nodules bursting from his skin, but still he struggled through the sucking rot even as his body was sloughing apart and exploding into the air, and when he came to the tree he saw it was not a tree at all but a monstrous toadstool, mottled and bloated and ribbed with gills that dripped viscous gray fluid, and when he thrust his hands into its putrid flesh his hands alit upon a body that he feared would be Jonboy's, but still he plunged into that horrid flesh, searching desperately, deeper—

He woke with a scream caught in his throat, his cramped body bathed in cold sweat. The carriage was empty except for the woman in the seat beside him. Carmine watched him from over the rim of a thick book.

"You were struggling in your sleep," she said, shutting the book. Dust erupted from its pages in such a way that brought Jacob back to his dream, to spores expelled from collapsing flesh.

"Where's...ah—where's Varish?" He asked, forgetting the scholar's name in his post-sleep fugue. The knot on his head throbbed with each anxious heartbeat.

"He departed at Queensroad Station while you slept. He charged me to give you his warm regards when you woke," she said, smiling.

"I thought his stop was New Razen." Carmine shrugged. "Who can truly know the mind of a scholar?"

Night still held the land, lit only occasionally by skeins of lightning. In those brief moments he saw that they had passed into lands lost to the Blight. Trees sagged beneath blankets of rot. The landscape lost its definition, was rendered a uniform, rolling gray.

"Wonderful, isn't it?" She asked, and seeing the look on his face, amended: "The Beast, that is." She ran her hand along the carriage wall as though stroking the flanks of hound. "Older than the Kingdom. The last great work of the Magi. And even now, in the midst of it, untouched by the Blight." Her eyes took in the soft vault of the carriage's ceiling. Jacob followed her gaze. Organic-looking struts flowed down to brace the carriage's sides at equidistant intervals. "If only the Magi could protect the land with the same passion they do their engine," Jacob said.

"Magic doesn't behave that way," she said, tracing the vein-like patterns on the wall with a lacquered fingernail. "To know something—to understand it down to its *essence*—is to gain mastery over it. Whether it's a flower," she said, and nodded to Jacob, "or a bolt of lightning. Or the storm that breeds the lighting. The Magi can no more control the Blight than they can the lightning, because they don't *understand* it. But they understand the *Beast*. And the Beast, Jacob, is older than nature." She stretched her long limbs. "There's no spell that wards away the Blight. The Blight *flees* before the Beast."

"How do you know this?" he asked.

"I read," Carmine said. She tossed him her book. Jacob scanned the cover: *Apocryphae of the Third Sumastrian Age: Fae, Beastes, & Demones High and Lowe.*

"This is one of Varish's books," Jacob said. Carmine shrugged. Her lips were very red. The strange, chevron-shaped birthmarks were no longer apparent on her milky skin. They were the barest suggestions of pigmentation, faded like ghosts of old wounds.

"So it is. He must've left it behind. He was quite the forgetful boy."

The atmosphere inside the carriage had become thick, swampy. It was an effect the Blight had on the air, Jacob knew, but it heightened the feeling of unreality that hemmed him in.

Dark needles of dream punctured his memory. A desultory flicker of lightning scattered across land and sky, and for a moment Jacob thought he saw the spire of a colossal toadstool towering in the distance. He remembered rot-moistened skin parting obscenely for his hands, the decaying *stink* of it. But now, in the matrix of mind where memory met dream, Jonboy's blue eyes peered out from the stem of the toadstool, his mouth wrenched down in a wordless howl of agony.

Jacob had told him a hundred times, a *thousand*, to stay away from the little shed at the northern edge of his gardens—had warned him every day of the dangers of meddling with anything that grew there. But Jonboy had his father's questioning nature and love for growing things, and the specimen of Blight Jacob had been studying for weaknesses—a tiny gray-capped toadstool encased in glass—had been left unattended as Jacob went to fetch a different mixture of fungicide.

If he had been thirty seconds sooner returning...

Jacob looked up with burningeyes. Carmine stared into them hungrily, longingly.

The Beast's whistle sounded in the depths of the night like the call of a creature searching the world for a counterpoint; the last of its kind, joined to the will of hungry men who understood and shared in the loss it felt.

Jacob would not remember the final leg of that journey. He would not remember passing beyond the Kingdom, leaving the lurching gray Blight behind. He would not remember glimpsing the pile of unclaimed books beneath Carmine's seat as he disembarked. He would not see the lad whose sunny grin had been so like Jonboy's, or remember his last vision of the lad—led away by the too-thin man into the boiling steam-and-smoke maw of the Beast, the engine restless on its haunches, trembling like a famished hound.

Transformation

They walked along the smooth stone of the Stragnos Way, the old road that wound a blue-black scar through green countryside. Carmine's voice unspooled on the buzzing spring air. It sounded half song, half whisper—a melody just below the electric hum of cicadas and the honeyed calls of birds. She wove a tale of grief and horror, elaborating on banishment to the Thin—that dark hollow between the worlds—and of return, aided by the stuttered summoning of one naïve, red-haired scholar.

And she spoke of hunger. Always the hunger.

"I sensed a companion in you," she said, brushing hair out of her eyes. "Your shadow is as dark as mine."

Jacob said nothing. He knew something about dark shadows, for the truth of it was, the Blight had been born in *his* gardens. He had bred down the most potent toadstools in all the land to better cultivate his soil—to enrich it and improve its clumpability—but soon discovered that this new species was something else entirely, an aggressive variant that shrugged off even the most potent of fungicides. It became his obsession to contain and control, and when it sprang into Jonboy's flesh a monstrous evolution was triggered, and then the land withered beneath it.

He felt despair gust through him. The task was too immense for him—his crimes were too great.

He had killed the land. Killed his *son*.

He felt Carmine's hand on his shoulder. Her green eyes stared levelly into his. One of his jars of Blight in her hand.

"To know a thing—to *truly* understand something, down to its *essence...*" She stripped away the wax seal with a slash of her lacquered fingernails.

Is to master *it*.

Her unsmiling lips did not part for word or breath. Jacob felt the force of that truth reverberate in the hollow of his heart, struck like a deep note from a drum. She handed him the jar. Blight trembled within, eager to find the wind.

In his dream, the stalk of that colossal toadstool had parted for his searching hands. There had been a body nestled there, a mockery of life enwombed.

It had not been Jonboy.

Perhaps this was the answer he had come north to find.

Glass shattered against the old stone of the road. From across the hazy distance he heard the Beast call out, forlorn and searching, as spores swarmed on the air.

Jacob closed his eyes for the last time. His flesh began to whisper like a field of husks stirred by a breeze. Carmine took his hand as fingers curled away. She kissed his lips as they peeled apart in a howl lost beneath an eruption of spores.

And as the wind broke and bore him beyond all grief and memory, what little remained finally began to understand.

K is for Kenosis

Megan Arkenberg

Easter 1818

The rain hangs in the air, a chill white fog cut here and there with diagonal shafts of sunlight, on the morning after she kills the doctor. The sea is calm. A salt-wind, more hesitant that she has ever felt it, catches in her skirt like a child's hand ushering her up the shore. She goes to church because the doctor would have laughed at her for it, would have scowled like an old woman offered bad fish and dismissed it as "foolishness."

The doctor dismissed most of the village as "foolish." *Foolishness,* she had learned, was a word he found infinitely more cutting than *superstition*—for the doctor was very nearly a superstitious man. He believed himself to be followed, pursued. He would not say by what. Their house on the little island is warded like a wizard's, charms of broken glass and filed metal guarding every aperture. She did not mock him for it; she even helped to string the lattice of fine wire across the windows, her clever left hand wielding the hammer, her clumsy right holding the nail.

(The left hand was a gentlewoman's, a lady who taught young women to play the harpsichord and piano-forte, turning wrists and raising palms with the gentle pressure of her fingertips. The right hand scrubbed potatoes day in and day out in a tub of cooling water, and knew little else.)

But foolish or not, superstitious or not—worthy of mockery or not—she has made up her mind to go. It isn't easy. The island is half a mile from the shore, almost linked at low tide by a wide isthmus of gravel studded with eelgrass, as treacherous by boat as it is by foot. The church lies another mile inland. A road had been tramped between the two, many years before, but its traces remain only in the rusty patches where neither grass nor flower grows. Rust from the nails in a fisherman's boots, she thinks, dragged day after day to prayer. Her own feet find the path unfamiliar.

(The left foot, a prostitute's, remembers soft sheepskin cushions, a warm hand beneath the arch, kisses pressed to the inside of the ankle. The right, a grocer's girl's, remembers pinched shoes and long hours treading the same length of floor.)

Inland, away from the muck of the tides, the air takes on a cleaner smell. She had rowed the doctor's little boat herself, quicker and smoother than the doctor ever did—both of her arms are thicker and stronger than his (used to carrying children and hot bread, used to pushing wheelbarrows of brick). Now she checks her gown for dampness, for splatters of salt or tidal mud. She owns two dresses: the one the doctor picked out for her, dark green, elegant; and this, a soft gray wool she stitched for herself, severe and clerical in its cut. (Her brain remembers Latin and deeply buried fantasies of convents: of clean white stone, gargoyles and stained glass; of herb gardens and rose gardens; of other women's hands.) A high collar hides the joint between her head and neck, and the seam across the top of her breasts.

But even the scars that are visible get only a passing glance from the faces she passes on the road. A farmer blinks at her, curious but not unkind. Life is cruel and demanding, out here beneath the cold sun and the frozen rain. No one gets by unmarked.

(No man here looks like the doctor, smooth and pale, his linen white as a bride's.)

Ahead of her now, the church's square steeple floats above the ridge like some fairy castle of sand and seaweed. Easter has come too early for lilies this year, but the door is hung with garlands of evergreen and hazel catkins, with red berries and delicate clutches of snowdrop. And at the very last, she falters.

This is no place for you, a voice whispers in her head. It is the doctor's voice, his cadence, his supple accent. *You're not one of them, not anymore. I have made you more—*

A hand on her elbow interrupts the thought. A child of three or four—boy or girl, she cannot say, with its big black eyes and rosebud mouth—has come up behind her, stood on tiptoe to feel the smooth wool of her gown. "Hello," she whispers, her mouth sore and stiff from disuse. The child giggles and darts back down the path to a waiting mother.

"Hello," she says again, louder. The child's mother tips her head in greeting.

After church, there is dinner at the young mother's house, and after dinner, there are hymns by the fire. It is late by the time she returns to the island.

The air in the little house has become close and warm, and the flies have gathered thickly over the things she left in the pail by the stove. She should fling them away, she knows, out into the surf before the smell attracts creatures worse than flies. Already the sheets on the doctor's bed are stained with blood and worse than blood, with the grease and fat of a body more accustomed to books and scalpels than to children, potatoes, grocer's shops. She will need to replace them before she goes to sleep.

She is not tired yet.

Hanging her shawl over the back of his chair, she notices that his head is not where she left it, perched on his desk amidst his glass flasks and copper coils. It has rolled off, leaving a thin ribbon of blood in the dust, coming to rest against the clawed feet of his bookcase. She picks it up with handkerchief and sets him on a shelf beside his tattered copy of Milton.

"Happy Easter, Herr Doctor." She greets the filmed white eyes with a smile.

The traps around the windows, the broken glass and wire, she begins to sweep away. She sings while she works, Easter hymns and scraps of Psalms, and where she can't remember the words, she fills the gap with humming. The only devil she has ever known is laid to rest at last, and the sunlight fighting down through the gathering fog is like the first light of the world. *I am Eve in the garden, then.* She smiles to herself. *I am afraid of no one.*

L is for Laboratory

Lilah Wild

Beef Wellington, thought Candace.

Her stiletto heels clacked along the Boulevard sidewalk as she rehearsed the night ahead: her dining room table, surrounded by a small corps of investors, hostessing duties played to perfection. Beef Wellington was not on her menu, but the image wouldn't leave her alone. Filet mignon baked in pastry, ludicrously extravagant and so hard to get right...it was an intentionally difficult dish from her mother's generation, picked to show the boss just how well a rising star's wife could cook, a challenge that proved a family's smooth fit with corporate culture. *Taste this pâté. Crunch through this puff. Know that we are the right kind of people, we deserve to ascend.*

What an old-fashioned display, what an adorably *vintage* way to show your worth, she snorted to herself—kitchen skills, *ha!*—as she opened the double glass doors to Jolique.

She was immediately assaulted by loud, sugary pop beats and the florals of a hundred perfumes, the signature sensory overload of the cosmetics megastore, packed with its signature crowds. Everywhere, the hot pursuit of beauty was underway. Aisle after aisle offered an excess of bright colors, quick solutions, irresistibly cute little packages. Shoppers paused before shelves of the latest products, their arms swatched in slashes of lipstick, their feet choking any hope of smooth passage. Guaranteed promises glittered like grails in a maze. So many, many grails.

Candace was here for the purchase of transformation. Nobody expected her cooking to be great, not anymore, when the best culinary skill one could flaunt was the choice of a highly elite caterer. No. The demands were different now. The language of good taste, expressed through her tastes in couture, certainly. The discipline of yoga, tightly sheathed by that couture. The self-control of dieting, a hard one, as a stomach growl punched through her willpower and demanded more than just the glass of grapefruit juice she'd had for breakfast. There had always been appearances to aspire to, she'd known that ever since her mother had pushed her onto the social stage and commanded her to climb. The appearances had merely evolved since the time of the decadent little meat cakes. Her manicure, her living-room sofa, so many choices would be judged during cocktail hour, all the details that told if you belonged. Jolique's array of seemingly infinite choices made her head swim; she needed someone to lead her past all the potential pitfalls and make her face up into the night's dazzling centerpiece. It was the last errand on her list, before the mad dash home to dress up, set the scene, and welcome her guests with a fearless smile.

The staff were outfitted in their smart Jolique lab-coats, canvases of tailored black that showed off each employee's specialty: liquid liner winging up towards an arched, powdered brow in a perfect cat's eye, lipstick applied in a gradient red-to-black fade like the edge of a rose. Toolbelts of brushes rode low along their waists, fluffy brushes peeking from their tiny holsters. They were salespeople, but salespeople steeped in glamour. Their immaculately drawn faces demonstrated their power. Their knowledge would whisk her straight to what she needed, and Candace had no time to waste among the idly browsing hordes.

Most of the artists were trapped in clusters of customer questions, and the free ones were quickly accosted. She tried to catch the orchid gaze of a professional bombshell, but was passed by for a trio of shrieking teenagers. Another walked by with firehouse lips, who did a quick admiring sweep of the eyes to Candace's trinity of shoes, bag, and hair, but kept going. Normally Candace couldn't make it five feet past the entrance without an artist swooping down on her. Today, well, it *was* a madhouse in here. She'd ascend to the realms of skincare and perfume, and probably have better luck finding someone. She passed by the cattle chute of the register, couldn't help but glance at the overpriced impulse purchases, and climbed the stairs to the mezzanine.

A security guard clad in the store's same fashionable black nodded at her as he monitored the chaos below, but it wasn't much better up here. She tried to make her way past a display of moisturizers, but the route was blocked by a bridal party. She turned around, and maneuvered through mists of fragrance, coughing as she pushed her way through the jagged terrain of other customers' handbags, mesh shopping baskets, and oblivious elbows. Cuts of tenderloin, Candace hungrily snarled to herself, look at us, dressing ourselves up in truffles, splashing ourselves with wine, too many delicacies crammed into the chic glass candybox of Jolique.

Another artist walked past her, heading straight for the bridesmaids. A tiny knot of failure began to coalesce beneath Candace's powerhouse emblems, the brand-name armor not shining through enough. A diamond flash of attitude blasted it apart. She had spent a lot of money in Jolique, qualified for their little VIP gifts countless times over, and it was obvious she was here to spend much more. Why weren't the salespeople fighting to wait on her? They were artists, yes, but retail was retail, and their first job was to serve the customer. She looked around for a manager, but everyone was in black, no way to tell a higher-up from an associate, a flattering shade from a terrible one, it could get so *confusing* in here—

"How many faces do *you* have?"

Candace spun around. A nymph in a Jolique uniform smiled at her. A blonde bob framed her glowing face and her eyeshadow blazed orange, matched perfectly to her lips. It was like being beamed at by a benevolent little sun.

Candace was about to protest. *No, no, I want to be waited on by somebody normal,* but the artist was analyzing her bone structure, bathing her in a haze of sweet chatter, guiding her over to the one vanity that was not taken up by other customers. Personal attention, finally. Candace exhaled, as she sat down on the makeover stool.

Atop the vanity, more tools of the trade: alcohol to sanitize, makeup remover to erase, a platter of wands and sponges and bits of foam on sticks to conjure gorgeous illusions. A box of tissues stood by, awaiting mishaps and rejections. Candace faced the mirror, large and round and ringed in lights, and presented the blank parchment of her face, ready for the artist's calligraphy of color and shadow.

"…such beautiful skin. You are so lucky, really. There are so many people who come in here, they have cystic acne, or flushing, or they're prone to breaking out all the time. They're coming in to cover themselves up, they want concealer, they don't get to have the *fun* of colors, you know? It's like they don't get to have faces at all. I'm Serena, by the way…"

Serena's hands danced around the table in a nimble ballet, readying brushes and swabs and cotton pads for the ritual. She pulled a square silver box from a pocket over her heart, and set it down in the center of this momentary altar. Candace had meant to ask for a tasteful palette of neutrals, the most appropriate yet fashionably on-point colors for business, but she found herself melting beneath the heat lamp of Serena's undivided attention. The noise, the crowds, the blasts of shrill floral scents, all receded behind her cheerful voice.

"But you, *you* could go swimming, and get out of that pool without a care in the world. You could wear *anything*…"

And before Candace knew it, one of her eyelids had been turned blue. Not what she wanted at all. At *all*. And yet…the sharp word rising in her throat was stilled by genuine curiosity, as she gazed into the lighted mirror. Blue eyeshadow was another relic from her mother's heyday, notoriously difficult to pull off with any dignity, an eternal joke of the fashion industry. But the way her eyes were peering through the hue of silvered skies, veiled through a cool shimmer, it looked…*good*.

"…this is called Moonlit Mermaid. It's really great for those night looks, you know? And normally I wouldn't pair it with something so dramatic for your mouth, but your features, ohhh, you are just so *blessed*. I *have* to see if I can make it work on you. It's called Vermilion Vampire…"

The shimmering blue and deep matte red should have battled against each other. Violently. They should have left Candace looking like a clown. Theatrical colors way, *way* beyond the workday, shades she had never considered for herself, *ever*…

Where was this strange harmony coming from? The palette itself, the challenging hues emerging one by one from the little silver box? The gentle yet clever hand that miraculously knew how to wield them? Fingers muscled from countless tutorials, cosmetics fortified with carefully researched ingredients, this was a rare individual whose mind and body were rich with study, Candace sensed. Someone whose every choice, no matter how tiny, held some degree of consideration behind it: someone she would love to work with, a perfect hire. The certainty with which Serena painted was amplified by the sleek silver rings on her fingers, arcane symbols of angles and lightning bolts, quirks of uniqueness. And her voice wove a comforting cocoon around the vanity, a tapestry of soothing words that walled off the frenzy of Jolique. She understood well the importance of all the little details.

"...we definitely can't do rouge, that's too much for even *me* to pull off, but I do want to give you an overall glow. This is called Fire Faerie..."

A thick plump fluff glided across Candace's cheeks, leaving behind a golden powder. The brushes honed in on her features like soft lasers, reached down past all the expectations and demands and appropriate beige blazers, and found the shapes of her shadows with ease. A salesgirl's hands zipping up the back of a business-casual dress, a manicurist's fingers cradling her still-wet French-tipped nails, moments of closeness abounded in the business of beauty. But makeovers seemed the most intimate of all: a bare face, a fingertip steady against a trusting cheekbone, the smallest of caresses as one person made another look better. Serena's tangerine eyes studied Candace like a work of art as she measured, blended, evened out. The regard, so different from the respectful distance that professionalism mandated in her day-to-day life, was intoxicating.

"Here. You can see yourself closer." Serena presented Candace with a hand mirror.

She looked beyond merely beautiful. She looked *astonishing*.

It was like some advanced technology in duochrome shades, the kind where your skin was pink at one angle, green when you moved an inch. Candace was the mermaid, cool and collected within the tempest of an overwhelming workday. But then she was the vampire, irresistible, sinking sharp sweet teeth into the wallets of willing clients. And then the faerie, laughing through it all, relishing the summer bonfire of midnight oil. She was something else, every time she turned her head. What would have been cartoonish on another face worked in perfect synchronicity on hers. A conjunction of facets that seemed brand-new to her, but a puzzle that had been waiting inside her all along, that might have been completed years ago—if only she'd encountered Serena's talent then! No top-shelf props, no luxury totems, the miracle was animated by nothing more than the raw stuff right in her skin, blooming with all her drive and determination, shining up from her freshly astounded soul.

Maybe this was how she should present herself tonight, this strange but intriguing Candace-creature, defying expectations, maybe show off some memorable quirks of her own in front of the investors. Not just a producer of results, but a personality. A *luminary*.

Serena picked up a spray bottle, a fixative mist to keep the colors from sliding away, and smiled down on her creation.

A ringtone interrupted from Candace's bag.

She looked down and rummaged around for her phone. It was essential to her career that she looked good, in all ways, and that included being ready at all times. Even if it meant a deference to someone else's desires instead of her own. Even if it meant being horribly rude to a retail worker waiting on her. Even if it meant being leashed to her phone, instead of living in the moment.

She had her thumb on the answer button when she glanced up at Serena.

The artist had frozen, the bottle paused in her hand. Her smile was gone. Her sunny eyes had gone somber, silently imploring Candace not to answer.

Her thumb slid into position almost by pure reflex, so conditioned to the summons, her eyes crinkling apology and her voice chirping *Hello.*

All the colors immediately dropped a degree of luminosity.

A different Candace started to surface as she spoke to the voice at the other end of the line. The expression she wore when aggravated took over, a bad-twin flipside that revealed little conduits of displeasure etched into her skin. She had taken herself away from the gift, and every word to the person who was not here, not in this present place of metamorphosis, shattered the glamour further.

She saw Serena gathering up her tools, putting the colors back into the box, and concluded her call quickly.

"I'm so sorry. Where were we? I'd definitely like to take the kit."

Serena paused, and gazed down at Candace, and smiled sadly.

"I *almost* got you there. I was *so* close."

Candace looked back down at the mirror, and gasped. This secondary face was showing through the paint, the façade unravelling its patchwork. Mermaid blue, meant as a calming force against the frustrations of her career, was now the skin of a blood-hungry shark that would never, ever know a moment of rest. Vampire red, a charm to conquer the tension of every meeting with charisma and wit, had become a slash of dried blood around the mouth of a hyena, driving every friend away. Faerie gold, innocence, the wonder of play, the reason for all this work in the first place... the metallic scales of a predatory snake, forever unsated. Her companion animals had turned on her.

She threw down the mirror.

"What the hell is this—"

But the artist had vanished.

Candace scanned the crowds for that blonde bob, but all she saw were other shoppers getting their faces painted, or squeezing plumes of perfume onto wrists. The heat lamp had gone out, and she'd been left by herself.

She glanced at the large round mirror, and stared hard at this other face she'd unwittingly been carving into her features. The azure and crimson and bronze, so lovely just moments ago, sat atop her skin like sparkling smudges. The prestigious logos of her outfit began to clash wildly with each other, heels versus bag, without her confidence to hold them together. Her reflection presented the unappetizing costume of trying too hard, and she had to be knitted back together again. She needed Serena, *now*.

Candace jumped up and startled the artist at the next vanity, who'd been demonstrating mascara to a septuagenarian with a stunning map of laugh lines. Brushes fell from his hands.

"Hey! What are you—" Violet-shaded eyes shot daggers at Candace, and then visibly recoiled.

"Where did Serena go? The girl who was just working on me?"

"I've never seen that girl before in my life," he said, picking his tools up from the floor. "Now if you'll excuse me..."

"But she had on a uniform!"

"Ask a manager. I'm really busy right now." He turned his back on her, and stepped further away, putting as much distance as he could between them. The woman in his chair stared openly at Candace. Heads swivelled in her direction as her face colored with heat. They could all see. Through the cracking cake, down to the furious meat.

Someone took her arm. She looked up into the stern face of a security guard and was led out of the crowds, over to the window.

"We can't have you disrupting the other customers," he said, toneless, almost bored, until he got a look at her face.

"I need to speak to Serena, she works here!"

The guard's features creased with slight revulsion as he shook his head. "Serena? There's nobody here by that name."

She broke away from the painful scrutiny of his gaze and glanced down at the sidewalk, and caught sight of a blonde bob, silver-ringed hands wadding up a Jolique lab-coat and tossing it into a trash can.

"There!" She pointed down at the intersection. The traffic light changed, and the orange face proceeded to cross the street within a swarm of people. "That's Serena! The blonde!"

The guard looked down, and let out a sigh. "I don't see any of our people down there. I'm sorry, ma'am. You should go home and lie down."

Candace's breath came quicker, as the horror dawned on her.

"Get me a manager!"

"All right, I'll say it less nice: you're being asked to leave."

"What the—you know I can sue you for this, right? I can sue you for letting in an imposter, not vetting your people, don't you throw me out—"

Her panic was cut short by the ringing of her phone. She fished it out of her handbag and glanced at the name. And the time. Oh, *shit*.

In her right hand, the future, the dinner clock had counted all the way down and one of the guests was calling her, wanting to know where she was. To the left, the advancing forms of two more security guards were coming for her. Throughout, a storm of noxious cologne made its way through the mezzanine.

Caught between righteous consumer anger and career showtime, scared out of her mind, and trying not to gag, Candace felt the trace of Serena's deft fingerprints all over her face. A stranger, not a salesperson at all, but...those orange eyes. They'd seen something in her and plucked her from the crowds for some surreal and breathtaking experiment, hands so enchantingly kind, a dormant trio of selves conjured up within tiny silver bolts of lightning. And better than anyone who worked here for real. Like that famous violinist who'd left the greatest concert stage in the world to busk on the street, just to see who'd stop and notice how well he played, amid the noise and haste...what else had been waiting for Candace within her internal landscape, the oceans and castles and woods and untold other worlds that glimmered behind her skin, wild spirits ready to be summoned by the palette, if only she'd just put down her phone...

Pure fear gave way to the agony of a blown deal. A poor performance before the waiting investors was only one pang in a much deeper loss, now. The mermaid had swum away, and the vampire had flown off.

She raised a hand to touch the glass, and even as the guards reached her, Candace turned her burning eyes towards the Boulevard, frantically searching the crowds for that bright yellow hair. The faerie's gold still splotched her cheeks like the dust of foreign coins, a blessing rescinded, as she ached to be back within that radiant concentration, never so alone as all of her faces softly dissolved.

M is for Makeup

Laura VanArendonk Baugh

Anastasios looked down upon the stone-paved circle and the white-haired soothsayer in mute horror. Had he dared to speak, he could not have done so.

"Your very words are treason against the Ivory Throne," pronounced King Kassander. His tall crown shone in the firelight and the reflected gleam of the gilded ceiling. "You will die on the horns of the festival, to wipe clean the stain of your lies."

"You know it is truth!" insisted the old man, a bit of spittle flecking his beard in his urgency. "You know it, my king!"

"Take him to the arena," ordered the king.

"She speaks in the flames!" shouted the soothsayer. Guards took him by either arm and drew him back. "She speaks in the flames!"

Anastasios stole a glance at his father, but the king's face was stony, unmoving, marked neither by sorrow for the soothsayer's sudden turn to madness nor discomfort at the dire predictions. It was as if all emotion had been wiped away, leaving one of the royal statues which marked the main streets.

"You must witness this," murmured his mother beside him, pitched for his ears alone.

Anastasios swallowed. He did not like blood, and the bull dances disturbed him with their frightful potential. With his father's sentence, blood was no longer a probability, but a certainty. But his mother would not allow him to show weakness. She drove him more fiercely than his father. A queen without children, she required more defense of her position and her adopted son's, and she brooked no possibility of weakness in the heir found to fill the place she could not.

She speaks in the flames. Anastasios could not guess what the soothsayer had meant, but the words had carried all the man's conviction.

The throne room's walls were painted with endless figures carrying tribute to the Ivory Throne. Ambassadors and emissaries in bright and splendid costumes, representing lands from Argos to the Adriatic tribes to the south continental peoples, offered gold ingots, chalices and coffers, clever machinery of bronze to calculate the wheeling of the heavens, jade, amber from the far north, slaves, and precious stones of all colors. Everywhere he looked Anastasios could not help but see the magnificence and prestige of his homeland.

The painted figures marched to a painted Ivory Throne, where the artist had set a king, stern and unsmiling. It might equally have been Kassander or any of the previous kings. They looked very alike once painted, Anastasios thought, with tightly curled beards and flat lifeless eyes and the elongated skulls which marked them as nobility.

Anastasios had not been royal at his birth, and so his skull had not been bound as a noble child's should have been. By the time he was searched out, a slave's brat got years ago by a king whose queen would give him no heir, it was too late to mold him to fit the crown.

The queen had ordered a special tall cap fashioned for Anastasios, stiff and curved and glittering with jewels.

Such trappings did not impress the soothsayer. "You have spurned the signs of the gods, my king," he had declared only the day before. "My warning is not the first, but the last." He pointed at Anastasios. "There is a sign, right before you and in this very court. Great king, you had no natural heir. When can any man recall such a thing in the time of the Ivory Throne? And a boy was sought among the slaves of this house and raised to a higher place than his birth. This defiance of a sign is sure to only further anger the gods."

"Anastasios is my son," King Kassander answered, steel glinting in the vowels. "I have sired him and I have claimed him."

"And you will put a born slave on the Ivory Throne," said the prophet. "And the consequences will be not on your head, but on every subject in your once-great kingdom."

"Once-great?" repeated Kassander, and the courtiers shifted their weight and their eyes.

"Do you believe, king, that a bastard slave could follow in the footsteps of your ancestors?"

"We are not so weak that a single stumble would bring us to our knees," Kassander said. "And this speculation does not credit your warning. Have you nothing more beyond your own disapproval?"

"There are many portents for those who have eyes to see." The prophet swept an arm to indicate the whole of the island and its people. "In the last two days alone we have been given many signs of ill to come. Birds are flying away in great flocks. Cats hiss and scratch at their mistresses, dogs whine by day and howl by night. Three of the royal elephants waded into the sea, as if to swim to Argos or Egypt. All of these are plain to see, mighty king."

"I assure you, I have eyes to see." King Kassander had raised a dismissive hand. "But I have no ears for this sort of malicious speech against my son and heir."

Yesterday, he had sent the soothsayer out of the court for speaking ill of Anastasios' ability, but today he had ordered the man's death for prophesying the kingdom was in imminent danger. Prophesying was his task and duty; why execute him instead of asking his aid?

And if the old prophet spoke the truth? Was Anastasios endangering them all by defying the gods, playing at prince?

The queen looked at him, her eyes probing for weakness. "We must go down to the arena now. Are you ready?"

Anastasios nodded once. "I am ready." Or at least, he could not be made more ready by delay.

The festival could not open before sunset, so even the streaked gold light was fading from the royal stands when the royal family entered in procession to take their places. The arena itself was lit with five bonfires spaced about the circle and torches at regular intervals along the wall. This curving wall of linked stone was the height and a half of a man, enough to nearly always protect the first row of spectators.

The crowd had come early to fight for choice seats and drink away the time until the rites opened. They were loud and anxious for the night's beginning, and the surprise of an execution before the dancing only pleased them more. There was the slightest of hesitations when the soothsayer was announced as the sentenced man, but the general enthusiasm and wine carried them through the moment and they cheered as he was pushed into the arena, his hands bound with golden cord.

The cord did not matter; had he the full use of his hands, he could have done little to save himself. The wall was too high to jump, especially for a white-haired prophet. And even the trained bull dancers who had dedicated their lives to the skill could fall before the sacred bulls. But the binding made it clear, as the bull was released into the circle and snorted at the bonfires, that he was a sacrifice.

The bull was white-skinned with a scattering of red-brown hairs blurring over its shoulders and legs. It shook its head at the first fire and then cantered halfway about the circle to look white-eyed at the shouting crowd.

The soothsayer turned toward the royal pavilion. "I do not die alone this night," he called, his tone somewhere between warning and defiance. "But I die by the ancient glory of the bull, while you perish in water and smoke."

His words seemed to catch the attention of the bull, which turned toward the soothsayer and shook its gilded horns in threat. When the man did not move away, the bull lowered its head and rushed at him.

The crowd screamed in horrified delight as the golden hooks caught the soothsayer's torso and lifted him into the air. He cried out, but the sound was lost in the universal shout. The body fell to the sand, and the bull knelt on it and twisted its horns into the still-moving dead man.

Anastasios kept his chin steady but lowered his eyes. On the golden chair beside him, he had seen his father's fingers tighten on the armrest—not at the goring, but at the soothsayer's pronouncement.

If the soothsayer lied, then executing him was just and necessary, but if he spoke the truth, killing him would not avert whatever fortune he had seen. If Kassander feared a true prophesy, then why was the man sacrificed instead of asked how to placate the gods and put aside disaster?

She speaks in the flames.

The bull, redder now over face and forelegs, left the corpse and began trotting about the circle again. A gate was opened and it cantered for the escape from the fire and shouting. With the door safely closed, slaves came out to retrieve the crushed body.

The arena was one circle within the greater circle of the festival ground. The temple was a circle of circles, and its innermost parts were concentric rings. In the innermost ring was an entrance, the Gate of Flames, where the priests and prophets might find portents.

Another gate opened, and the crowd began to cheer as the dancers entered. There were eight of them, four male and four female, dressed in spare, simple garments which left arms and legs bare and with unrestricted movement. Two carried poles a little taller than themselves, decorated at each end with colorful streamers the length of a man's arm. The dancers formed a line at the center of the ring and prostrated themselves fully flat, faces in the sand, to the king.

Another bull was let into the ring, this one a uniform deep brown, and the crowd whooped. The bull snorted and bolted along the wall. The dancers sprang up from the ground and the bull sprang away, startled by their sudden appearance. Then it charged.

The first man dove to the side, rolling safely away across the sand. The second planted his beribboned pole and vaulted to the other side, his feet skimming just above the gold-painted horns. The next dancer was a girl, her hair drawn high and descending in two braids. She crouched as the bull approached and caught a gilded horn beneath her armpit, bracing one hand against the horn and the other against her opposite forearm. She let the bull's upward thrust launch her into the air, stretching her hands to balance briefly on its back before flipping to land in its hoof prints. The crowd whooped its approval.

Anastasios' palms were sweating. At least once dancer died each year, an accepted sacrifice to the honored ritual.

The priests were all in attendance at the arena, watching the bull dancers. Afterward, they would drink like everyone else and would retire. The temple would be guarded, of course, but there would be no one of sufficient rank to challenge a prince.

One of the dancers slipped and fell, and the bull wheeled and drove into her. She screamed horribly as it pushed her across the sand and into the ground, bearing down. The two with poles prodded at the bull and dangled the streamers before it so that it drove forward, pushing its horns at the ribbons as a dancer whirled in place to tease it away, and three others seized the broken woman and half-carried, half-dragged her toward a gate.

Tonight, Anastasios would find the Gate of Flames and see if *she*—whoever *she* might be—was yet there and yet speaking.

The temple lay between the palace and the arena—by day, an easy walk for a slave, but a more difficult reach for a prince who would be observed and marked with every step. It was long past dark by the time the bulls had ceased and the arena had emptied, but Anastasios waited another hour after the festival sounds had slowed. There would be much drinking in the city below the palace, but the temple itself would be deserted by even the most dedicated of worshipers, and this night he would be unremarked.

He put on his own sandals, something he had done rarely since becoming a prince. He tied the laces, checked the tall cap which would grant him admission to the temple if challenged, and left his rooms.

The temple and palace sat on a hill overlooking the city on one side and the sea on the other. A very few orange lights still gleamed, but the festival's carousal was winding to a close, and the night's drinking had mostly ended. The temple itself was dark and quiet. He crossed the grounds by the light of the half-moon, sitting partway up the curve of the sky. Anastasios was halted by two guards with bronze and copper armor who extended spears to block his path. "The temple is closed at this hour," one said.

Anastasios pushed his hood back enough to reveal his face and artificially tall cap. "It is not closed to me."

The guards snapped upright, spears drawn to parade position. "My apologies, prince. I did not recognize you in the dark."

Anastasios nodded and went past them.

The temple was dark but for the flame ever-burning upon the altar, casting long, flickering shadows upon the tiled floor. Stone columns stretched upward into the shadowy ceiling, decorated with brightly colored motifs to illustrate the kingdom's wealth and power as well as the bulls present on nearly every temple surface. Anastasios moved toward the altar, which still bore the charred remains of the festival day's bovine sacrifice as well as a little flatbread half-baked on the edge, and pushed on into the corridors beyond. He would have to guess his path from here.

He kept one hand on the wall and eased forward into the dark. He stayed near to the wall, but after a dozen steps he shuffled into a chest and gasped with surprise and pain. He knelt and felt for the lid, grasping inside for the lamps he hoped he would find. He was not disappointed, and after a few moments of fumbling he stuck a spark and lit the little lamp.

He heard a small sound behind him, and he turned with the sudden knowledge that he was not alone in the room. A young woman looked back at him, dressed in the short, efficient garb of a bull dancer, with her hair in two descending braids and a darkened bandage about her upper left arm. She looked at him, wide-eyed, and it occurred to him that perhaps she was not supposed to be here either.

"I was offering a sacrifice," she said, confirming his suspicion. "I did not expect anyone else so late."

"It is late for a sacrifice," he agreed. He had learned, watching his father in court, that agreement without explanation could accomplish much. "And there has been much sacrifice already today."

"This was a personal matter," she said. "Euanthe was badly injured in the bull dancing tonight. She will never dance again, may never stand straight again, but one might still ask that she may live."

"The bread," he recalled.

She nodded.

"I too am here on a personal matter," he said.

She started to answer, hesitated, and then looked at him more closely. Her eyes widened, and she flung herself to the floor. "My lord prince!"

She had not easily recognized him, and why should she? His face was on no coins, no statues, no paintings. Self-consciously he felt again for the weight of his elongated cap. "Rise," he said. "I seek the Gate of Flames."

She sat upright and looked at him in surprise. "The Gate, prince? Why?"

He had not anticipated her questioning him. "Need I explain? I wish to see if there is indeed a portent there." Belatedly he realized he had explained, after all. Quickly he added, "Do you know the way? If so, you might be of use."

"I am a bull dancer," she said, "and the path to the Gate of Flames lies outside the dancers' quarters."

He thought back to when he had been a slave's child instead of a king's. "That does not mean you do not know it."

She smiled, recognizing the subtle change in his voice. "That is true."

"Then, if you will keep my secret of coming in the night, I will keep yours of taking me to the Gate of Flames."

Her smile broadened. "Of course, prince."

He gestured her to her feet. "What is your name?"

"I am Casta." She turned. "This way, prince."

The gate was not a door, but a well. Stone steps spiraled down about the outer wall and disappeared into the dark.

Casta looked dubiously down. "I don't like it," she said frankly. "It feels like the earth is breathing."

It was an odd phrase, but Anastasios agreed. The air here was warm and darkly scented, dangerous in some way he could not define.

She speaks in the flames.

"The priests and prophets come here," he said, "so it must be safe enough. Let us go down."

The steps were narrow, both in depth and width, and he kept one hand on the wall as he descended. Casta followed behind him, leaving enough room that a slip would not send them both tumbling to the unseen bottom. The odor increased, sulfurous and foul like a midden. Anastasios' eyes began to sting.

The stairs ended in a passage which was no longer dressed stone, but more carved half by man, half by nature. It was tall enough for Anastasios to stand nearly erect, but too narrow for Casta to walk beside him. The passage curved away into the dark, untouched by the feeble reach of the lamp.

"This is the way," Casta said, her voice low in the dark. "A labyrinth to enlightenment."

He lifted the lamp, showing the rough stone wall's curve darkly golden in the lamplight. Concentric circles, again. "Do you know the way?"

"I know there is a way. That is not quite the same." But she took the lamp, pressing past him in the narrow corridor, and started down the passage.

There were no branching paths, for which Anastasios was grateful. This was a labyrinth, then, and not a maze. Troughs ran along the floor, deep and narrow grooves parallel to the curving walls, and Anastasios could not guess their purpose.

The path doubled back on itself, working back and forth but ever inward. He kept close to Casta, and she stayed near him, as if they somehow needed each other's warmth in this warm dark.

The curves became tighter and tighter. And then the passage opened into a wider space and Casta stopped so abruptly that Anastasios bumped into her from behind and jostled the lamp. She did not look back at him or speak.

Beyond her, something was in the dark. He could feel it, sense it, a disturbance in the air and a presence against his skin. Casta lifted the lamp, and eyes shone green back at them.

They leapt backward, Casta stumbling against Anastasios, and he caught and steadied her.

Anastasios steeled himself. "Who's there?" he called, and his voice wavered only a little. "Your prince asks."

There was a rustling sound, as of leather or scales brushing stone, and a soft laugh. "Not *my* prince," came a low voice, resting just a bit longer than usual on the final consonant.

Anastasios swallowed and took the lamp from Casta. *Be confident and assertive,* his mother had admonished him, *and demand their respect. They cannot refuse you.* He put a hand on Casta's shoulder and stepped past her, raising the lamp high. "Who are you, then, if not my subject?"

Light spread forward, and a lion's face stared steadily back at him from the shadow.

Anastasios flinched backward, but Casta's hand caught him between the shoulder blades. "Stand still," she whispered, her mouth close to his ear. "Quick movements enrage or entice. Be still, and offer no threat."

She would know how to face dangerous animals. He froze, his knees nearly trembling with their rigidity, and waited.

The lion's lips curled in a cat's smile. "Your female is clever," it said, its mouth forming about the words as no lion's mouth could do. "But you live by my forbearance, not by her wisdom. I have something to say to you, prince."

Anastasios swallowed. "How can a lion speak to me?"

"A lion." The cat sounded disdainful. The big head turned, showing a thin mane which did not conceal the ears. The mouth opened, and the beast spat forth a stream of fire.

Casta and Anastasios screamed together. Fire lit the passage, making them shield their eyes, but Casta against Anastasios' back kept him in place despite his fear.

When they looked again, the floor trough was full of fire, burning invisible fuel in a long line about the outer edge of the round chamber. In the center stood a creature, a beast beyond comprehension. It was a lion, or at least the front part of it was. A goat's head rose from the withers and watched them over the lion's thin mane. A long tail moved restlessly behind the lion body, but it was not a tail, it was a serpent with its own head for the tail's end, eying them.

"Trikephalos," breathed Casta.

The goat head spoke, its voice thinner and higher than the lion's. "Someone has schooled you well, girl."

Anastasios recognized the sound of the word as the language of the eastern peninsula, Athens or Argos or one of those, but he did not know its meaning. He could not appear less educated than a temple girl, however. "You said you had something to say to me."

The lion's ears tilted back in annoyance. "Foolish prince, I am the Khimaira. If you asked your girl, she would tell you that I am a portent, an ill omen. I foretell disaster and ruin. You should take care in demanding news from me."

Anastasios raised his chin. "If you bear ill news, then all the more reason I should hear it promptly, so that I may address it. For what is an omen, but a warning, and what is a warning, but an opportunity to evade ill consequence?"

The snake head rose and looked down upon them. "I birthed the sphinx, cleverest of creatures," it spoke, sibilant. "What gives you to think you can play word games with me?"

"You would not come to the temple only to mock me with a warning you will not give." He hoped this was true.

"You would not require my warning if you opened your eyes to the omens Nature herself has given you," snarled the lion. "Think, boy."

Anastasios swallowed. "My father had no natural heir, and I had to be found to bear the prince's crown."

"No," said the goat, irritated, "as if you were so important. Look around this place. The air which sinks can be set afire. What air sinks and puddles like water, and what air burns?"

Anastasios looked around the circular room as if the answer might lie against the curved wall. Fire licked about the edge of the floor, an ankle-height ring of flame. Another concentric circle.

"Your father knows," said the serpent's head, tongue flicking as if to taste Anastasios' response. "Your father killed to keep this secret."

Circles within circles. "The soothsayer," Anastasios said. "He spoke the truth."

"How could he not? For I had given it to him."

"Then all the portents—his ill omens—something really is coming."

The lion's lips curled upward. "Oh, yes."

"The earth," Casta said, her voice uncertain as she interrupted a prince and a monster. "The earth breathes out contagion and flame and death. The very earth will strike against us."

The goat seemed pleased. "I said she was clever."

"How do we stop it?" Anastasios looked from Casta to the beast, his pulse racing. "What sacrifice is needed?"

Must they kill many bulls? Bull dancers? Even the false prince? What would soothe the anger of the fiery earth?

The lion shook its head, ruffling the mane. "Not every crisis of earth is the act of an angry god," it said. "You cannot soothe what is not angry."

Anastasios' heart leapt. Had the soothsayer been wrong as well as right? Was the false prince not an abomination to the gods?

The lion was still looking at him. "I came to speak warning, but it is not to tell you to turn the disaster aside. It is to tell you to escape it."

Anastasios swallowed. "And this is what my father refuses to do."

"If he leaves, he is a king without a kingdom. He will live on the crusts of mercy tossed by those he has ruled. Instead of demanding their tribute, he will plead for their aid. It seems he believes it is better to die a king than to live a beggar."

"And is he wrong?" asked the serpent, head swaying seductively. "What is a man worth, when he cannot be what he was?"

Casta shook her head. "But there are thousands in this city," she said. "Tens of thousands, and more over the island. What about them?"

"A great king is always buried with grave offerings," said the serpent's head, faintly satisfied. "He is given slaves to serve and food for feasting and ornaments for amusement. Your King Kassander will have the greatest grave of all great men, the mightiest and most glorious tomb of all time."

Anastasios shook his head slowly, trying to grasp this. "He—he could not—he would not allow the kingdom to...."

But he would. His father was proud, unyielding, and fiercely protective of their dignity and the Ivory Throne's. Rather than become a beggar at the table of kings he had once subjugated, he would die in wealth and splendor.

"When?" he asked, and the word cracked in his throat.

"Very soon," the goat said.

"Tonight," said the serpent.

Anastasios' throat closed. Tonight? But that was too soon—there would be no time to convince his father....

The lion turned, and Anastasios saw it in profile for the first time. Two goat's udders swung swollen beneath its belly as it turned. It sat, and the dugs left thin trails of moisture where they brushed the stone, vanishing in the heat.

"You have a—" Anastasios stopped. A cub? A kid?

"A child," supplied Casta. "You are a mother, and not afraid to leave your child when you perish here. That means you must know a way of escape."

The three heads looked approvingly at her. "Very good," said the goat. "It is true, I will not be here when the earth splits and pours forth molten rock and death."

"Then tell us how we can escape with you!"

"Oh, clever girl," said the lion's head, "you are not clever enough. My father was the winter storm, my mother was disease. How could you travel the paths I walk?"

Casta shook her head, tears lighting her eyes with reflected fire. "But there must be a way. You would not come to warn us if there—there has to be a way. If we cannot take everyone, we can take some."

The fires around them flared, and the ankle-height flames leapt unevenly. Far, far below them, a sound more felt than heard pressed upward, a terran growl of discontent.

The lion's head swung to face them. "Run," it said.

Anastasios did not wait to argue further. He seized Casta's wrist and pulled her back, turning to retrace their path through the winding labyrinth. The oil lamp fell and shattered, but the trough-fires lit their path and led them forward.

Casta pulled free and sprinted, and Anastasios knew she would have passed him if not for the narrowness of the passage. "Hurry!" she pressed. "We can yet warn them!"

The labyrinth uncoiled before them and at last they burst through to the spiraling well of stairs. Now Casta did pass him, heedless of his rank, and dashed up the stairs first. "I'll beat the temple shield," she called back. "You order everyone to boats."

Anastasios did not question her order, but its effectiveness. He was a prince, yes, but not the king. If the king had decreed the soothsayer's words false, how could the prince gainsay him? Who would act on such treasonous words? But perhaps if they heard the temple shield—

They ran through the temple and past the altar, still smoldering, and out to the great porch. Casta took up the mallet which hung from the wall and ran to the enormous bronze shield which hung between the columns. "Go to the palace!" she shouted as she heaved the mallet into position. "Warn everyone!"

It was a simple instruction, yet so difficult. How could he warn everyone? Who would not believe him mad or treasonous? If they did believe him, what would he order them to do?

Casta swung the mallet and struck the shield. The metallic clang cut through the air and then faded to a low rumble which rolled through Anastasios, shaking his belly and his blood and burning inside his ears. He bolted for the palace as she wound back and struck it again, sending waves of sound out across the sleeping city.

He reached the palace gate before her fourth gong. The guards, jolted from their nocturnal watch by the sound, started toward him and then held their posts. "Who are you?" they demanded, and then, "My prince! What is the matter? Why does the temple call at this time of night?"

He hesitated. How could he say this? "We are in danger," he said. He held up a hand as one of the guards turned to signal another on the tower. "Not from attack—from below. The earth will split and destroy us. We have to leave the island."

They stared at him. "The earth will split?" They could not argue, not with the prince, but he saw their disbelief plain in their expressions.

"I spoke with the Khimaira!" he snapped. "She spoke to me in the temple, beyond the Gate of Flames!"

The gong's resonance had built to a steady roar of sound, and lights were being struck in the buildings below and in the palace windows above. The guards were surprised to hear of the monster's appearance, but they were not yet convinced. "And if the earth itself should wish to swallow us, what must we do to placate it?"

There was a short, feminine cry of protest, and the shield's boom ceased. The temple guards must have reached Casta. Anastasios wanted to scream with frustration. "We have to flee! She said it would come tonight!"

The shield's last tone still resonated, a deep sound which rolled under them and made Anastasios' bones buzz. It did not fade, but rose, threatening to drown even his shouts, and he realized it was not the brazen shield but a sound from the earth, deeper and louder than anything he might ever have imagined. One of the guards seized him, sheltering him with his body against invisible attack, as the very stone trembled beneath their feet.

Anastasios shouted over their curses. "We have to get everyone off the island!"

The guard not holding Anastasios shook his head. "Impossible, my prince. Even if we have the time, we haven't the boats. Our merchants and our fishers and our warships together could not carry everyone. And we would need food, and supplies, and—"

The earth bucked beneath them, throwing them to the ground. Anastasios pressed his hands to his ears as the city shook. Stones and dust showered around them. Down in the city itself, the buildings seemed to wave as if they sat upon the sea instead of upon rock, and then they parted, wrenching aside as a gap opened like a new street, cutting the circles.

Anastasios pushed to his feet as the shaking stopped, running forward a few steps to stare down at the city. The noise stopped, so now the cries and shouts could be heard. Lights moved in the dark as people searched for children or spouses, and scattered flames showed where oil had spilled and caught during the rocking.

A new sound, familiar and yet out of place in the dusty chaos or the palace's porch, was rising. Anastasios ignored it as he turned toward the temple. It was yet standing, though clouds of dust showed it had been shaken with the rest. Had Casta been harmed? Where was she now?

One of the guards began invoking deities in rapid succession. Anastasios turned and saw moonlight reflecting on the waves, waves which never should have been so near to the palace. Water was washing into the city, rushing toward the great new crevice in its center.

"Sound all the bells," Anastasios said, though he knew even as he spoke there was no point. No alert remained to call after such a shaking and booming. There was no one who was not aware of the danger. But they had to do something. "Sound all the bells, for the people to get to safety."

But where was safety? The ground had gone from beneath them and the sea was coming into them. There was no safety but in boats, far from the swirling maelstrom this would become.

He left the guards as they still spoke and started toward the temple. If Casta had been seized, she must be released. She must flee the island.

But the temple guards were staring down at the city with her. One held the mallet in his fist, the other had a hand on Casta's shoulder, but it was clear any thoughts of detaining her for beating the shield were forgotten. "Casta!" he called, and she turned to him.

"It's terrible," she said, her voice hardly more than a whisper.

He came to the edge of the porch and looked down with them. The first of the sea reached the rift and poured over the edge in a thin sheet, white in the moonlight. A moment later there was a hiss like a world-sized serpent and enormous clouds of steam burst into the air. The fissure boomed through the clouds rising to obscure their view.

If it had been him—if he had been the cause, he might have been able to stop it. He could have fled in a boat, or died in the arena. But he could do nothing.

Anastasios reached for Casta's hand. "We have to go," he said. "We can try to reach the docks. My father's ship will be there."

"Your father—"

"If he will not use his ship, that is no reason we cannot," Anastasios said sharply. "I am his prince and heir. If he chooses to die, then I inherit his ship and may ride it to safety."

The temple guards looked briefly disturbed at this frank speech but did not argue. Below, screams were rising as the steam rolled across the houses nearest the rift. One guard nodded. "And we will watch you, my prince," he said. "Let us go to the ship."

A clever way to ensure his place aboard, but Anastasios could not begrudge him that. He nodded. "We must hope the docks are yet standing. And that the water has not yet risen above the length of the anchoring lines." If the ships could not rise above the flood, they would sink as the dock lines pulled them under or break free to float away in the torrent, leaving Anastasios and the others trapped in either case.

Casta wrapped her fingers about his and they started along the temple porch. One guard stopped to retrieve a torch from a holder, and Anastasios was glad of the supplement to the moonlight. The water below was deeper now, too strong to be resisted, and people and crates and animals were carried thrashing down the streets and into the black crevasse. Their shrieks and bellows, and the screams from those watching from the roofs, made Anastasios wish for the earth's roar again.

They came to the stone steps which led down toward the docks, curving along the upper border of the city. Dust and loose stone lay over them. On either side, scattered over the hill, tiny vents spat steam or smoke like the breath of hidden demons.

The guard started down the steps, testing each foothold, and a few stones shifted beneath his weight, but the steps generally held firm. He was about twenty paces below them when he turned to call upward, "It is safe to descend, prince."

Anastasios, Casta, and the remaining guard started forward. A tremor ran through the earth, and they each froze, but it passed. Casta and Anastasios looked at one another and then hurried down the steps.

The scouting guard ran ahead, kicking a few stones from their path and testing each step for stability. They came to a passage cut through the hill's shoulder, a luxury to spare the king climbing and to display his wealth to ascending guests. The earth rumbled again, and dust and small stones showered from the dressed walls on either side.

The foremost guard hesitated and then drew a copper bull figurine from somewhere within his clothing. He held it close to his mouth for a moment, glanced over his shoulder at them, and then started forward again.

The earth remained still, and the dust in the roofless passage began to clear. About ten paces in, the guard began to cough. Anastasios at first supposed it was the stone dust, but the man's cough grew fiercer. He stopped, and Casta and the second guard with him. He remembered the sting in his eyes and throat as they descended into the Gate of Flames.

The coughing guard looked at the bull in his hand and recoiled. He spun to face them, his wide eyes streaming. He pulled at his throat, as if something invisible tightened around it, but Anastasios stared at his breastplate, where all the copper symbols of the temple had blackened.

Casta gave a little gasp at the sight of the dark bull and armor. The guard choked, stumbled, and went to the ground.

"Nereus!" shouted the second guard, and he rushed down the steps toward the passage.

Anastasios remembered the Khimaira turning to spit fire into the floor troughs, and all the room and passage lighting at once. "No, stop!" he shouted.

The guard reached the passage and ran directly into the ground, as if he had fallen asleep midstride. The torch leapt and the air itself erupted into flame, engulfing both men. There were no screams.

Casta snatched at Anastasios, pulling him back along the path. "Come away!"

They ran back toward the temple. The earth roared again and they went down hard as the shaking began. It was like the ground wished to shiver them off, as a bull might a fly, and they clung to each other as if that might hold them to the earth.

An enormous metallic clang reached them even over the booming of the earth cracking open, and Anastasios looked up to see the temple's great bronze shield rocking and shuddering where it had fallen. First the blackened bull—and the fallen gong—just now the soothsayer's accusations of defying angered gods seemed as credible as the Khimaira's talk of a disturbed earth.

The tremor ended, and they got to their feet. Anastasios had lost his cap, and his hair hung over one eye. The palace had fallen, stones tumbled inward. The temple stood half-erect.

Anastasios looked down on the city. The steam was fading, but now the rising sea carried buildings as well as people. "We have to reach the ship. We cannot stay on this island."

Casta shook her head. "If we keep to the hill…."

He pointed to the seawater rushing through the city. Only the rooftops were visible now. "The water is still rising. Who can say if there will be a hill by morning?"

She swallowed and nodded. "Or docks, or a ship."

But the inward rush of the sea was slowing, it seemed. The fissure had been filled, with water or buildings or bodies, and though the water was high, it was no longer pouring into a steaming cauldron. It was now a treacherous shoreline, waves slapping against the reefs and boulders of half-crushed houses and floating debris.

Anastasios looked down the porch toward the path they had tried. "But if we cannot go to the docks, then I don't know—"

"The shield," she said. All courtesies of rank had gone. There was no time for spare and pretty words. "We will ride the shield."

"What?"

She was already hurrying to the fallen gong. It lay with the rim turned upward, a wide dish with a raised lip. "We will use this as a boat," she said. "We can take it out to the docks and find a proper ship. Hurry!"

It was madness, but madness was all around them, so why not? He crouched and began shoving with her, grinding the great bronze shield over stone.

The temple porch fell away to a steep slope, where the palace and the temple could look down upon the city and the tributary sea. "You first," said Casta. "I will be better able to leap in as it runs."

That was undoubtedly true. Anastasios tucked himself into the shield, pulling the remnants of the hanging chains inside so they would not drag behind or snag on debris. "Now you," he said.

Casta gave a mighty push, and the shield slid over the porch's edge and started downhill. She sprinted alongside and leapt into it, catching her arms about Anastasios as the shield tipped and veered. Then it stabilized and sped downhill, sliding smoothly over the grassy slope.

There should have been people on the hill, Anastasios thought. They should have climbed to safety. But the earth's assault had come in the night, when all were drunk and spent after the festival, and almost no one had been awake to flee.

"Lean back!" he called to Casta. "We can't let the lip dip into the water!"

They shifted back as best they were able, lifting the leading curve of the shield like a prow, and it struck the water with a jolt which snapped Anastasios' teeth hard enough to pain the back of his head. But the shield bobbed and floated, and they quickly scooped out most of the water which had splashed inside.

"Now, to the south," Anastasios said. "Toward the docks. We'll find someone there."

The currents were confused and twisted about the shattered city, and they had only their hands for paddles. They were swept at the sea's whim despite their best efforts. But they were afloat. After a time, they ceased wasting their strength and waited for the tide to turn, if it would.

They leaned together for warmth and for the stability of their makeshift boat. Anastasios wondered where he might have been now, had he not found Casta in the temple in what seemed a lifetime ago. Where she might have been, had she not found him. They drifted among the debris, moving through the city. They passed a broken wall where a mewling bedraggled kitten perched, and Casta stretched to seize it and folded it into her lap.

The hill began to crack as the city had, splitting narrowly between palace and temple, and the fallen buildings began to tumble down the slope. The fissure steamed, a ghost in the moonlight of all that lay beneath the surface.

He had been first a penniless slave of the city, and then a rich slave to an ill-fitting crown. Now he was a penniless prince—except perhaps he was not even that, not now. The Ivory Throne was nothing now, and for the first time, he owed obedience and obeisance to no one but himself. It was a curious sensation.

"Look," Casta said quietly. "The dawn."

"Look," Anastasios said, pointing to the south. "A ship."

It was not the royal ship; that, like the docks, was nowhere to be seen. It was a fat-bellied trade vessel, possibly out of Athens. He rose on his knees and shouted. "Hoy! Help!"

An answering hail came from the ship. "Come this way, if you can!"

They paddled as best they could, and then a rope was tossed from the ship and they snatched at it. They were pulled close and then over the side, the kitten clinging to Casta with all claws. Two sailors went down to tie ropes to the shield's chains to draw it up, as such a fortune of bronze could not be sacrificed.

"Poseidon had an eye for you," said the captain. "You're the fifth and sixth we've picked up." He gestured to a cluster of refugees sitting together on the deck. "That's not much for a city."

Anastasios nodded.

"Have you seen anyone of the palace? King Kassander? We've been watching for his ship, but there's been precious few vessels seen."

What is a man worth, when he cannot be what he was?

Casta opened her mouth to speak, looking at Anastasios, but he answered first. "No one from the palace," he said. "The palace was taken in the earth-shaking. We alone were saved."

N is for New Beginnings

Milo James Fowler

And to the clockwork man was given a heart of flesh agreeable to the gears within him, to pump his oil like blood through a wrought iron body; and over his heart was mounted a glass door hinged with brass and padlocked shut, so that all in the town could see he bore an organ much like their own.

Dr. Horstmann saw what he had made, and he pronounced it good, tucking the lock's key into a front pocket of his waistcoat. It would take only a single bullet to shatter the glass and puncture the clockwork man's heart, leaving him rigid as a statue. But the good doctor considered it worth the risk, to allay the fears of superstitious townsfolk. His creation was no monster; it was vulnerable, as anyone could plainly see. And it served a purpose, taking the place of a beloved blacksmith who had passed away that winter: Dr. Horstmann's only son.

Then arose Asaph, itinerant man of the special cloth, who rode across the barren wastes into town and saw an abomination which the townsfolk had considered a thing of dread curiosity. Asaph's will was a thing of steel; no one questioned him. He commanded good Dr. Horstmann's ankles and wrists be tied with stout lengths of rope to four different horses in the town square.

"This is what we make of your devilry!" Asaph cried, and he fired off his Colt revolver, two explosions in quick succession.

The horses bolted wide-eyed. The townsfolk screamed as Dr. Horstmann's arms and legs tore loose of his torso, trailing behind the animals' hooves in a screen of dust. All could see what was left of the doctor, bloody and wrong, as he thumped across the ground and rolled over in the dirt. Yet death did not come to him quickly.

Standing in the shadows of the smithy shop, the clockwork man watched through eyes like marbles. They carried swirls of blue, contrasting with the black iron of his face and the limbs that protruded from frayed denim overalls.

"You thought you could play *GOD*? Replace a man with a *machine*?" Asaph's boot heel rolled the doctor onto his back. Chest convulsing, Dr. Horstmann gazed upward, meeting the eyes of his judge and jury.

The blistered townsfolk crowded around the spectacle like thirsty horses to water. The man of the special cloth held up a hand, and they froze in place.

"Listen now," Asaph said. "The instrument of Satan speaks."

Dr. Horstmann's head jerked forward, and he spat a mouthful of blood onto his waistcoat. "Don't fear—my child," he gasped. Then his head fell back into the dust, and his mutilated torso lay still.

"What's that he said?" murmured the crowd.

The man of the special cloth had heard, though he knew not what the good doctor meant. The clockwork man had also heard, and he understood the meaning of the words, for he knew the origin of the pulsating organ within him.

"Now for the creature!" shouted Asaph, spinning on his heel with the Colt raised. He stood head and shoulders above the townsfolk who pressed close around him, and when he came halfway through a complete revolution, his eyes caught sight of the clockwork man lingering in shadow.

The townsfolk turned to follow Asaph's gaze, and they released strangles of horror as the machine emerged carrying a massive hammer in his iron fist, his joints clanking against one another, sunlight glinting on the glass door that contained his thumping heart of flesh.

Dr. Horstmann had not gifted the creature with speech, but even if he had, the clockwork man would not have known what to say, seeing his creator lying in such disarray.

"Do you see?" the man of the special cloth called out, and the townsfolk nodded as if they knew what he meant. "It knows it should die." He cocked back the hammer of his revolver and took aim at the quivering organ behind glass. "As should every abomination."

He fired. The townsfolk cringed at the blast of the .45, and some of them let their astonishment be known as the clockwork man brought up an arm to deflect the round. It glanced off him like granite. He did not slow his approach.

Asaph eyed the blacksmith's hammer in that iron fist and pulled the trigger again, twice, shots as close together as before. When the clockwork man deflected them as well, the townsfolk scrambled to turn tail and scatter. Only the man of the special cloth remained rooted—either by fear or determination—with one last bullet in the cylinder of his Peacemaker.

"Come meet your doom, golem!"

He did not fire, not until the clockwork man had come within three yards and dropped the hammer into the dirt, reaching with his right arm of iron for the shoulder of his left.

That was when Asaph emptied his gun of the last shot, shattering the glass door and puncturing the heart of flesh inside. Oil splattered outward, and the clockwork man's gears shuddered to a halt. He froze like any clock that could no longer run.

There he stood. Transfixed in time. The gap clear to see where he had torn his left arm free. The blue marble eyes focused not on the man who had shot him, but on the good doctor lying forgotten in the dust without arms of his own. His creator. His father.

The man of the special cloth stared as if he himself had been turned to rusted iron.

O is for Offspring

Brittany Warman

Documentation Related to Case #688: E9-1 to E9-6
Detective Robert Sanland—*For Immediate Processing*

E9-1
Case #688

"Of Gods and Cameras: Interview with Tom Boland, Creator of the
Chimera Photograph Manipulation Series" (excerpt)
By Kathy Harkness : *Text & Pictures Magazine*
09/05/2026

[*Unpublished*; redacted due to events of 10/26/2026-11/05/2026]

Tell me about how you got starting taking pictures? Did you always like it?

I've always loved taking pictures, ever since I was a kid. The precision of framing things just right, the satisfying click of a shutter, it's all a kind of taming of magic and horror to me and that's... exciting I guess. It always has been. Here, let me give you the world anew, let me give you the same thing but different. Let me show you how things *really* are. That's how I got into photo manipulation—at some point it got to not be enough to just give people more of the same, more of what was *actually* there, I wanted to find some way to see beyond what was before my eyes and reach some deeper, more terrifying truth. Something beyond sight. A core truth, I guess.

And then?

Well yeah, so that's when I starting blending and merging the pictures with my computer. The first one I did was this woman I was on a train with who was complaining and complaining about her commute. I thought it sounded like barking, her whining and nagging, so I gave her the mouth of my neighbor's dog, whose picture I'd taken just after he had stolen a slice of meat from one of the picnic tables at the park across the street. I switched her eyes with the buttons of my wool coat because she didn't see anything around her but her own problems. I gave her the boots of the man sitting three seats down from her, because the greatest thing anyone could ever give her would be to walk a mile in his shoes for a change.

It's a stunning image you've created, so lifelike. Really all of them are. What would you say your favorite one is?

Um, well, that's a hard question, I mean, most of them are so... horrific. They're really the stuff of my nightmares [*laughs*]. That's what they should be though, right? I mean, art is supposed to provoke change. I think the most satisfying one though is the one that started as a picture of my boss at the awful job I had before the pictures started taking off. I replaced his head with the head of a hyena, laughing without joy at everything. I gave him the bottom half of the girl who worked in reception... because it was the only thing he ever seemed to notice about her, despite how insanely pretty her eyes were, especially each day around 4:30PM when the sun hit the windows in this specific way. They would light up, you know, I guess partially because she just had to wait that final half an hour before she could go home. I hated that he was always just checking out her ass. So yeah, I made him ridiculous, but I did give him the tail of one of the scorpions at the zoo too... the man could certainly still sting when he wanted to and he knew it.

I think that really gets to the heart of the... unsettling nature of your work. They aren't just parodies of people, they strike the audience as really biting, powerful commentary on the truth of their souls, of our own souls.

Well, thanks, I mean, I want people to see that. I want them to be uncomfortable. This is who we are, these mash ups of objects and people and animals and whatever. We're not really more than that.

Don't you ever worry that you're misrepresenting the people you "re-create"? Certainly there's more to the dog smile woman, for example, than just the complaints you heard. Perhaps she was just having an off day?

No, yeah, I mean... yeah. Maybe. A photograph is just one second in time, one moment. The mix of things we're made up of is always changing, isn't it? That woman may have gotten home as a totally different person, all kneading cat paws and knitted blankets, who knows? But I like to think I revealed a truth deep inside her, a truth no one really wants to see. And those are the ones we have to expose, as artists. And anyway, it's just moments, just photographs.

You sound kind of sad about that?

Do I sometimes wish my chimeras were more than photographs of things from my imagination? Sure, what artist doesn't want to live in the world they create? Plus, if you *became* what you projected, don't you think people would think more about what they put out in the world? I mean, it would be horrible and wonderful at the same time wouldn't it?

I think I'd lean toward horrible myself! [laughs]

Yeah. Yeah, I guess so *[smiles]*. But it would change the world.

Mr. Boland's photographs can be seen in the Stiller Gallery on 5th Ave from October 25th to December 31st.

E9-2
Case #688

"Chaos in Central Park: Sutherland Body Found in Gruesome State"
CCC News Corporation
10/26/2026

[First Incident]

Police are now confirming that the body discovered this morning by an eight-year-old child is indeed that of well-known political analyst Barbara Sutherland. Mutilated almost beyond recognition, Ms. Sutherland's remains were found in the Conservatory Gardens on the east side of the park.

Though the incident has been officially ruled a suicide, rumors from those on the scene attest that the corpse's eyes were removed and replaced with large black buttons, while her mouth was slit almost from ear to ear. Both injuries are inconsistent with self-harm and authorities are reportedly questioning the series of events that led to the famous commentator's death.

Curiously, the boots Sutherland was wearing were visibly several sizes too large.

Sutherland's office could not be reached for comment.

E9-3
Case #688

911 Call from Christine Roberts [transcript]
10/31/2026 – 10:57PM

[Third Incident – Note that details of the second incident are classified at this time due to the high-profile nature of the victim]

911 Dispatch: 911, what's your emergency?

Roberts: Please, please help, my husband, he's… oh my God…

911: Ma'am I'm going to need you to calm down and tell me what's happening.

Roberts: I'm in the bathroom, the door's locked but I can hear him, he's in pain, I don't know what's happening to him. I hear him outside, he's... his whole body was... I think someone else is out there? Oh my God, he's screaming, please send help!

911: Where are you?

Roberts: I'm at [REDACTED]

911: Police are on their way. Please try to remain calm.

Roberts: Oh my God, oh my God...

E9-4
Case #688

11/02/2026

[Public Safety Announcement]

THE FOLLOWING PUBLIC SAFETY ANNOUCEMENT APPLIES TO ALL AREAS OF CENTRAL MANHATTAN

On 10/26/26, 10/31/26, and 11/02/26 three incidents similar in nature occurred in the immediate Central Park area. Police are on high alert this evening and suspect the events are connected. Citizens are advised to stay indoors if at all possible and avoid the park while police investigate.

Anyone with information regarding these crimes is encouraged to call the NYPD tip line at 212-555-TIPS.

IF YOU KNOW OR SUSPECT YOUR PHOTOGRAPH IS PART OF THE TOM BOLAND EXHIBIT CURRENTLY APPEARING AT STILLER GALLERY PLEASE CONTACT THE POLICE IMMEDIATELY

E9-5
Case #688

"The Unbearable Weight of Artistic Inspiration"
11/04/26

[Boland Personal Statement on Blog]

I likely have very little time to post this and I doubt all that many people will read it before forming their own opinions. I expect the police will be able to put together the pieces of the puzzle quickly, but mystery was never a goal of mine. Indeed I want the facts known. I want to be recognized for what I really am. I am only the beginning.

Artistic inspiration is a terrible burden. It eats away at your soul while the rest of humanity wanders freely from fast food restaurant to movie theater, from shopping trip to picnic. The urge to create something lasting, something powerful… it devours you. And nothing satisfies it, once you've fixated on a creation—it haunts your dreams until you can bring it to life in the way you imagine. Anything less is simply not good enough. This is art, its curse and its beauty. Nothing can grip a human life more, not even love. We are all selfish creatures really.

You're likely following my blog because of your interest in my photographs, but this is not my art. This is nothing. Blurry, ephemeral images of seconds in a day cannot possibly create the effect I truly intended, an effect that is lasting, something that *changes* humanity. A photograph you can forget. A human body transformed into its truth... *that* no one will ever forget. *That* is art.

Death and art have always walked hand in hand. All art is dead, is it not? If it is ever to have any chance of living, for even a moment, sacrifice is necessary. But often death was my project's choice, not mine. They were unable to see the beauty in what they had become, the sacrifice they had made for the betterment of the world, they only saw the horror. Yes, there was pain—for them, for me—but I have created thirteen masterpieces and my legacy will be unmatched. My gift demanded nothing less.

When you hear the stories, when you see the pictures now... now perhaps you'll think twice about what you have decided to be. We are all made up of so many different, changing things, but maybe you'll want to be one of the beautiful chimeras, not one of mine. My art will change the world. There is no other way. I have always seen the real you and I am not the only one.

E9-6
Case #688

"Tom Boland: Serial Killer or Inspired Prophet?" (excerpt)
The New York Times
11/10/26

[Editorial; Anonymous Writer]

The events of late October to early November have undoubtedly rocked the nation in numerous ways. The circumstances of the death of Mr. Boland at the hands of the NYPD on November 5th, 2026, combined with the horrific states of his alleged victims' bodies, are not likely to be soon forgotten. There remains too, of course, the matter of the seven as yet unidentified victims mentioned in the artists' blog.

But I don't want to talk about Mr. Boland's crimes. I don't even want to talk about how he was able to accomplish them, though that too remains in question. I want to talk about why he did them. We are a culture that values both artistic expression and violence. Is it any wonder that those things would eventually combine? Is it any wonder that Mr. Boland saw himself as an inspired artist, a prophet bringing the truth to the masses?

No. And I, for one, won't be surprised when it happens again. For we *are* mutilated, chimerical creatures at heart. We are uglier than we appear. Showing the world what we're really made of… what could possibly have a greater chance of changing the world than that?

P is for Photography

Michael B. Tager

The master had weak bones and could not dismount the mule without assistance. The student—Dana in another life—jumped off her own stoic beast with a joy of movement that she tried to suppress, given the circumstances. She tugged at the buckles and ropes that held the heavy bag to the mule's back until it fell to the rock-strewn dirt then slung it over her back, groaning. She had put on muscle weight since joining the monastery; before, she could never have lifted it. The bag was as tall as she and stuffed to bursting. When she was satisfied with the pack's position, she then hurried over to the master and offered her hand. With a withered palm the master accepted and, working together, was soon on the firm, barren ground.

It was a soft spring day, still cold high in the mountains but with the promise of warmth and light. When the sun poked through the heavy cloud cover, the master sighed and grinned, turning sightless eyes to the sky. "The sun is our Mother, no?"

She-who-was-once-Dana nodded. She had half-expected a lecture. The monastery was silent except for when the masters gave their long speeches on the way of the world and for meals, though it was understood that the supplicants would discuss their learning.

The master continued. "The sun gives us energy and life. We bask in it; our skin is warmed and tanned by it. Seeds grow due to its love and animals thrive in it. What else nurtures us besides mothers?"

After a silence, the student realized she was expected to answer. "I don't know, Master. Water, perhaps?"

A short nod and a twitch of withered lips. The master was hairless and so wrinkled it was impossible to tell what sex they were. She guessed the master was a woman, but couldn't be sure. "Not a bad answer, child." The master lead over the rough terrain.

"Thank you, master."

"Child, for the rest of the trip, formalities can be eased in this case, I think. No need to call me master."

"What should I call you?"

The master opened her mouth, paused and then shook her gray hair, cheek bones sharp against dry skin. "My given name would sound odd after so long unspoken. Give me another name."

She-who-was-once-Dana thought for a moment, her palm growing warm in the old woman's firm grip. She said, "My old teacher, before I came here, her name was Lenore. May I call you that?"

A bark of laughter. "In my old life, I'd call that a dancer's name. But yes, call me that."

They were on a cliff overlooking a deep valley. Wisps of moisture that weren't quite clouds roiled beneath them. Small birds flew in circles. A few hardy plants grew horizontally from the cliff face. Far below, mountain goats clutched at invisible paths. She would never get used to seeing that, even if she lived there until she was one hundred.

At a slow, measured pace, they continued forward, the student lending her strength. Near the edge of the cliff a ladder was attached to the earth by heavy, stout metal pylons wrapped in cracked leather. She was careful when she began her descent, testing each rung until she was sure it could hold her weight. Only once a year did anyone visit this spot and there had been accidents in the past, or so she had been told. This was her first trip.

Several rungs below the top, she waited until Lenore began her own climb down. It took several minutes of careful placement and the student became aware of the strain on her arms, the sweat drying instantly as howling winds tore at her with playful hands.

When Lenore had one foot on the rungs, "Water has energy, yes. It carries the power of *qi*, as we do, who carry the power of the sun in our bones. Without it, we are nothing. But to me, water is masculine. It carries us places with steady, unrelenting strength, does it not? When it rages, it is a tempest and then calm. Is that not a man?"

When she was sure Lenore was secure on the earth, the student began down the ladder, her sandaled feet slow and deliberate on the rungs. Lenore climbed one rung at a time taking long breaks in between. The ladder had been there a very long time. Centuries perhaps. She said, "A woman can rage, too."

"I would never dare test the fury of the sun. I was in the desert once, far south of here, when I was young. It was quite something. But really, it isn't about masculine or feminine, it is about power and energy and life." Lenore waved a hand and sparks flew from the tips of her ragged fingers and floated, exploding in small bursts and light where they touch they ladder. "It is about what we harness. Why we are here. Why we live in a temple above the clouds, learning to master the energy in our blood. You know what it's about." Lenore waited for her to speak.

"About *qi*."

"Yes, child. About *qi*. With it, we can move the moon. Of course, I am old and weak. You are young and untrained. But there is a balance. Demonstrate what you have learned. Show me." A heavy breath and

Lenore's shrunken feet touched the rung above her head. The master's toes were heavily bruised, toenails long and jagged.

She gaped up at Lenore. "Now?" The wind tugged at her and a fat drop of rain crashed into the rock beside her.

"Now. Show me."

With a sigh and concentration, she summoned the life within, focusing it in a single finger that she outstretched from the ladder. She felt tension in her head, tightening in her throat. With a grunt, she released the energy into an eruption of light. Harmless, barely solid, it flew by Lenore's turned back and exploded on the rock. Her breath returned in a glorious inhalation.

They rested there for the span of fifty breaths. The backpack weighed her down and seemed to want to drag her into the abyss below. She kept her spine straight and when Lenore spoke again, she latched onto the words, hoping for distraction. She was disappointed. "Well done. No more talking, I think. Not until we're there."

While she regained energy, the student chanced a looked down, past her flowing amber robes, past the next fifty yards of ladder, to the jutting outline of their destination. The ancient cold metal of the ladder burned through her sandals and into her callused feet. The wind howled and she, unable to help herself, glanced down at the roiling depth below her. There were wisps of clouds and her stomach threatened to rebel. She repeated the mantra of the monastery. *Life is the illusion before death. We were nothing before we were lived. We will be void again.* The quaking in her gut subsided.

When the master was ready, they continued. It rained briefly, a harsh, cold rain that set their teeth to chattering. She missed her long hair that would have kept her degrees warmer and wished for better under things than the shapeless rags under her robes. But she repeated the mantra over and over. She was not special. She was part of the world.

Finally, after what seemed an interminable time, her feet found solid purchase again and she lifted her hands to help Lenore. The old monk was gray with exertion, but grinned nonetheless. They faced the sky and the endless mountains around them. It was forbidding and, she thought, beautiful. She said so.

Lenore's face was angled to the sky. "Do you know why this trip is necessary?"

She thought of her teachings. "Life comes from life, though death comes to all."

A wink and the snap of fingers. "You are a sharp one. You haven't been with us long, eh? A year? Two? How long have you been drinking of the water of life, which flows from beneath the stones? Eh, do you know, girl?"

She felt the old woman's sharp fingers as they jabbed into her ribs. She squirmed away and said, "It was three years this past summer. Twelve hundred and ninety-six days, to be exact."

"So long? Heh. Life moves quickly." Lenore shivered and pointed to the black cave behind them. The rain had started again, fat drops that splattered with a loud hiss. They shuffled inside and moved carefully until their eyes adjusted. "It moves quicker than you think when you're young, when your blood is strong and thick and runs like fire. When you're old, blood is thin and tired and comes out in trickles instead of a gush. It seems like yesterday when I was here last, guiding my old master in this same trip. I might have been even younger than you. How old are you?"

"I don't know," she said, feeling her way through the darkness. There were no torches and once they turned a corner, no outside light. But it wasn't full blackness, not true dark. There was light coming from somewhere, somewhere deep down the cave. *Time is an illusion, a chimera. We are here, we live, we are gone.*"

Lenore grunted and exhaled, like a bull about to charge. "You don't have to quote scripture at me, girl. Regardless. Blood is water and sun mixed. It carries the power of the world, the energy of life. Like your moon's blood. Like arterial blood. It's what keeps us animals, keeps us grounded in the world. They eat us, we eat them, we return to nothing while feeding the life and joining the water and the sun." The master was breathing heavily now, every step a bare shuffle. "You know, every initiate comes here once with their master. You knew that, yes?"

"Yes Master." When the woman glared at her, she stammered and said, "I mean, yes Lenore."

"Good, good." Lenore grunted and a small smile stole over her lips. Another exhalation and her weight dropped on the student's shoulders. "I'm quite tired, girl."

The student shifted so that her shoulders supported the master's weight. With her left hand, she reached across her body and took the master's right hand. They walked forward, linked. She thought for a moment on her master's words and said, "Don't we want to be more than animals? Isn't that the goal?"

The further they went, the brighter it became. It was warmer, too, and stank. She wasn't sure of the smell. It was partially animal, partially just *heat*. The chill from the water and winds had subsided and she'd begun to sweat. But Lenore still shivered and coughed.

Something wet and foul-smelling left Lenore's mouth and smacked against the rock with a thick splat. It was tinged with red. She could see now, Once-Dana realized. She looked forward into the tunnel and could not quite make anything out beside the smooth stone beneath them, worn by countless steps and years. There were no sounds of bugs or anything live. When Lenore spoke again, she jumped. She'd forgotten her question.

"Bah. We are animals more than we're not animals. We eat and drink and shit and fuck." She cackled at her student's reaction. "Oh, shush. You've heard the words before. Do not think we are better than the people below. We may read more books and we may drink from the water of life but we are them and they are us. Our numbers swell from the people's castoffs, we partake of their men when the time is right and our initiates wish it. We are merely dedicated to a different ideal."

"Yes, Master," she agreed. She had to remember, she was not better, she was not better, she was not better. She muttered the mantra to herself as they continued. It helped calm her, but she found her heart beating again the further they walked. The heat was growing, as was the light. She felt her pulse in the vein of her neck.

The master faced her, expressionless. "You are not frightened, are you child?"

She knew she was blushing and was thankful the master couldn't see her. If the master could see at all she'd have seen the cave brighten considerably. A regular, deep sound could be heard as well, like raspy breathing. The smell was becoming worse, almost overpowering. It was definitely offal and rot. "I am," she admitted. "I am trying not to be."

They moved around a final bend and the cave opened into a cavern. The master stopped and leaned into her, gasping. "It is right to be afraid. We are animals. Their blood is the same as our blood, a marriage of water and sun. They would be afraid. We are afraid. Come." They shuffled through the entranceway, Lenore almost carried by the tiring student.

Inside, the darkness faded away and she could not help but gape. The cavern was large and stretched away for hundreds of feet, shadows enveloping the corners and high, naturally vaulted ceiling. The ground gently sloped downward before them and extended to either side for what seemed like miles. Enormous eggs, almost as tall as she was were spaced haphazardly about the chamber. They were membranous and glowed with an inner light. Together, they lit the cavern and the heat and stench they gave off was akin to a hundred camp fires. She couldn't stop staring before her, at the deep river that flowed by, at the island in the center of it, at the dais and the animal chained to an enormous stone and the nest of bones and hair and cloth where it lay.

"What is it?" she asked in awe. The creature was like nothing she had ever seen.

It was monstrous and beautiful, but its eyes, large and liquid, burned with intelligence. It was an animal, but it understood. And it stared at them and licked its thin lips with a thick, wide tongue. It purred and stepped forward, waiting.

Every nerve in her body screamed at her to run away but Lenore nudged her and they approached, stopping at the edge of the river, far from the creature. The master asked her to describe it and she did so as the distance decreased. It was large, far larger than their mules had been, larger than any horse she'd seen. It didn't have fur or feathers, but something in between, an iridescent green over thick scales. It had four legs, weirdly jointed and as she watched the creature's forelegs bent in amongst themselves as it crouched and cocked its shaggy, large-eyed head at them. When it opened its mouth, she saw rows of sharp teeth. It was powerfully muscled and she was glad for the thick chain around its long, sinuous neck, though it looked ancient.

She asked again. "What is it?"

"A relic of a time when it had a name. Who knows what it is? We don't. But it has been here for as long as we have, longer. It is our master and we guard it and it rewards us with its attention." The master's eyes, blind as they were, were full of love and admiration.

"Why is it here?" she asked, fear bubbling inside of her despite her best efforts to control it. *We came from nothing.*

The master's head shook side to side. It was the wrong question and the answer was simple. "Why are any of us here?" From the depths of her robe, a long knife emerged with a bone handle. It was curved and sharp. The student took it with a shudder. "We have records of when the first sister arrived. The creature and the monastery were here already. The monastery was broken then, exposed to centuries of weather, the creature withered. We nursed it to health and it, in return, gave us power."

The creature, sensing what was to happen, reared on its hind legs and screamed. The sound was sharp and hard and pierced Once-Dana to the core. A thick stream of black urine erupted from a dark cavity and sizzled into the slow-moving river before being swept away toward them.

Lenore pushed her in the small of the back. "Now. This is half of why we're here. Drink."

She started. "What?" she asked. "Now?"

The master's face hardened, her mouth turning down. "Don't be a fool. Obey me, *disciple.*"

At the command, she knelt and put her mouth to the river, drinking the tainted water in large gulps, her disgust pushed away by years of conditioning. The water tasted sour and clean at the same time, pure somehow, though filthy. She drank and drank until she could drink no more.

Gasping, she leaned back and felt a surge in her belly, of nausea and something else she couldn't readily identify. Her eyes closed as heat rushed through her, into her eyes and fingertips. She remembered suddenly when she was sixteen and in the throes of her first orgasm; she thought of her lost twenties, snorting whatever she could to be high; she was a child, lost in the sensation of her own body as she ran in circles, laughing. She gasped and held her head in her hands.

When it was over, she held out her palm and blinked. A ball of energy formed, its core white-hot, the edges crackling with fire. She let the ball rise and then she flicked it away to the ceiling of the cavern, lost in shadows, where it burst in a cascade of sparks. Bodies of bats fell, burnt, to the ground, some splashing into the water. A few fell into the creature's open mouth.

She watched the creature unfurl vestigial wings and regard her with intelligent eyes. "This is where our power comes from?"

Lenore chuckled. "Our water is its water and we imbibe of its strength. Do you not listen? We are all one. Are you not stronger, wiser, more patient since you have joined us? And are you not even more so now?"

The student clenched her teeth and resolved to remember her teaching. She said, "We are all one." She stood and touched Lenore's elbow. They walked again, following the riverbed. The creature paced, tracking them the whole way.

There was a rickety bridge crossing the river, made of simple wooden boards and leather. It was rotting in places. The master clucked tongue against teeth and mumbled about needing it to be fixed. "Everything wears out. Us especially."

When they crossed the bridge, the master elbowed her and she stopped. She was still breathing heavily from her experience. Her eyes wouldn't stop moving, her fingers twitched. She removed the straps from around her shoulders and the backpack, forgotten, slid to the ground. She opened it and removed large hunks of meat, salted and smoked. She eyed the creature. It watched her from the dais, its tail slowly moving above its eggs. She shivered and took the knife in hand.

"It is so beautiful." Lenore stood facing the creature, trembling. "So beautiful. It's funny. When I was here, with my master, I was terrified. It is powerful, so full of life and energy. Now, it's like seeing an old friend." She pointed at the eggs. "When I was here before, it had just clutched. My master told me that it had clutched once before in her lifetime and that none hatched. No one could get close enough to help the eggs. It attacks the second it can. It knows the borders of its prison."

"Prison?"

"Maybe sanctuary." Lenore sat in the earth and traced images in the dirt, nonsense symbols and pictures, loops and swirls she then destroyed with the wave of a palm. "What's the difference? All its energy is focused in this one place. It sees rushing water and cannot swim away, though it can drink." The master pointed to an offshoot of the river, a little stream, that ran through the dais. "It can never be free and its children die before they can be born. There are records of many clutches. No records of children. It has not seen the sun in recorded history, felt the touch of Mother's sunlight. Maybe someday we can free it, when its eggs blossom and they can go forth once more. Maybe that is our purpose. I do not know the answers." She coughed and said. "Do what you are here for," and gestured at her.

The student faced the creature and took the knife from her belt. She held it in her left hand and extended her right hand out. She traced the knife from the tip of her middle finger in a straight line across her palm, right to her wrist, to the edge of the vein. She cut deep and gritted her teeth against the stinging pain. When drops fell into the dirt at her feet, she reached into the pack and removed a small piece of meat wrapped in butcher's paper. It was fresh and a choice cut. She held the stream of lifesblood over the meat until it was well saturated. She looked up; the creature watched her with its large liquid eyes. It knew what she was doing. She knew it did.

When the meat was sopping, she tossed it underhanded. The animal's long, sinuous neck snapped forward and the meat disappeared into its mouth in one bite. It licked its lips and grumbled, almost a purr. It sniffed and its lips pulled back in what would have been a grin on a human. The student only saw teeth. It knew her now.

She wrapped her hand in gauze and waited. Time passed in silence. Eventually she began to toss the creature the meat she had carried. It watched the gifts arc toward the dais, and ate them with darting movements, but evidently took no relish in its meal. Instead it focused its attention on the master, who continued to draw in the dirt.

Finally, she said, "Will this be enough food?" The last piece had disappeared down its gullet.

The master waved a hand. "It doesn't eat like we do. Once a year it feeds and then it mostly sleeps. It'll keep." A sigh. "I used to love to draw in the sand. I lived on the beach and in the winter I'd play there, with the sound of the surf, drawing in the sand. We come from nothing, we will be nothing, but in between, we live. There are payments to be made for life. And we live well, full of power and song. Our women go forth into the world to spread stability and joy. We are peacekeepers and queens and warriors. And from our old, we give back to our wellspring. It is fair, is it not?"

"Yes, Master." Once-Dana bowed her head.

The old woman drew one more picture in the dirt and then stood. Holding head high, the master stepped forward, one shuffling step at a time until, with a howl, the creature moved. It was a blur and it wasn't until the chain snapped tight she realized it had already reached her master. Lenore didn't scream and with a shake of the beast's head, she was dead.

She forced herself to watch until the master was gone, until the blood that was the marriage of water and sun drenched the cavern floor, drops even falling on her feet, one on her cheek. She lifted a finger and ran it through the blood, bringing it to her lips. It was salty and tasted of life.

When it was over, the creature settled back on the dais and looked to be resting comfortably, though its eyes were focused on her, its strangely intelligent eyes. Her cheeks wet with tears, the student turned to leave—*we come from nothing, we return to nothing*—and heard the loud rattle of chains and a quiet voice filled with gravel and the tenor of souls, "I will see you again."

She turned and the creature's eyes grew, its muscles tensed. It jumped and roared, leaping toward her. She started and screamed, her hand flying up and sparks of light bursting from her palm. But the chains held and the creature stopped yards away. It patted at the ground and a dry, hacking sound came from its throat. Was it laughing at her?

Not your time, child. The voice sounded in her head and the student cried out. Then the beast looked up with its huge, human eyes and her own eyes met them and she was enveloped. The depths were brilliant and deep and they swirled and she felt herself falling into the past times. She felt heat and thirst and desire for freedom and a thousand voices inside, all screaming in rapture. They were all a part of the creature, the nameless one in chains. They were sacrifice, communion, a return to Godhead, though it was only a beast, if an eternal one. She searched for the master and found nothing but felt a thousand hands upon her head and she wanted to scream and join, but then the creature blinked and she stepped back.

She who was not-Dana shook her head until it was clear. She wanted to rush forward and lay her head on the ground before the beast, but it wasn't her turn. Someday it might be, when the eggs were ready to hatch and the creature could join the world again. She raised a hand in farewell. The creature opened its mouth wide, looking for all the world like a cat yawning, or grinning, and then closed its eyes, heavy rumblings a prelude to a long sleep.

Q is for Qi

L.S. Johnson

1.

There was a point every evening when Elsa would look around and realize that the dinner rush was over, indeed had been over for some time. It always took her by surprise, even after months of working at the chophouse. Like everyone had sensed her exhaustion and up and went at the same time to give her some peace. She liked to think like that, liked to think that the customers were her friends, visitors in her large, wood-paneled living room, and she was just making sure they got a good square meal. It made it easier to deal with the jerks; it let her pretend that the large tip she got was for her kindness or her cooking and not because her uniform was too small. And when would Doug order her a new one anyway?

She could ask Mary, but Mary didn't like to be asked; she left the day-to-day managing to Doug, said she didn't have the head for it. Still, Elsa thought if she could just find the right moment, she could get Mary to do something. The skirt rode up when she bent down, and depending on the time of the month the buttons would strain and gap. The last time Elsa had asked Doug he'd *yeah, yeah*ed her and added, *it's not doing you any harm, though*. And it wasn't; God knew she needed the tips. Her job was the difference between a good dinner for her husband and son and being on relief, and she had sworn never to go on relief again.

Still. As she cleared the table she looked at Mary out of the corner of her eye. All of the other waitresses were young and single, flirting with the cooks while the busboys flirted with them. She and Mary were older, and they both had little boys; if Mary were another waitress Elsa knew they'd be fast friends. Too, every now and then Mary would stand her a cup of coffee at the end of the night, and they'd chat a little, mostly about their sons. Elsa looked forward to that more than she could say. To be herself again, even in her cheap uniform.

A little more time, she figured. A few more good chats, and she could lean in close and say, *Mary, do a girl a favor, can't you get me a uniform that doesn't make me look like a sausage?*

As if in answer to her thoughts, a catalog suddenly appeared in front of her, and she felt a large, warm hand rest on the small of her back. *Uniform Supply*, the cover read, framed by a smiling waitress and chef. She turned to see Doug standing over her, his shadowed face unreadable.

"I can't let you take the catalog home," he said, "but if you stay after closing and pick out what you want, I'll order it first thing in the morning."

Elsa smiled as broadly as the waitress on the cover; it felt as if a huge weight had been lifted from her shoulders. "Of course I'll stay," she said.

She phoned Robert and told him she'd be late, and then settled into the stock room with a cup of coffee and the catalog, squinting at the pages in the dim light. The styles were line drawings so she couldn't quite tell which one matched the chophouse uniforms, and there were both half and whole sizes, and she couldn't find the sizing chart, she kept flipping and flipping... She heard Doug saying goodbye to the others, heard the shutters coming down.

Her last clear memory was of planning to tell Doug to forget it, she couldn't make heads or tails of the thing; everything afterwards came in flashes. Being held down across the boxes. Doug spitting words in her ear, dirty words no man had ever said to her before, and behind them a roaring noise like she was drowning. Choking on her sobs. He was so strong.

And when it was over, and she was fumbling with her clothes, why didn't they go on right, why couldn't she dress... when it was over he told her in his normal voice that if she told anyone he would fire her, and she would never get work in another restaurant, and he would tell her husband and her son and everyone in the entire damn city just what a goddamn slut she was.

Her journey home was a blur; she felt almost insensible until she finally managed to close the apartment door. Only then did she begin shaking. She dared not enter their bedroom, she knew that Robert would know and what would happen then? Instead she dragged blankets onto the couch and buried herself inside them, pulling them over her head until she was cocooned in a hot darkness, shivering as if she was riddled with fever.

There she lay, all night, fighting back tears, terrified lest she make the slightest noise and wake her husband and son.

When she heard the alarm ringing she made sure she was covered from head to toe, closed her eyes, and pretended to be asleep. The sounds of her son running around, Robert shushing him, it all made her feel sick and then ashamed of herself, for feeling so about her family.

Robert came into the living room to get his watch and she made herself limp and kept her breathing steady. But when he bent over her and touched her forehead she cringed and he whispered, "Coming down with something? You feel pretty warm."

She nodded.

"Do you want me to phone the restaurant? I can call from the job site."

At once panic filled her. "No," she croaked, her voice loud. "I'll call."

"Tell Doug you need a day off. It's the least he can do for keeping you so late." Robert laid his hand on her shoulder, caressing her through the blanket. "He better make it worth your while. I don't like you missing dinner. It's not good for Bobby, you know?"

As he spoke her mouth filled with bile. It was all she could do to nod again.

"Get some rest," he finally whispered, kissing her forehead.

There was the murmur of their voices, Bobby's distant *bye Mommy feel better* that she could not bring herself to acknowledge. She didn't want him to *see*, she didn't want either of them to see her. Only when she heard the door shut did she let herself start sobbing, waves of grief so violent as to choke her.

She was still crying when she managed to get herself to the bathroom and onto the toilet. The feel of the toilet paper made her feel sick and lightheaded. And then she smelled it, it was everywhere, and she tore off her clothing and climbed into the tub and opened the taps completely. She cried again, though she felt empty of all tears. At least in the water she couldn't smell herself, couldn't feel herself.

The phone rang out, echoing in the tiny apartment. The noise jarred her; she realized the water was up to her neck, rushing out of the overflow as fast as it poured in. She needed to do... something, yet she could not think what, could only think that if she just stayed in the water nothing more could happen to her.

When the hot water turned cold she finally closed the taps. Her fingertips were shriveled. She could not look down at herself.

The sudden knocking felt like physical blows, making her mewl in fear.

"Elsa?" a female voice said.

Mary.

Elsa lurched out of the tub and seized her thin bathrobe, wrapping it tightly closed, then wrapped a towel over the robe until she felt cocooned.

Mary knocked again, three short raps and then a pause, followed by three more. Elsa started for the door only to hesitate. What if Mary knew, what if she had come to accuse her, even attack her? What had Doug said to her, what was he saying to everyone?

"Elsa," Mary said, "I know you're in there." She paused, as if weighing her words. "I know what he did," she said, her voice barely audible. "For God's sake, let me in."

Before Elsa knew what she was doing, she was across the living room, unlocking the door and flinging herself into Mary's arms.

The smell of frying eggs made her stomach knot, but she could not bring herself to speak. Mary moved around the kitchen with tight, efficient gestures that seemed to indicate either unease or a barely contained anger.

"I knew when you didn't show up this morning," she said as she slid the eggs onto a plate. "I knew then. Before—" the word came out so clipped she paused to swallow, then repeated, "—before, with the young ones, half of them would get on the next bus home, the other half would try and blackmail him." She put the plate in front of Elsa. "I honestly thought you were too old for him."

She stared at the plate—the eggs swimming in grease, the toast almost as yellow as the yolks—and tasted bile again.

"What did he tell you?" Mary asked.

She could not look up at Mary; she was terrified of what expression she might find. "That I'd never work again if I told anyone, and he'd tell Robert I'm a…" Her throat closed around the word like a fist.

"Eat." Mary sat down across from her, folding her trembling hands one atop another. For the first time Elsa realized just how smooth Mary's hands were, how pristine her manicure, yet her engagement ring was as tiny as Elsa's own. She took up the fork and managed to get a piece of white between her lips; the scummy texture made her gag.

"I want to divorce him," Mary said in the same tight voice. "I can divorce him, if you'll sign a statement saying what he did."

Elsa looked up at her then, and wished she hadn't. The grim face staring at her was terrifying. "A—a statement? Mary, I can't… I haven't even told Robert, I couldn't bear it if he knew. How could I face him—"

"I've looked into it before," Mary said, speaking over her. "I could do it by myself, but it would be costly, he would fight me tooth and nail. It's really mine, you see. Doug manages the restaurant and that's our income, but he started it with *my* money." She stared at her clenching hands. "The divorce is useless to me unless I can keep the restaurant, and he'll fight me for it. Unless I can show a judge what he really is." She met Elsa's gaze squarely. "I'll make it worth your while, don't you worry."

"But I can't tell Robert," Elsa said. She had started weeping again. "I couldn't last night… and if I tell him now he'll ask himself, *why didn't she tell me when it happened?*" She looked beseechingly at Mary. "Please, I just want to forget. I don't care about the job, we'll get by. I just want to forget."

"Then Doug will say he fired you, and he'll spread it around that you propositioned him." Mary spoke the words flatly. "I know how he works, I've seen it before. I married an animal," she added under her breath. "A goddamn animal."

Elsa understood the words, understood what they meant, but still she couldn't quite believe it; it felt as if it was all happening to someone else. Finally she asked, "Will I have to appear in court?"

"No. Just tell my lawyer what happened. Once you sign the papers you'll be done with it all."

"And the police? Won't they want…evidence?"

Mary snorted. "Who said anything about the police? There's no point in telling them anything. You washed away all the evidence." When Elsa began crying harder she took her hand, holding it as if she was unsure of what to do with it. "Look, Elsa. Even if you hadn't cleaned… you know, we both know that wouldn't have been enough. They'd have wanted to see bruises, ripped clothes; they'd want witnesses who heard you hollering for your life. You know it, I know it, and God help us, Doug knows it."

Elsa stared down at the shimmering white and yellow on her plate. "I don't know," she whispered. "I don't know."

"I'll tell you what I know: what I'm offering you is the only thing that will get you out of this without putting your family on skid row." She suddenly squeezed Elsa's hand, so hard Elsa yelped in pain. "You can't survive without two salaries. I can see it just by looking at this place. I'll pay you what you were getting, and you won't even have to work for it. You just have to help me get rid of him."

Elsa's fingers were starting to go numb; only then did she notice on the back of Mary's tightly gripping hand was a spray of fine, red bumps like pimples, each with a tiny black center. Where had they come from?

"What about your little boy?" she whispered.

Mary's grip increased. "Better he grow up without a father, than be raised by the likes of him."

The taste of egg in Elsa's mouth was like something rotting. She couldn't think on what to say or do, she could only sit there, her eyes endlessly leaking and her hand tingling and throbbing. At last she nodded, and sighed with relief when Mary let go. Quickly she brought her sore hand to her chest, massaging it to bring the blood back to her fingertips.

And then she held out her hand between them, staring as a rash of red dots broke out across her sore knuckles.

She stayed home sick for three days.

On the fourth day Elsa told Robert she was going to the doctor, but instead of going to their family doctor she went to a specialist. There she handed over her small savings and took off her blouse, showing him the bumps everywhere: patches on her back, on her arms, all with different shades of brown at their centers.

She did not tell him how she opened one with a straight pin and teased forth a tiny brown feather, wet with a clear liquid, spreading its miniscule barbules as it emerged into the light of the bathroom.

The specialist gave her a cream that cost her the grocery money in her pocketbook, suggested she change her laundry detergent, and sent her on her way.

On the fifth day Elsa told Robert she was going back to work, but instead she put on her best day dress and dark stockings and a long-sleeved jacket and gloves and went to the heart of the city, where she met Mary at her lawyer's office. There she told what had happened in a small, sobbing voice, ashamed to raise her eyes despite the lawyer's gentle tone and the hand he laid over hers. While they typed it up properly she drank a very strong cup of coffee and wondered why everything felt so wrong: why she didn't feel better for telling, why Mary still looked so grim, why everyone else looked so pleased at hearing what had happened.

When the typist brought in the clean copy she reached for a pen to sign it, only to be stopped by Mary, who touched Elsa's gloved hand with her own. "You're sure it's enough?" she asked the lawyer. "To get *everything*? I want to break him, not just divorce him."

"Mrs. Phillips," the lawyer said with that pleased smile on his face, "with all your evidence, and now this? You're going to clean him out; he'll be lucky to leave the courtroom with the shirt on his back."

Slowly Elsa picked up the pen and signed. Beside her Mary exhaled, as if releasing something that she had long held inside; at once, though, her sigh became a hacking cough. She hunched over in her chair, coughing and spluttering, waving away the lawyer's offer of water; Elsa leaned over her and pressed a handkerchief into her hand.

"Thank you," Mary muttered. She stayed hunched over, coughing into the handkerchief and dabbing at her eyes and face. At last she sat up and tucked the handkerchief into her purse, so only Elsa saw the black feather gummed to the cloth.

2.

Elsa slid the raw eggs into the pan, careful not to break the yolks. Bobby liked his eggs just so, he liked to eat all the white right up to the edges of the yellow circle, then cut a single small opening in which to dip his toast. He was like his father in this: the precision with his habits, wanting everything to be just right.

Elsa knew she was no longer just right; she was becoming less right with every passing week. Neither the doctor's prescription nor her own lotions had done anything to stop the rash that now covered her from head to foot. She had tried vitamins, powders, baths with salts and baths with oils; still the bumps spread and swelled, some with white heads now, some with nearly black ones as well as brown. Her family believed she must have eaten something poisonous, she would have to be patient and let it work its way through her; when they said this Elsa had thought *Mary* but kept her mouth shut.

Had Elsa's mother still been alive she might have said something different. Her mother had often told her bedtime stories that weren't in books, stories from *the old world*, stories her mother's mother had told, and her mother before that, and so on... Stories of women who were changed into things, river rocks and fleet deer, nightingales and sparrows and tall, twisting trees: always they were betrayed by someone and then swiftly changed, to save them from a worse fate. *And then she was no more of this world,* her mother would always finish, and then she would pretend to show Elsa something from the woman in question—a leaf, a feather. But such endings had never felt like escapes to Elsa. They felt like condemnations, and her dreams would be filled with monstrous images of animals with women's faces, their silent mouths screaming endlessly.

Only now did Elsa understand her child-self had been right, that those stories weren't fantasies. They were *warnings*.

She wasn't escaping anything; she was being imprisoned in her own body. The bumps kept spreading, and her joints ached. Her fingers and toes curled when she rested, and her elbows were becoming stiff. What would happen if she became too sick, too strange-looking, to go outside? Who would help her, who would care for her?

She knew in her heart it would not be Robert, and she would not so burden her son.

As she arranged his food on the plate she looked at Bobby's bowed head, and beside him her stony-gazed husband, still staring at the front of the newspaper like it was the world. Mary's lawyer had called to discuss her statement—Elsa hadn't expected anyone to call her, she had thought once she signed the paper it was over—and Robert had taken the call. His first rush of anger had been horrible but also a relief, she had spent so long anticipating it; what she had not anticipated was that he already believed her to have been unfaithful with Doug, and the statement merely confirmed what he had *heard*.

So much said in the days and nights since, that could not be unsaid.

She could only think of two people who might have told him such a thing, and only one who could have done so without getting punched.

She put the eggs before Bobby, kissed his head, and hurried back into the kitchen. The smell of her son in her nostrils. Robert slept on the sofa now, and only responded when she told him basic things: what was for dinner, who had phoned during the day. All the money was in his name, and if he started talking to a lawyer—? Only now did she see that her statement might work against her just as it had worked against Doug.

Even if she could afford a lawyer of her own it would get ugly quick, and she would have to relive it all. And Bobby… to put him through all that, what would it do to him?

Could she bear to let her son go?

She began washing the pan, watching her reddened hands in the water as she scrubbed, her knuckles flexing white with the effort—

—and then stared, open-mouthed, at the line of erupting bumps along her hand and forearm. Small brown tubes jutted out from her irritated skin, their tufted ends waving like tiny ferns in the water. She raised her hands, turning them one way and another, and then ran a soapy finger along the lines of feathers, marveling at their plastic feel, at how the tufts were already drying and softening.

Only then did the enormity of it hit her. She pulled at a feather, trying to remove it, but the pain was swift and shocking: it was *in* her, it was part of her. Still she raised her hand to her mouth and bit down hard on the shaft, wrenching and pulling until at last it came free. At once the wound began to bleed, not the bleeding of a normal scratch or scrape but freely, copiously bleeding, splattering red across the countertops and sink, dyeing the dishwater pink as she fumbled for a clean towel and pressed it to the wound.

Elsa bent low over the sink then, swallowing her sobs so Robert and Bobby would not hear, for she understood, at last, how everything she had ever imagined about her life to come had been lost the moment the first bump appeared.

She had expected another apartment like her own, a tiny, cramped space among dozens like it, but as she made her way to Mary's address it was as if she had crossed into another world. Here were large, sprawling Tudor cottages, with actual lawns and pruned shrubbery; here were flowers, spilling from pots and twining their way around railings. Elsa had never known the neighborhood existed. Even the city noise seemed muffled, as if she had passed through some kind of bubble to reach this place.

She found the house and was again surprised: it was one of the largest, with gabled windows and a quaint little turret. It was something that belonged in a wealthy suburb, not here.

It was all my money. How much money did Mary actually have? Until now Elsa had been debating her approach, because she hadn't believed, couldn't believe, that Mary would utter such a lie, and to Robert no less. But this storybook house, the pristine lawn and the lace curtains and the driveway, that she actually had a car—oh, it made something grow hot and tight in Elsa's stomach, made her hands into fists so that she had to punch the doorbell with a reddened knuckle.

When the door swung open she pushed her way in before Mary could protest, storming into the silent, pristine living room and rounding on her. "What did you say to Robert?"

Mary shut the door and locked it.

"He's filing for divorce, Mary. He's filing for *sole custody*." She was trembling with anger. "You said nothing would happen. No trials, no police, just make a statement. You got what you wanted. Why did you *do* this?"

Mary looked at her levelly, then angled her head. "Drink?"

"Damn you, answer me," Elsa ground out. Her own tears were blinding her; she wiped at her eyes with the back of her hand, only to yelp as the tip of a feather poked her.

"Well, I'm going to have one." Mary went to the little cart in the living room; in the silence there was only the sound of Elsa's shuddering breath and ice clinking against glass. At last Mary said, "I didn't intend to say anything to Robert. He came up to me in the playground the other day, my son was standing right there. What was I supposed to say in front of him?" She downed two fingers of Scotch and poured another. "They've been teasing him at school, saying things about Doug... so I thought, there's no reason for him to know the truth about his father, not now. So I told him and a few of the other mothers... I said it was an affair, I just meant to soften it a little. And then all of a sudden Robert was there, I mean he came to my son's *school* for God's sake, and all those snoops were listening to us, waiting to catch me out." She suddenly rounded on Elsa. "What would you have me say?" she yelled.

"The truth," Elsa yelled back. "The goddamn truth! What about *my* boy? Robert's taking him away, Mary, he says I can't be trusted!"

Mary took another long sip. "You know," she said in a normal tone of voice, "I think I did you a favor."

The words brought Elsa up short. "What?"

"You heard me. I did you a favor." She took a step closer to Elsa, her eyes narrowing. "I think you didn't want to tell him because you knew, deep down, that he would never believe you. What kind of husband believes a stranger over the woman he supposedly loves? What kind of husband lets the mother of his son go to work each day looking like a slut?" She finished the second drink and wiped her mouth on her sleeve. "And then he comes to me—to *me*—asking if there was any funny business between you and Doug? In *public*? In front of my *son*? I don't think he gives a damn about you. I think you're just a thing to him, like a car, and you're just not running right anymore."

With a cry Elsa flung herself forward, hitting Mary as hard as she could; they tumbled onto the carpet. She pushed herself up to sitting and brought her fist down, once and again, trying to beat away the smirk on Mary's face.

On the third blow, there was a cracking noise; Elsa froze, her hand raised. Behind the blood and the bruising weal on Mary's nose was something else, something black and shell-like. She looked at the hint of beak, then at the blood on her own spotted knuckles, and sat back with a whimper.

"Maybe we deserve this," she whispered. "Maybe it's a curse, we brought it on ourselves, all this deceit and ugliness..." Her eyes were running, running. "God, why didn't I just tell him that night..."

"Because he's a man," Mary said, her voice garbled; she rolled her head to the side and spat blood, then propped herself up on her elbows. "Because you know that no matter how you explained it, he'd never touch you again. Not after *that*." She made a cutting gesture with her hand. "We're changing because of men, Elsa. All the gods are men. All the doctors are men. All the cops and the judges and the shrinks are men. If Doug had done that to a man they would have hung him from the nearest lamppost; if a man suddenly started spouting feathers they'd have a cure within a year or worship him like he was the goddamn Second Coming. Us? Oh, we're hysterical, we're crazy, we can't be trusted... and when we try to say *no*, this is what we get." She staggered to her feet, touching her nose gingerly. "If you ask me, this is just an allergic reaction to all the men in our lives."

The furious outpouring made Elsa cringe, but not as much as it would have, once. "You shouldn't speak like that," she said to the carpet. "You should think of your boy—"

"My son hates me," Mary said flatly. "Thinks I drove his daddy away." She tapped the black spot with her fingernail, wincing at the clicking sound. "He told me the other night either I let him live with Doug or he's going to leave the day he turns eighteen and never see me again. He's started getting into fights at school... now I have to decide whether I want to raise a delinquent, or let Doug raise a monster."

She went over to the cart and poured two more Scotches; when she held one out Elsa got to her feet and took it. The amber liquid burned her throat. Robert never let her have liquor…

But Robert wasn't around anymore; Robert would probably never be around again.

"You always think you're different," Mary said, her back to her Elsa. "You get married and you see other women's husbands and you think, *not me, my guy won't ever go around chasing skirt like that.* You have a son and you think, *not my boy, he'll never go bad, he'll never be disrespectful or cruel like those other kids.*" She looked at Elsa and her eyes were red. "My son is going to leave me all alone like this!"

She shoved her sleeve up to her elbow, revealing lines of molting feathers, small and fine like new blades of grass.

Elsa stared at her; and then she smiled. "For the love of Christ, Mary," she said, "why would you ever want him to stay?"

When she returned home the apartment was dim and quiet. There were a last few boxes of Robert's things by the door; the bedroom suddenly seemed large without Bobby's narrow cot against the wall. The silence pressed in on her, it made her skin crawl, and with a racing heart she hurried into the living room and turned on the radio. The familiar orchestration, the first crooning words, they all soothed her:

And now the purple dusk of twilight time
Steals across the meadows of my heart

She moved around the room, turning on lamps, smoothing down her hair as she prised off her hat and coat. Her whole body was tense;

she realized she was listening for footsteps in the hall because she hadn't made any dinner, and what would Robert say if he came home and there was no dinner waiting?

But she didn't need to worry about that anymore.

Love is now the stardust of yesterday
The music of the years gone by

As she went to hang up her things in the bedroom she paused before the dresser mirror, staring at herself. Her face was mottled with bumps like she was a teenager again, but even more frightening were her eyes: they were veined with black, as if a pen were bleeding into the whites. Her eyesight was fine—better than fine lately, the world had taken on a purplish tint that seemed to yield a new sharpness. Now as she gazed at herself she realized that she could actually see it, she could see the black feathering outwards, it was filling her eyes—

she clapped her hands over her face like a child and when she looked again it was still there, though now her reflection swam from her tears.

But that was long ago
Now my consolation
Is in the stardust of a song

Elsa stood in the little bedroom and cried, her coat and hat slipping to the floor. She cried for herself, for Mary; she cried for her son and the lies she had told him to ease their parting; she cried for her empty room and her empty arms and her body that was leaving her, for her own fear and loneliness, for all the women who had ever been hurt so, for all the women made birds.

3.

The knocking, loud and sudden, made Elsa squawk with fright. It took a moment to calm her fluttering heart and turn down the television, a complicated process of hooking the dial with her fingernail and nudging it. She had always been proud of her hands, how small and shapely they were, but they were nearly gone now. Her fingers had first become painfully stiff, then fused into three clawlike digits. Now calluses were growing over what had been her finger joints, just before the first line of feathers.

She waddled to the door, trembling with both nerves and hope. It was the wrong day for her grocery delivery, and rent wasn't due for a week yet. Perhaps Robert had brought Bobby to see her at last, or perhaps it was Mary, perhaps with all her money she had been able to find a cure, something to undo it all.

But when Elsa looked through the peephole, there was nothing.

She turned off the overhead light, then seized the chain with her beak and tested it, making sure it was securely fastened; only then did she open the door a crack.

Before her, on the ratty welcome mat, was a paper grocery bag with a note clipped to one side. Elsa couldn't see inside the bag, but she could smell it: meat and spices and something that she had only recently learned to identify.

Seeds.

Crouching low, she eased one clawed hand through the gap, hooking the bag and pulling it to the door. The note wasn't a note but a postcard, a picture topped with fancy calligraphy: *Philomela and Procne*. The light in the hallway was dim, but in the last few weeks Elsa's eyesight had become nothing short of remarkable, the world taking on a purple-tinted sharpness that let her see even the gnats that made their way through her window screens. Now she tilted the postcard to see the whole image, only to cry out.

Two women with the heads of birds, their spread arms sprouting wings.

"My Nana was like you," a voice said from the left.

Elsa jerked backwards, terrified; she tried to shove the door closed but it caught on the bag.

"I'm sorry! I didn't mean to frighten you. I'm Doreen, I live downstairs." A housedress and apron suddenly appeared, filling the gap between door and frame. "I—I saw you the other night," she continued, dropping to a conspiratorial whisper. "Taking out your trash. My Nana went the same way, and I just thought…"

She trailed off; Elsa could see her hands wringing atop her apron. Slowly she rose to standing, taking in Doreen's wide-eyed face, the flush in her cheeks.

"My momma used to make that meatloaf for Nana, she always liked it." Her blush deepened. "And I thought… my husband's away for a few days, and you don't seem to have anyone who can do for you."

Still Elsa just looked at her, her breath coming in whistling gasps through her beak. As frightened as she was, she could not stop staring at Doreen: there was a strange mottling on her arm and jawline, some kind of discoloration.

Elsa could think of very few things that would mark a woman in just those places.

"Well," Doreen said, ducking her head. "I'm, ah, I'm downstairs in 2B, if you ever need—"

"Wait," Elsa said quickly.

That is, she meant to say *wait*, but it came out as another squawk; still Doreen paused as Elsa worked the chain off and opened the door completely. Only then did she realize she was letting this woman see her, really see her, when she could barely look at herself and dared not go out save in the dead of night.

But Doreen just smiled. "You look like her," she said. She reached out and stroked Elsa's shoulder, and the sensation made Elsa's eyes well, made the purple world shimmer for a moment.

"Coffee?" Elsa asked, and this time she didn't wince at the sound of her own voice.

"Really?" Doreen's smile grew warm, open. "I'd like that."

She bent over, picking up the bag, and Elsa saw it then: how she flinched at some pain in her arm, how for a moment her skin rippled with the first hint of a rash that just as quickly faded. For now, but what might happen when next he struck her, or hurt her in some other way? Or when someone else—a friend, a relative—talked her into paying him back, only to use her for their own ends?

There could not be so many Marys in the world, Elsa could not believe it; yet she could *see* it in this woman, like something sleeping.

But if she could see it, maybe she could stop it.

She stepped aside and let Doreen in.

R is for Rare Birds

Beth Cato

"Be careful out there, Tiger," Doctor said, as she did every day when she let Tiger Boy out through the narrow basement window.

"Tiger *Boy*," he corrected, as he did daily.

"Yes, Tiger Boy." Her smile was more wobbly than usual.

He knew she didn't like letting him out by his lonesome, but he couldn't stay pent up for days and days on end. He started to get restless and toy around with things, and that was really, really bad in a laboratory. She used to joke that she wasn't sure if his mischief came from his Tiger or Boy nature, but she hadn't said that in a long time.

She didn't say too much at all, these days.

Tiger Boy pulled himself through the window and then hunkered there in the bushes, watching Doctor in the basement. She pushed herself around in her wheelchair as she went from machine to machine. She worked awful hard. There might be more people alive out there, she would say. People who survived the virus, like her.

People who could become immune if she added cat DNA, like with Tiger Boy.

Doctor wasn't sick-sick now, but she didn't look so good. Her brown skin had gone pale like newspaper left out in the sun and she coughed a lot.

He was on a mission today. He was going to get her some medicine.

The shaggy grass was warm through the gloves that Doctor made him wear as he bounded, on all fours, from the bushes. At the top of the rise, he stopped to roll around. His shirt lifted up and the sunlight on his belly felt so good that on any other day he could have stayed there for hours. But not today.

Doctor had him fetch things so he knew the neighborhood pretty well. After he woke up months ago he brought a lot of food and water back to the basement. He could read well enough to find food that Doctor liked, but trying to understand more than a few words in a row made them all twirl in his mind. It made Doctor sad sometimes. She had wondered if he had always had difficulties or if making him into Tiger Boy had hurt his brain. That didn't make sense. His body might hurt after running around, but not his *brain*.

He stayed on the grass or dirt as much as he could as he padded down the street. The road was still packed with cars that hadn't stayed in straight lines like they should. Lots of skeletons still sat or lounged around, too. There were even some small ones at the playground.

Tiger Boy always stopped there. That was one of the few things he remembered from when he was just a Boy—coming home from school, the store or anywhere else, you had to stop at the playground. It was tradition.

He went to the swings first and flopped his belly atop the black band. He swayed a few times then pushed himself over and ran to the slide.

The ladder up the slide was hard because he really was better on all fours now. Doctor didn't want him to do anything dangerous like climb or eat things he found outside or play in cars. "You're all I have! You can't take risks."

The slide was extra special, though. He did it before everyone got awful sick. He could still do it now, just on his belly.

He made sure he was extra careful for Doctor as he made his slow, steady way to the top. He tipped forward onto his chest, and wiggling his hips, pushed off. The metal slide was sleek heat through his shirt then his hands met the soft sand at the base, and he galloped on.

His old apartment wasn't that far away. Doctor said brains were interesting like that—that he remembered places all around, even if he couldn't remember his Boy name.

"Sorry, Mama!" He always apologized when he entered the apartment. She always hated when the door was left open or unlocked, but door knobs were hard on his hands. Besides, she didn't gripe at him now.

Mama sat at the couch. Well, she leaned these days. Most of her skin had sucked in close to the bone and she wore her favorite shirt, the one with a beer logo on the front.

Here, he thought of himself as more Boy. Mama didn't like cats, after all. He made himself stand on his back legs. His body looked mostly the same from when he was a full Boy, but he was a lot different inside. Doctor said that he acted more like a Tiger than he really should, but if he was happy and it helped him cope after everyone died, that was okay.

Doctor helped him feel better. He really needed her to feel better, too.

The bathroom cabinet had medicine in all those funny bottles that he couldn't open. That was okay. Doctor could do it. She could do anything except climb the stairs. Tiger swung his backpack off and parted the magnet tabs that Doctor had rigged. The bottles dropped in like the shakey-shakey instruments they used to play during music in school. He let the flaps pull shut again and shimmied the pack on. Leaning on the wall, he waddled back to the living room.

"Mama, Mama, Doctor is sick. What else can make her better?" he asked.

Mama just looked at him in her lop-sided way. The table in front of her had her little mirror tray and rows of white powder that he could never, ever touch.

"That's it!" he said, and added meow of triumph.

He went to her bedroom. There were baggies of white powder still in her dresser. Those he could touch, because he'd bring them when she asked. Mama said they made her feel good. Maybe they'd help Doctor, too.

His backpack loaded up, he said bye-bye to Mama. He dropped to all fours once he was in the hall and headed outside. A brisk wind chased him to the playground. He hopped up on the bench. Another body his size sat there.

Tiger Boy remembered that he used to sit up like that all the time. At his school desk. On the bus. On Mama's lap. How long had it been since he'd tried to sit like that outside of the old apartment? He frowned. Time was weird. He missed Christmas. The whole year used to be divided by before Christmas and after Christmas. Doctor said they couldn't do Christmas in the basement; there was no way to get a tree down there. That made them both cry.

Tiger Boy looked at the other body on the bench. The medicine rattled in his pack as he twisted around to sit like that. "I'm still a Boy here, too," he said to his playmate.

If he was still a Boy at the playground, maybe he could go down the slide the old way, too.

Doctor's words echoed in his mind. "You're all I have! You can't take risks."

"I can be a careful Boy," he said out loud.

He climbed up the ladder oh so slowly. At the summit it got all confusing. How was he supposed to get his legs up on top? Where did his hands go? Was he supposed to grab hold of something up high, or down low? He fumbled and knotted himself and leaned back and suddenly knew the utter strangeness of grasping nothing at all. He was falling.

He twisted around, the pills pinging in their bottles, and landed in the sand on all fours like a Tiger. Pain stabbed up his hands and knees and he yowled, but after a few seconds the shock was gone. He shook out his arms and legs. He was okay. Good. Doctor wouldn't be mad. He lowered himself to the still-warm sand and breathed heavily for a few minutes, then eased himself up again.

"I'm still a Boy," he whispered. "I am. I just have Tiger, too. The Tiger in me knew how to land."

The Tiger in him saved the Boy. That's what Doctor said happened in the basement, too. That he was stronger, better, because of the change in his DNA.

He padded around to the landing area of the slide and sat up on his haunches. The slide looked huge from down here—a big sleek, silver mountain.

Going down on his belly was lots of fun. Had sitting up really been the better way to go down the slide, back before everyone got sick? Some part of him thought so. There had been more air in his face as he slid down. More of a view of the whole playground and all the people. The kids had laughed and talked and ran every which way. He remembered that, the joy of it.

The wind caused the swings' chains to twist and creak.

Tiger Boy fell back onto all fours. Maybe he shouldn't do the slide anymore. Maybe Doctor was right, and things like that were too dangerous now.

That made him feel strange and sad inside. He shivered, despite the sunshine, and the pills rattled in his backpack. Oh! The medicine!

At that, he trotted toward the basement and Doctor. The medicine in his backpack was music to every stride. He'd help her feel all better. That was the right thing to do. It was a Boy thing to do.

S is for Slide

C.S. MacCath

Before the ancient stars coalesced into brightness, in the vault of the foregoing universe, there were sorrows too great for any being to bear, and the greatest of these was the sorrow of ending. Not the end of a day, with its sundown promise of another sunrise, and not the end of a life, while memories of the dead remain and there is hope in some hearts for the soul's journey onward. No, this sorrow was vast, cold and complete, and it spanned the void of space among the last rough fragments of matter strewn in terminus.

Who was there to grieve in that heat death? Scripture tells of three; supermassive singularities at the end of their gathering in, brooding upon the cacophony before and the quiet ahead, sacrificing radiation to become chimeras of the wonders they once devoured. There was Face-of-Time, in whose mouth a trillion tongues cried out in languages long extinct. There was Skin-of-Suns, fat with the orbits of planets given to memory. And there was Feet-of-Entropy, fevered with a dance of creation fallen to stillness.

One day (as they understood days, these black-eyed watchers of epochs), Face-of-Time strode into the void on a legion of legs; each one a transit system between the stars, a glittering city, a hut in the mountains, a burrow where mothers of beasts gave birth to their young and spoke the deeds of sentience. "I mourn the loss of minds," it said in all those tongues. "There was a poet once, a being of fire and ammonia, who gave the brief flame of xyr life to the search for a perfect word and spoke it as xe died. Who will remember the poet, the word or the many who held it on their lips for a thousand years? There was a pilgrim too, a piercer of the spacetime veil, who matched the speed of light and yet prays in a shrine where time and motion cease. Who will call him away from that devotion? And what of the cow who hid her calf to save him from the slaughtering knife? Who will tell the small tale of that good mother when I am gone? I mourn the loss of minds," it said in the languages of the dead and retreated to its fading accretion disk.

Skin-of-Suns shone into the vacuum then; a hundred billion solar nebulae casting planets like dice into the hundred billion galaxies of its flesh. A gravity well opened its throat in a threnody for the celestial, captivating the last two listeners in the universe. "Exquisite, they were," it sang, "elliptical, spiral and irregular, extravagant civilizations of matter and the kindred supermassives they contained. Their jewelly stars are extinguished forever now, and even the knowledge of them will perish when I am dead. Incandescent, they were, those daughters of hydrogen and helium, audacious mothers of worlds and moons. What became of their children, the fertile descendants of stellar ignition, whose bodies were the nurturers of life? Disintegrated in the blasts of supernovae. Burned to cinders in the long, slow fires of solar giants. Left to freeze while their primordial foremothers huddled, small and white, in the unremitting dark. I sing of them all," it whispered in a broken strain of grief. "They were exquisite."

"How they moved." Feet-of-Entropy embodied the inception of the cosmos; nihility, infinite density, an outward rush of power. "From no-place, no-time there came a pulse, unconstrained, a wild expansion that brought the first builders into being." A fire burned upon its belly, radiating out, and in it the forges of the elements worked. "Light and heavy, they were made and sent forth into the black, fallow night to blanket infant worlds and combine. There was breath in that union, and water, and in time, there was life." Bacteria spread across the vastness of its body, now brimming with a myriad sunlit cradles of evolution. Hosts of beings swam in the oceans there, crawled forth to stand on claws, hooves, paws and feet, launched into the air on tremulous wings. "Some survived, adapted, and of these a blessed few traveled out again to greet the universe that gifted them so richly. I was there, a necessary sorrow, from the origin of things; a putrefactor of flesh, a quencher of forges, a cold, killing equilibrium. The dance has ended now; for them and soon for me. But oh, how they blazed, how they soared, how they moved."

A trillion years they spun thereafter; silent, pensive, dying. Scripture tells us nothing of that time, nor do we know who chance favoured in that bleak, forbidding night with an insight that would bring an end to endings forever. Perhaps there had been a universe before, and perhaps some weaker God therein had offered what it could to the one that followed. Such a thing was probable. But Face-of-Time, Skin-of-Suns and Feet-of-Entropy were three, and they were not yet consigned to dissolution. A measure of strength remained in their colossal accretion disks and in the depths of their inky singularities. So it was when together they chose a minute point in spacetime and poured all they had gathered into it; every perfect word, every civilization of matter, every swimming, crawling, standing, flying being. They lost the chimeras of their bodies, and in time, they lost their lives to that pouring out and into infinite density. But in the moment of their deaths, a new universe was born, one that remembered.

This is why we know them; three Gods who paved the Way of Perpetual Arising and embedded awareness of it in each particle of the cosmos. The leaf, the river, the cloud, the planet, the comet, the star all carry fragments of the same primordial tale. Have you heard it in the howling of the wind? In the crashing of the wave upon the shore? In your dreams of other times, distant places, foreign people? By the triune constellation marked upon my face from birth and its mirrors in the skies of every world where we evolved, by the marks my brethren bear from every species we have met, I speak a truth already singing in your bones: You are an heir of spacetime, and the memory of you will never die the heat death.

Now this telling comes to an end, but there is much left to be told; in the wise cells of your body, in the skillful combination of elements, in the practiced fusion of their creation and in the Gods who will send them forward into universes unending. Go now, and live a life worthy of their sacrifice.

T is for Three (at the End of All Things)

Author's Note: Many thanks to the Tribe of Physicists for its help with the science of this story.

Samantha Kymmell-Harvey

Claire picked at her freshly applied nail polish while she waited. The sterile smell of the hospital waiting room made her stomach turn. *Final soma-therapy injection,* she reminded herself, trying to push the memories of her cancer surgery from her mind. *Then I get my life back.* The double doors swung open.

"Claire Evans?" the nurse looked up from her e-registration.

Claire stood. "Coming." She tucked the polish back into her bag.

"Just place your finger on the pad, please," said the nurse, holding the pad out. Claire pressed her index finger against the glass and watched as the device opened the full record of her life, her DNA sequencing summary, her cancer surgery, even her first skin regeneration when she fell from her bike as a child. The Bureau of Genetics knew more about her than her own mother.

The nurse smiled and tucked the pad under her arm. "Right this way," she said, pushing open the double doors.

Her feet faltered momentarily as she took her first of her last steps down that dark hallway. Claire planted a hand on the wall to steady herself.

"Everything ok, Mrs. Evans?"

"Just nerves," she said. *I hope.*

A guttural cry echoed from one of the examination rooms. Claire gasped as she saw a man emerge and limp down the hallway toward her. The nurse scurried past her, waving her arms at the escaped patient. His cries muffled anything the nurse might have said to him.

His wide, dilated eyes locked with Claire's raising goose bumps on her arms.

"Anna!" he murmured, reaching for her.

Claire watched him teeter toward her, arms outstretched. Run! She told herself yet at the same time, there was something so sad about this bizarre man. Something that made her pity him rather than fear him.

"Stop him!" Dr. Benson yelled over the cacophony, white coat billowing out as he hurried toward his patient.

The madman locked hands so hard her fingers hurt. His touch sent an electric jolt through her bones. A wave a heat flooded her body as a dizziness overcame her.

Medi-lights, glinting needles, numbness.

"Anna, I see you in there," he said, caressing her face with his gruff hand. "Don't let them take me from you again! Remember me! Remember!"

Hazel eyes. A bright light. I can't see. They're hurting me!

The images vanished. Claire blinked as the hallway came back into view. Only their pinkies remained interlocking as the doctor pried his hands from Claire's. Her lungs burned. She realized she had been holding her breath.

"No! Let me go!" he pushed the doctor to the floor. "Pinky swear, Anna! Pinky swear!"

The nurse came up behind him and plunged a needle into his thigh. Within moments, the man silenced, his body relaxing under the influence of the drug.

"I'm so sorry about this, Mrs. Evans," Dr. Benson said. "I'll be with you as soon as I can."

Shaking, Claire watched as the man was escorted back to his examination room. Dr. Benson closed the door behind them.

"Soma-therapy doesn't usually have that affect on patients," she said. "He must be doing something else to his body."

The nurse escorted Claire to the end of the hallway. The strange man's moans echoed between the walls. Claire sat on the examination table and the nurse shut the door.

"Any problems with your soma-therapy injections?"

"No, not at all."

"Your body seems to be adapting to the new sequencing very nicely," she said with a smile. "Dr. Benson will be happy to hear that. He should be here momentarily."

Claire said nothing but picked at her nails again. Her thoughts drifted back to the scene she'd seen in her mind when that man had grabbed her. Her arm even vaguely ached from a phantom injection. She rubbed a finger over her imaginary sore spot. It had felt all too real.

She didn't like to think about where the genetic material for the soma-therapy was harvested from—the Genetic Bank. Whoever the material was harvested from, it had cured her of her cancer.

One more injection. You can do this. The stranger's touch still tingled on her skin. She clasped her fingers together and squeezed. *I hope I don't end up like that guy.*

Claire waved to her husband and flashed a grin. He stood up from the cafe table and kissed her cheek.

"There's my shiny, new wife!" he said, pouring her a glass of water from the carafe.

Claire smiled. "I'm not *new*, just not sick anymore. I'm certainly ordering dessert."

"You can eat whatever you want, my dear," said Tom. "And I think we can finally discuss our procreation timeline. The Bureau's extension will probably be discontinued now that your treatments have ended."

Procreation timeline. Claire winced. *How loving.* But that was the accountant she'd married—logical and always in control. Even though their marriage had been ordered by the Bureau just the same as everyone else's, Claire still felt lucky. Her husband was reliable and responsible.

"I don't think we should rush into this," said Claire. "After all, I'm just getting used to the idea of having a future."

Tom shook his head. "And risk being uncoded? No, I don't think so."

"We're not going to be uncoded because we're not going to disobey the Bureau's orders," she said. "But I'd love to renew our extension. It would give us some time to adjust to having normal lives again."

"Why wait? I already have an idea for the nursery. What do you say—" Tom swept up her hand and kissed it just like the knights of old in the movies. "—m'lady?"

All Claire could feel was the subtle electrical current of that crazy man's touch, still pulsing over her skin. She flexed her fingers in an attempt to rid herself of the sensation. But she found she only wanted more of it. She nodded mechanically. "I love it, I can't wait."

"Hey," Tom said, suddenly leaning forward, staring intensely at her face. "I think your eye is changing color."

"What?" Claire dug around in her handbag and retrieved her compact. The mirror reflected back eyes she hardly recognized; one her normal blue, but the other hazel and growing darker.

Claire pressed the link on her com-pad to Dr. Benson's office.

"Yes, that can be a side effect of the soma-therapy," said the nurse. "But your normal coloring should return within a day or two. Call if anything gets worse."

"Okay." Claire hung up.

"You okay?"

She nodded. "Everything's fine."

Wake up, something's wrong.

Claire jolted up from the bed. "Who said that?" It was a woman's voice, one she didn't recognize. She took a sip of the water on her bedside table, and let the coolness wake her and wash her dreams away. *It was just a dream,* Claire thought, *See? You can still think in your own* voice. A bit of laughter escaped and Claire shook her head. "I sound crazy."

Help me, please!

The other woman's voice again, tense, sharp, sad.

Stop it! Claire untangled herself from the bed sheets and hurried to the bathroom. She flicked on the lights. Her two different colored eyes stared back at her.

This isn't real. She blinked, but her eyes did not change. Splashing her face with cold water didn't help either. *This is just a side effect. It will stop. It will stop.*

"Tom?" Claire shouted. No answer. Had he left for work already? "Tom!"

I have to call the doctor, Claire thought.

Don't. The woman's voice quickened.

Claire perched on the edge of the tub. *I'm not having this conversation with you. You're not real.* Her blood thumped in her ears as she rocked back and forth. *Please don't let me be like that man...* His wide, drugged out eyes stared vividly in her imagination.

What man? she asked.

Claire sighed and opened the cabinet. *Goodbye, side effect.* She popped open the headache medication and tapped two pills into her palm.

I'm trapped. I need to find something... someone? I can't remember.

With a swig of water, Claire downed the pills. *It's all just a bad dream.*

There was something almost therapeutic about unpacking all the boxes Claire had tucked away in the guest room. They'd stayed tucked away, like promises of a future yet to come. But now that she was cured, Claire's future could finally be opened. With each slice of the exacto-blade, she made more space for the nursery.

She removed a tin of candles from the box. They smelled like her college dorm, like lavender and vanilla. Those scents had fueled a hundred essays. Maybe they'd calm an infant, too? *What if I'm not good mother? What if I get sick again?* Claire thought of the crazy man, of the voice she had heard in her head this morning. *Stop doubting yourself. One box at a time, Claire.*

Wading through the boxes further into the closet, Claire then squatted beside a small cardboard box whose inked label had faded. With a swipe of the blade, the box opened. But Claire didn't recognize the piles of microchips inside. That technology hadn't been used since early days of the New Eden Renaissance after The Accident, when the Bureau of Genetic Husbandry was first begun. Claire hadn't even been born yet.

She plugged a chip into her com-pad. A folder opened revealing hundreds of image files. *These must be Tom's.* Claire knew he had been married before, but he never really talked about it much. He said the memory his first wife's death was just too painful to discuss.

She opened a few of the images. None of the people looked familiar to her except for Tom. He was very young, his hair still sandy brown, his skin still smooth. *When had these been taken?*

Stop, the woman's voice returned. *Let me see that.*

Claire screamed, dropping her pad on the floor. *I've had enough of you! Whatever you are, you're making me crazy. I'm calling the doctor.*

No! The doctor can't help me. Only you can. Just help me remember who I was before being in this body.

Blood rushed to Claire's face and the room began to smear around her. She sat down and put her head between her knees.

Her words realized Claire's fears. The genetic material in her soma-therapy had come from an Uncoded.

You were uncoded, weren't you? Claire asked. *I'm infected by an Uncoded.*

I think so, the voice said. *I must have been.*

What did you do?

I don't remember.

Who are you?

I don't remember.

Claire groaned. *Of course you don't remember, you're only a part of who you used to be.* She picked up her pad and examined the photo. It was of a tarp slung between two trees. Gray mist of smoke rose above a newly doused campfire. *Look familiar?*

The voice didn't say anything for a long while. Claire flipped forward another photo. This one was of a clearing in a forest.

I lost someone there, the voice finally spoke. *I need to go back and look.*

"Where is this place?"

It was on the edge of the city.

There was a small natural park on the edge of New Eden the City Council finished a few years ago. It may not be the exact forest this woman remembered, but it was the best she could do. *If I help you to find what you've lost, will you then leave me alone?*

If it works that way, then yes.

Let's go then, said Claire.

The crisp May wind brought goosebumps to Claire's exposed arms as she stepped awkwardly onto the path. She hadn't gone on a hike since her diagnosis. She inhaled and closed her eyes. Smelled like dirt and dankness.

Look for the circle of oaks, said the woman.

With each step, Claire went further into the forest, never questioning the path she walked. A stinging sensation of panic teased her stomach. A branch broke beneath her feet.

They'll never find us here. We'll be safe if we just stay. Claire saw a tent, a little brook trickling by. Angry voices echoed in the distance. The tent vanished as Claire spun around. There were nothing but trees. It had all been a distant memory.

Am I crazy?

You're finally waking up, said the other woman's voice. *Keep going, it's just ahead.*

Claire took a deep breath before treading further into the woods. Reaching a thicket, she pushed through and emerged into patch of grass surrounded by oaks. It matched the photograph; only the weeds and three-headed dandelions were much taller. The wind skated over her skin like fingers. Its touch reminded her of the strange man. Why did she keep thinking of him?

Here. I lost something here...

A flood of images overtook Claire. Head throbbing, a face appeared in her mind. His dark curls tangled, his eyes full of fear and love. Not Tom's face. He hooked his pinky with hers. "Pinky swear, my love. We will never be parted."

Ethan. The woman's voice again, sad, desperate.

Overcome with dizziness, Claire sat in the moss and closed her eyes. Her arms burned. Long red streaks ran up her forearms. They bled. Her breathing quickened, the forest folded in on itself. Claire screamed and opened her eyes. Her arms weren't bleeding, they weren't even scarred.

"Stop this!"

You must remember. The voice urged. *We must find him.*

"No, no. We are not 'we.' I am me, you are you."

We are one now, Claire. You promised you'd help me.

"That's back when I thought you lost something. Something easy, like a watch or a locket. Not a person. That's dangerous. Chances are, he was uncoded like you."

Which means he could be alive in someone else, like I am in you.

Claire's mind drifted back to the crazy man at the hospital. If he was hearing a voice in his head, then of course he was going crazy. She'd be next if it didn't stop. "It's impossible. I'm sorry. But it is. I'm going home, I'm going to see my husband, and I'm going to enjoy this second chance at life I now have."

Is this not my second chance, too?

"You don't get a second chance. You're a criminal."

For once, Claire enjoyed silence all the way back home.

"I've had the weirdest day." Claire curled up beside Tom in bed, playfully entwining her foot with his.

"Oh really? Tell me about it." His lips kissed her forehead then her cheek before finding their way to her neck and exposed shoulder.

"I was..." Eyes closed, Claire tilted her head back. Her words vanished from her thoughts as a new memory manifested. In her mind, she lay beside the dark haired man underneath the tarp. She ran her fingers through his curls, picking the dead leaves from them. He smiled, his dark eyes free of worry.

"Wait," said Claire, wiggling free from Tom's grasp. *I don't need this right now, whoever you are.*

I'm not to blame. It's your body.

"What's wrong?" Tom kept kissing her.

Claire sat up. "Stop. I have to ask you something."

"You look very serious," Tom said, sitting up and wrapping his arms around her. "Is this about your weird day?"

Claire exhaled sharply. *Just ask.* "I was cleaning out the guest room today."

Tom nodded. "And?"

"I found some old microchips. I wasn't sure if they were mine or yours, so I popped them into my com-pad. They're just some old photographs. But one in particular seemed out of place."

"It's this one," Claire said, showing him the campsite.

Tom's face paled as he averted his eyes. "That's just a picture from one of our family vacations." He handed the com-pad back, chewing his lip ever so slightly.

Claire's stomach twisted. She grasped the com-pad to keep from showing her hands were shaking. "I thought you didn't like camping."

"Of course not, but my father loved it."

He's lying, said the voice.

I know. Leaving the city was illegal in his father's time.

In my time, too. The Accident was still affecting nature then. They didn't want to risk more death.

"Excuse me," Claire left the bed.

"Wait, Claire, what's wrong?"

She shut the door to the bathroom and clicked the lock. Gripping the counter, Claire stared down her alien reflection in the mirror.

This has to stop, she said. *Tomorrow, we are going to the doctor and you will be removed from my head.*

I'm not the problem, Claire.

Yes, you are. I had no problems until you came along.

Tom's the problem. He's a liar. We must find Ethan.

There was a knock at the door.

"Claire, you okay in there?"

"I'm fine. I'll be out in a minute." Claire turned back to the mirror. *Get out of my head!* She fumbled in the medicine cabinet. The bottle of pills cracked on the tile floor.

"Claire! Open up!"

Don't open the door, I'm scared of him, said the voice.

Claire bent down and started scooping up the pills. *If you do not get out, I will force you out.*

"Claire!" The door vibrated, thumping against the frame.

In her mind, Claire heard fists against a metal door. She was laying down on something cold. The room was dark. The shadowy outline of a man's face looked through the circular door at her. His clenched jaw she'd witnessed many times.

"Claire, I swear I will break down this door!" Tom yelled.

Don't do it. The voice said. *Your mind is just unlocking us.*

I hate us. Claire took a handful of pills and swallowed.

From the bathroom floor, Claire watched the door bend unnaturally outwards. Then Tom hung over her, cold hands on her hot cheeks.

"Claire, can you hear me?" Tom's cradled her head in his lap. "You don't know what you're saying. Don't worry, everything will be okay. I'm here."

Ethan!

The voices faded, leaving Claire in a deep sleep.

The doctor's office was over air-conditioned. Claire shivered in her gown, clutching her arms. Tom sat in the chair across from the bed holding her hand. The door clicked open.

"Mrs. Evans," said Dr. Benson. "I'm glad you're doing okay. I was distressed to read your husband's report when you came to the hospital last night."

"All of this started with the eye color change," said Tom. "She hasn't been herself."

Claire listened for the woman's voice in her mind, but she didn't speak.

"She's having strange nightmares," Tom continued. "Or maybe they are hallucinations. I don't know. Our deadline for children is getting closer. I don't want my wife to be both sick and pregnant."

"I certainly understand your concern, Mr. Evans."

Do you get a say? Her second voice said.

No, because you are the reason I'm here being treated like that crazy guy. We both stay silent.

The blue vein in Tom's neck bulged as he spoke. "Your treatments have done this."

Dr. Benson shook his head. "Soma-therapy does not create what you are describing."

"Maybe we need a psychiatrist?" Tom talked about her as if she wasn't even there.

He's so desperate to drug me up. What is he trying to hide? "I'm not crazy, Tom."

"I'm not calling you crazy, Claire," his tone sharper than it needed to be. "I'm just trying to help you."

"No one thinks you're crazy, Mrs. Evans," said Dr. Benson. "But you did try to harm yourself last night."

"I wasn't feeling well, I didn't mean to take that much," said Claire.

He was going to kill us, said the voice. *I don't trust him.*

Stop talking to me, you'll only make it worse. I have to think of a way out of this.

"Let's have a look at your eyes," said Benson as he switched on the ultra-light.

No! the voice screamed.

The examination room washed white as Claire was consumed by another memory-dream. The lights extinguished with the exception of one bright light overhead. Black shadows shaped like nurses surrounded her.

Where is he? Oh God! Let me go! her second voice shrieked.

Claire turned to see the nurse's gloved hands holding a syringe. It glinted in the spotlight. She tilted her head up. This wasn't her body. She was in someone else's body.

Wake up, it's just a memory. Wake up, Claire. She thought as she writhed, desperately trying to wrench herself free but the restraints dug into her wrists too tightly. A face on the other side of the doors looked in through the small square window, his jaw clenched. A younger Tom, eyes red and puffy, stared in at her torture. They made eye contact. He shook his head unapologetically. *It was Tom who had her uncoded.* Claire began to weep. *He killed her.* Then Dr. Benson appeared, gas mask in hand.

"Claire!" Tom's voice. "Claire!"

The memory-dream ended and the doctor's office sharpened into view. No nurses, no needles, no bed straps. She clawed at her chest, struggling to catch her breath. Dr. Benson held no gas mask.

I remember now.

"What did you do to her?" Tom pushed Benson away. Wrapping his arms around Claire, he rocked her.

He uncoded me, my husband, said the woman's voice.

Tears smeared down Claire's cheeks. "I…I don't know what happened." *Stay calm or he'll have me uncoded, too.*

Dr. Benson glanced from Claire to Tom.

Tom's eyes narrowed. "That's not even Claire's voice."

Claire shivered. Their secret was out. "I don't know what's happening to me."

Dr. Benson tapped a few buttons on his cell phone. "I've sent you the name of an expert. I suggest you go see him."

Tom tucked the card into his jacket pocket. "Doctor, you think she can be saved? They won't have to uncode her, will they?"

No one can save me from him, Claire thought. *I know too much.*

"I thought I was done with this mess." Tom's face flushed crimson, blue veins still bulging. He shoved Claire into the kitchen as he slammed the front door. "I cannot lose a second wife. Do you know what that would do to me?"

Claire shook her head. "I saw you there, Tom. In my memory. I was in an operating room."

"I didn't know you when you had your cancer surgery."

"It wasn't me on the operating table. But you know who it was. Who did you have uncoded, Tom?"

Tom clenched his fists, jaw set. "No, we are not having this discussion, Claire. Can't we just go back to the way things were? We were normal, we were happy. I deserve a normal life."

"So do I!" Jaw trembling, Claire tilted her head away from him. "But your ex-wife is inside of my head all day every day. Her memories are mine, her feelings are mine and I can't make it stop."

"That can't be true. You're not *her*. Anna."

My name, said the voice. *I remember my story.*

Claire spoke, her voice melding with Anna's. "I met Ethan when I was just a kid. We grew up together. Had our first kiss together. But when the Bureau matched us up with different people, we ran away into the wilderness. You turned me in. The authorities found us at our campsite homestead."

Claire thought of the photo she found, of the clearing in the woods Anna's voice had led her to. It was all true.

Tom's face flushed pale. "How could you know any of this?"

"Look at the evidence, Tom. Your ex-wife gets uncoded. Her genetic material taken from the uncoding is stored in the bank for medical uses. I get sick with cancer. I undergo soma-therapy and her genetic material proves key in my treatment, so I'm injected with it. That's why the Bureau matched us together, Tom. You were matched with her and since she is part of me, we were placed together. You were always going to be matched with *her* no matter what."

Tom released her, fists clenched. "She was never even my ex-wife," Tom spat bitterly. "She stood me up at the altar. But she's right. I found her. It wasn't that difficult. I knew she'd been unfaithful to me. She'd never loved me." He plunged his fist into the cabinet. The door split, the knob clanked to the hardwood floor.

Murderer, Anna said.

"You made her pay with her life," said Claire.

Tom didn't look at her. "Anna chose to break the law. It is the law that uncoded her, not me."

Claire kept her distance. "And now I'm your imperfect wife. Will you have me uncoded, too?"

"No," he said circling her, eyes swollen with tears. "I can't go through that again." He cradled his bleeding knuckles against his chest. "I can't lose you, Claire. I love you."

Claire said nothing. Her head swam in a million thoughts. All of Anna's previous memories were unlocking.

Run away, get away. Find Ethan. Anna shouted.

That was your life, Anna. Not mine.

He'll uncode you if you stay. He wants a wife that doesn't exist and never will.

Tom wrapped Claire in a bear hug, leaving bloody knuckle prints on her collar. "I will save you, Claire."

Anna, maybe we can both get what we want if we work together.

Ethan?

And freedom.

Pinky swear, Claire?

Claire smiled as she remembered Ethan and his unruly curls. He'd hooked his pinky with Anna's, just like the crazy man had in the hallway.

We'll find him. Pinky swear.

"Tomorrow, we're going to get you to the specialist and we can start over again. I can still save you." He began to sob into her hair. "I will save you."

"It's too late for us," said Claire-Anna.

We are kept in a white room with nothing but paper-based books and notepads. We haven't seen such relics since before the Accident. The doctors tell us to write down our memories.

"Mrs. Evans, you have a visitor," says the nurse as she opens our door.

Do we want to see him cry again today? we think. *It wastes our time.*

We say nothing to the nurse as we walk down the white hallway past the rooms where the others like us are being kept. Maybe Ethan is here, too. We haven't been able to search. They keep us separated.

The nurse escorts us to the plastic booth at the end. The nurse knows we don't speak much anymore.

"How are you feeling, Claire?" asks Tom. His eyes are red and puffy.

"We don't need to be here, Tom. Why won't you free us?"

He flinches when we say "we." Tom's cold hands grip ours. "There's nothing I want more than for you to come home. Don't you understand? This is your last chance. The Bureau has told us that we family members need to make decisions. Either we commit you here for life or we terminate you."

Terminate. The word sits on us. It mutes us with its power. No more second chances to live.

Tom keeps talking. "That's why you have to get better. You can have a normal life, if you choose to."

He sounds like he's repeating whatever Dr. Benson told him. It makes him feel like he can control us. We've already made our choice and Tom is going to help us. It can be his penitence for what he's done to us.

"We can hope," we say. "Goodbye, Tom. See you next month."

We stand and walk away. We hear Tom screaming at us. But we turn our head from him and scan the windows we pass. We know what he looks like, we remember him from before we merged. Ethan awakened in his new body before we did. The feel of his pinky is still a lingering ghost on our skin. But only blank faces look back at us from their holding cells. He isn't here.

The nurse returns us to our room. "Don't forget to write your notes, Mrs. Evans. Dr. Benson will be interested in your memories from your conversation with Tom."

We nod and smile, but we have other plans.

We hear the nurse's rubber-soled shoes thumping toward our door. Tom is a week early for his monthly visit. That's how we know he's made up his mind about us.

"Please come with me," says the nurse as she opens the door. "And bring your journal." The door hangs wide open as she waits for me. She scrolls through the messages on her com-pad, magni-card dangling from the plastic band round her wrist. Our good behavior has been paying off.

"Ready," we say, careful of our words.

"Follow me, Mrs. Evans."

Instead of escorting us back to the plastic box, the nurse turns the corner of the hallway. Her pace quickens. We know we're actually headed to Dr. Benson's office.

"Mrs. Evans," the doctor greets us as we enter the examination room. Tom sits on a small metal stool in the corner. His face is tinged a light shade of green. Our eyes drift to something glinting beside the examination table. A metal tray with three syringes. Today is the day. They'll have to make us lie down if they want to kill us this time.

Dr. Benson takes the journal from our hands and gives it to Tom. "Look for any evidence of recovery," he says. Tom can't look at us, won't look at us.

"Sit up here," Dr. Benson pats the examination table.

The nurse, now gloved, forces me to sit.

"How are you feeling, Mrs. Evans?"

We watch the nurse go linger beside the closed door. She plays nervously with her magni-card.

We touch Dr. Benson's hands. He's known the both of us from the very start. "Isolated," we say.

Tom looks up from leafing through the journal, eyes wide. Hopeful.

Dr. Benson speaks, "We've let you down. I suppose we didn't test soma-therapy long enough, but we needed to do something. The Accident would have killed us all off without genetic intervention."

We glance to Tom. His fingers tremble as he turns another page. We wish he would go faster. We've written something for him on the last page.

"The Accident happened generations ago," we say. "You've created a new generation. A stronger one."

Dr. Benson's eyes narrow. "No, Mrs. Evans," his voice lowers. "We've created a genetic pool that can never procreate. We've squandered our genetic resources to make people like—you."

Us we think, but we don't correct him out loud.

"As your acting legal caretaker, Tom has reached a decision regarding your care," says Dr. Benson. "Right, Tom?"

Tom picks at the corners of the pages. "This decision wasn't easy, I agonized over losing you. But then I realized, I already lost you a long time ago."

Pathetic, Tom. Two lifetimes and still he doesn't understand. Like a spoiled child bored with yet another toy, he throws us away.

"Turn to the last page, Tom," we say.

"Lay back, Mrs. Evans," says Dr. Benson. "You'll only feel a pinch. You won't suffer."

Tom's face pales. He looks away from me.

"Tom, please," we say as the nurse grips my arms. "It's not too late."

Dr. Benson plucks the first syringe from the tray. It clanks, heavy with serum. The nurse turns her face from me, her hands still firmly planted on my shoulders. Her magni-card rests against my neck.

We hear something heavy thud against the tile floor. We hear Tom cry out. We smile. He's finally found our message.

"Stop, I've changed my mind." Tom wraps his arms around Benson, wrestling him away from us. "Look what she wrote! She is cured."

Dr. Benson reaches for our journal. "Impossible," he says. "We've been monitoring her daily. There is no reason to believe she is cured or even can be cured."

Tom clutches our journal to his chest. "You are too blinded by your own experiments to see your patients' own progress. You have cost me two wives," Tom says, tackling the doctor. "She is cured and you would have had me kill her!" They tumble to the floor, knocking the tray of syringes over. They roll and scatter, shattering as they strike the cinder block wall. The journal falls open to our message: You are loved, Tom.

We smile. The nurse gives a shout. As she reaches for the doctor, we grab her wrist. She slaps us and screams, but we rip the magni-card from her plastic band.

"Thanks for helping us escape," we say to Tom as we swipe the card. The door clicks open. He starts to say something but Benson punches him.

As we sprint down the hall, we swipe that card in each and every door.

"Ethan?" we say.

They shake their heads as they push past us. Freedom is more pressing to them. We are a wave, a revolution. The nurses can't stop us, we are too many. The doctors can't stop us. The doors can't hold us back.

We emerge into the glimmering white light squinting. It's heat hugs us. We are free. We are free.

We've set up a tarp-lined utopia in the wild outside of the city. There are so many of us, we are our own city. We help one another to build and to remember. Yet still, we cannot find <u>him</u>.

We watch our first sunset in a very long time. The crimson-orange glow radiates throughout the forest. To think, we used to fear what is natural. The trees cast an elongated shadow, like an arrow. It points to something bright deeper in the woods. It crackles and flickers, like a campfire.

Our feet remember the cool squish of the mud, our skin remembers the cool breeze, our ears remember the peaceful birdsongs. We retrace our steps deeper into the foliage. The afternoon sun dapples the trail in gold. We remember where it all began.

We emerge from the thicket. Someone waits for us in the circle of oaks. His face is tanned from hours in the courtyard, his body lanky from the institutional routine. But behind those multi-colored eyes lies a shared memory. Tears blur our vision. It makes him look like an angel with a halo of smeared light.

"We promised we'd find you, our love." It is still Ethan's gentle voice, after all this time.

"We've never forgotten you," we say, playing with the buttons of his flannel shirt.

"We never stopped loving you."

We hold one another in the shade of the oak tree, our skin tingling like little sparks. It's as if two lifetimes never happened. He's still our second skin. Our lips hungrily find one another. He holds our hand, thumb rubbing where our daisy wedding ring once was. Our pinky fingers hook together. We grin.

"Pinky swear," he says.

"We swear," we say.

U is for Uncoded

Steve Bornstein

Melick picked his way along the river's edge. His sword was an unfamiliar weight on his hip, rattling against his leg and throwing off his balance on the already unsteady ground.

The cool air coming off the water was a welcome respite from the heat of the mountain summer, and he stopped next to a water-polished boulder to rest and refill his water skins. He shucked off his pack and swordbelt and left them on the rock to keep them from getting wet. He had another day and a half before he got to the valley where the trolls were supposed to be camped and he didn't want to spend that time with wet gear.

One more time he thought about how stupid this errand was, and one more time he reminded himself that he had no choice. They'd taken the only thing of his father's he had left and even though the barrel had grown steadily more empty over time, he still needed it. There were still ashes enough for years of work.

He was lost in thought, staring across the river at the woods on the opposite bank, so the sudden crash behind him startled him so much he slipped and fell to a knee in the shallows. Melick floundered and spun around, his spray-wet hair splattering across his face, and stared right at the giant lion standing where it had emerged from the forest not twenty feet away. Then a goat head looked up over the lion's mane, and he saw a thick snake twisting behind the beast. Not a lion, then. A chimera, and probably the death of him.

Melick's heart slammed against the inside of his chest and his knees weakened. The chimera watched him, sniffing the air. Melick glanced at the sword still propped against the boulder, halfway between the two of them. The beast hadn't attacked him yet, maybe he could get to his sword in time to have a fighting chance. The wind whipped up behind him, shocking him with the river's chill.

The chimera sniffed again and snorted. "I'm not goin' to eat ye, if that's yer worry," it grumbled. "Leather, aye?"

Chimeras could speak? He'd never heard of such a thing, just the odd story of how some hero saved a maiden from one of the ravening beasts, cheap tales told by bards looking for a bite and a bed as they passed through town.

Melick blinked and stared as the beast sauntered over to the water's edge and lapped at an eddy pool. It was close enough he could see the way its fur laid, where yellow gave way to gray, where lion turned to goat turned to snake. It smelled like a buffalo, and a wet one at that. The goat head looked around, bored. The snake that was its tail peered at him and flickered its tongue, tasting the air.

"Wh-what?" he said, shivering with chill.

"Yer a leatherworker, aye?" the chimera said as it stood again, water draining from its chin. The runoff was stained with threads of red. "I can smell it in ye, the tannin' and the dyes. Makes yer skin taste all nasty-like. I'm full anyway, s'not like I'm starvin'. Ye look stringy anyway, hardly any meat on them bones."

Another hard shudder ran through Melick. The chill of the wind on his wet clothes was reason enough, but the chimera casually discussing the pros and cons of eating him wasn't helping. He slowly waded through the water to the rocky shore, half-worried that the chimera would start to chase him like a mad dog drawn to movement.

"Oh, umm, yes I am..." Did it say it just ate? "Th-thank you, I..." His sword wasn't too far, now. Maybe he could still get to it before the chimera could get to him...

The chimera let out a low rumble, like a dog watching someone inch towards its food. "Ye know I can see ye, right? I'm being all polite here just havin' a drink. Ye go for that sword and I'll have to put ye down. I said I wasn't gonna eat ye, not that I couldn't kill ye dead."

Again it talked about killing him with as much emotion as he'd have shown swatting a fly. Melick took a panicked step back and felt his foot slide on a slick rock. Off-balance, he flailed and went down hard on his backside. The beast chortled. It *laughed* at him. Melick felt his ears burn.

"What are ye doin' out here?" it crowed. Melick felt the chimera's heavy footsteps through his bruised bum as it walked over and sat, towering over him. "Don't ye know there's monsters in these woods? Ye better run along home before one of 'em finds ye."

"I do know!" Melick blurted. The chimera looked as surprised as he felt at his outburst, but with it came courage. "My town was raided by trolls yesterday. The Treecutters never bothered us before but they swept through breaking and smashing their way through town. They broke into my shop and got my dragon ashes, I need those!" Melick panted, fuming and full of renewed purpose.

The chimera looked down at him with a smirk. "Ye say ye killed a dragon? Didn't yer pappy tell ye not to fib?"

"My father's the one who killed it," Melick said, getting to his feet. Suddenly the chimera didn't seem so imposing, now that it had reminded him what he was supposed to be doing. "It was the last thing he did before he retired, taking down the great wyrm Dimante. He gathered up the ashes that were left and bequeathed them to me when he died."

The chimera leaned forward a little and squinted. "Yer pappy was Malin?"

Melick nodded, running a hand through his wet hair to slick it back. "He was, and I've been using the ashes for tanning. My wares are the best around because of them, strong and supple. Those damnable trolls made off with all I had left, the whole barrel!"

The chimera sat up again and snorted. "And yer going to get them back, is that it? All by yerself? Where's yer war party?"

Melick huffed and walked over to the boulder for his pack and sword. "They're all cleaning up from the raid. They wanted to wait but I know those trolls are probably selling them, or eating them, or..." He threw up his arms in disgust. "I can't wait!"

The chimera snorted again. Its goat head looked bored and its snake tail had coiled up on the ground behind it. "One gamey leatherworker against the Treecutter tribe? Aye, I'm sure ye'll make 'em a fine snack, trolls like gnawin' on bones."

Melick buckled the swordbelt around his waist and settled its weight on his hips. "What else can I-" He blinked, his rant stopped short by inspiration. "You could help me!"

The chimera leaned forward again. "Help ye?"

"You could help me!" Melick said again. "You're a chimera, with your help I could get my ashes back!"

The chimera spat on the ground and stood. Its snake tail uncoiled with a sharp hiss, curling up over its back. "I'm only passin' through these woods," it rumbled. "I don't have any quarrel with the Treecutters and I don't want to give 'em any reason to have one with me. Never know when I'll be back this way again and trolls got memories as long as their arms." The beast turned and started to saunter back to the treeline.

"I'll make it worth your while!" Melick shouted, grabbing his pack and hurrying after it. "I can, uh... I can make you saddlebags!"

The chimera stopped and turned, eyes narrowed. "What?"

"I can make you saddlebags!" he said again, nodding frantically. He couldn't let this chance get away from him. "With the ashes they'll be strong and durable and they'd last you forever! You could, uh, you could put, uhm..." The silliness of what he was proposing finally occurred to him, but he kept going regardless. "You could put food in them, or things you wanted to keep with you..." His voice trailed off, withered by the chimera's skeptical gaze.

The chimera just stood there for a long moment. Melick waited for it to start laughing at him again. "That's nae bad idea," it finally said.

Melick's heart swelled. "Yes! Thank you, oh thank you!" He stepped forward to hug the beast but a warning hiss from the snake head brought him back to his right mind. He shuffled his feet and put on his backpack, trying to make it look like that was his intention all along. "Thank you." He cleared his throat and started back along the river. "This way."

Melick slept surprisingly well, all things considered. The chimera had been almost silent after agreeing to join him, and by the time they found a clearing for the night Melick was wondering if it was just some elaborate ruse to eat him after all. He bedded down on the other side of the clearing from the chimera with his sword close at hand, but the next morning he opened his eyes to find the chimera returning to camp with a bloodied mouth.

Melick scrambled out of his blankets and grabbed for his sword, looking around for the attackers. "Is it the trolls? Where are they?" he shouted, trying to gather his wits.

The chimera just stared at him.

Melick spun around a few times, sword at the ready, but no marauders or trolls came barreling out of the trees for them. He looked expectantly at the chimera, then understood. "You just ate," he said, lowering his sword.

"Aye?" the chimera replied. Melick sighed and picked up his scabbard, resheathing the sword. "Do ye always wake up ready for battle?"

Melick sat on a fallen tree, rummaging in his pack for some jerky. "I woke up and I saw your face, I didn't know what was going on." He waved a hand around his mouth, his ears hot.

It took the chimera another moment to understand what he was getting at. "Oh! Aye, and it was a fine plump doe too," it said, beaming proudly. It tilted its lion head back for the goat head to groom the doe's remains from its face. Melick stared, fascinated at this glimpse into chimera habits, but quickly returned his attention to his jerky and waterskin when he saw the snake head staring back at him.

They were only about a day's hike from the Treecutter tribe. Melick pondered his options as they broke camp and started off for the day. Fighting the trolls to get the dragon ashes back? Maybe if the chimera attacked as a diversion and he snuck in to steal the barrel... But then, could he even carry it off? He was people-sized, not troll-sized. Still, he knew his odds were much better with the chimera at his side than they were when he was alone.

It was almost midday when Melick finally broke the silence. "I didn't know chimeras could talk."

"Yer a funny lad," the chimera replied, chuffing.

"Honestly!" Melick said, laughing at the beast's reply. "All the stories are just about how chimeras are savage monsters and a hero has to go out and claim their treasure or rescue some damsel or the like. None of the bards ever sang about one having a chat in its lair with the maiden it'd kidnapped."

"That should tell ye somethin' right there." The chimera waited a moment and glanced at him when Melick didn't reply, and saw the man's blank look. "Chimeras don't keep lairs unless they're mating," it continued.

Melick blinked in surprise. "They don't? But where do you live?"

"I live right here," the chimera said with a grunt. "And in a few minutes I'll be livin' up there on that ridge we're headin' towards." Again it let the silence draw out for a moment while Melick absorbed that. "Ye wanna know where I'm from, I know. I tell ye, it don't matter where I'm from or where I'm goin'. I leave when there's no reason to stay and I get where I'm goin' when I get there."

He looked up at the chimera's goat head as they followed a path through the trees, watching it look around, and suddenly realized that the creature's lion head had been doing all the talking. The stories he'd heard always spoke of how fearsome a beast with three heads was to fight, so if they could all fight by themselves then weren't they independent?

Melick saw the goat head notice him and blurted out the question. "So does the goat head speak too?"

The chimera's goat head looked ahead and its lion head turned around to look at him. "Eh?"

Melick gestured up at the head that had taken over watching where it was going since the chimera turned to speak with him. "You're the only one who's talked so far. Doesn't that one have anything to say?"

The snake head hissed quietly from behind him.

The chimera snorted, a great bassy sound somewhere between a snuffle and a ruff. "I might as well ask ye what yer hand thinks of the jerky ye had this mornin'. Just because a goat uses a goat head to talk don't mean that's what I use a goat head for." The snake head hissed again.

Now Melick snorted, smirking back at the chimera. "Goats don't talk."

"Chimeras don't talk either," the chimera replied with a toss of its mane.

They broke camp early the next day, just one ridge over from the Treecutter camp. The chimera had woken him when it returned from hunting again that morning, not quite as bloody as its previous meal. Melick finished off his apple and wiped his hands on his trousers. "So I think you should go down there and attack them. That'll get them moving, right?" He stopped next to a rotted tree trunk and stuffed his pack inside. He knew that barrel was heavy; if he was going to have any chance of lugging it out of there he needed to carry as little as possible, maybe even dump out some of the ashes to lighten the load.

The chimera pointedly watched him buckle his swordbelt around his hips. "And ye'll just slay anyone who gets in your way, eh?"

Melick set his jaw and nodded, gripping the pommel of his sword tightly to keep his hand from shaking.

The chimera chuffed and walked past him, towards the top of the ridge. "Let's get this over with then."

It wasn't a very deep valley. From their spot overlooking the camp, they could see how the huts and animal pens were arranged in a rough circle around an open courtyard, with a much larger hut on one side of the circle. Melick thought it looked important. A few trolls walked through the camp but not as many as he thought there would be. He couldn't tell what they were doing, but there were none of the guards he expected.

"I'll check in there first," he said, pointing at the larger hut. "Maybe that's the chieftain's home or something. I think I can sneak in through the back and take a peek, maybe it'll be in a storeroom."

The chimera chuffed again and shook itself. "Aye then. Get yerself down there. I'll watch from here and when I see ye ready to go in the back I'll come runnin' in."

Melick nodded, suddenly aware of how dry his mouth was. Once he started down the slope, there'd be no going back. He carefully picked his way through the trees, watching for any wandering trolls. Once he made it around to the side of the camp, near the edge of the treeline, he waved for the chimera's attention and watched.

The chimera stood lazily, but its roar echoed off the valley's sides. It bounded down from the ridge, roaring again when it reached the valley floor at a dead run and raced into the camp. Trolls shouted and bolted for cover. Melick started out from the trees for the back of the camp's big hut and was halfway to it when all the commotion suddenly stopped.

He rushed up to the cabin and peeked around the side, worried the chimera had been killed but what he saw just didn't make any sense. The chimera was sitting squarely in the middle of the camp's courtyard, its snake tail curling like a cat's. There were a few trolls around it with spears, but none of them were trying to stab it and it wasn't trying to eat any of them.

"I'll be speakin' with yer chief," the chimera called out towards the large hut. Was this the chimera's idea of a distraction? A discussion? Was anything he'd been told about chimeras true?

Melick heard another small commotion inside the hut and then a gravelly voice call out. "And what brings you to the Treecutter tribe, wanderer? I'm afraid our hospitality is thin these days, many of us are ill." He cracked open the hut's back door and snuck inside when he saw it was empty, ducking into the first room to search for his prize.

"Aye," he heard the chimera say through the thin wall. "I can see that, and I'll not trouble ye any more than I must. I'm here to parlay for the dragon ashes ye stole three days past." Melick smacked his head. Was the beast insane? He opened another door to a storeroom full of barrels and started going through them as fast as he could. "Ye'll also want to catch that man going through yer hut there. Please don't hurt him though, I'm here for him too."

Melick froze, his blood icy. He heard the hut's door slam open and fumbled frantically for his sword. The storeroom's door crashed open and the doorway was filled by a huge troll, its green warty skin pocked with red lumps.

Melick drew his sword with a cry, but before he could get it halfway out of its scabbard the troll seized his arms. "No! No!" he said, struggling as the troll growled and dragged him out into the courtyard. Another troll tore the sword from his grip and he was shoved into the center of the courtyard. Melick tripped over a stone and stumbled, falling in front of the chimera.

"Traitor!" he spat up at the beast. "They'll kill us both now!"

The chimera frowned and knocked him over onto his belly with a massive paw, pinning him to the ground. "I owe ye no allegiance, lad," the chimera rumbled. "Now shut yer mouth before ye turn out right."

Melick flailed about for a moment but had neither the strength nor the leverage to get out from under the chimera's careful weight. He stopped, panting, and wiped the dust from his face to see the trolls gathered around them. Some held spears at the ready but most seemed to just watch. Again, there were fewer than he was expecting, and though some looked healthier than others they were all obviously in some kind of distress, with red blotches standing out against their dark green skin. Even the chieftain, standing proud in a headdress and feathered cape, had splotches across his face.

"We can't give you the ashes," the chieftain said. "My people have firepox and the unguent we make from the ashes will cure it. They are ours by right of conquest."

"Those ashes are- Nnngh!" Melick's rant was cut off as the chimera carefully pressed the air from his lungs, leaving him gasping.

"Aye, you did take the barrel," the chimera said, its goat head nodding. "And aye, the town did fail to protect it and your war party did claim them. But this lad needs those ashes too. They're his livelihood."

"Then he should have protected them!" the chieftain said. "What he needs is not my concern. I must attend to my tribe, not the needs of soft men."

Melick took another breath to start shouting but had it promptly squeezed out of him by the chimera's paw. "Aye, he's a soft one all right, but he's brave too. This lad was coming here all by his lonesome to take that barrel back. Got that from his pappy Malin, I wager."

The chieftain squinted at Melick. "This one is the son of Malin? A leatherworker?"

How many people knew of his father?

"Aye, so he claims and so I can smell. Says his pappy gave him the barrel, the remains of the wyrm Dimante." The chimera's goat head nodded again. "Now ye see why the lad wants it back, eh?"

The chieftain's grey eyes widened. "Dimante's ashes? Malin did everyone a service when he destroyed that beast." The troll's face clouded, then hardened. Melick was afraid he was about to reject the chimera's plea again, then the troll spoke. "Ashes from such a powerful wyrm should be most effective against our firepox," the troll said with a slow nod. "I had thought even what ashes we claimed would not be enough to save the whole tribe but knowing this, we will not need so much salve after all. When the disease has been cured, we will return the remainder to the son of Malin."

Melick blinked, mouth agape. Just like that, he was getting his ashes back. Not all of them, but he'd been thinking he'd have to dump some of them anyway to get the barrel back to town. "Th-... Thank you. Thank you!"

The chimera lifted his paw from Melick's back and sat up straight again, bowing all three heads to the troll. "Yers is a just and wise decision and we thank ye for it."

The chieftain growled something and the trolls lowered their spears. The small crowd started to break up. Melick rolled onto his back and sat up, looking up at the chimera. "I, uh, didn't expect it to go like that," he said, feeling awkward under the chimera's smug gaze.

"'Course not. They attacked you so you had to attack them, aye?" A couple of trolls were cautiously wandering up to the chimera to gawk but it paid them no heed. "I knew yer pappy too. He helped me out when I needed it, a long time ago. He wasn't like most adventurers who just attack a beast because they look evil so they must be evil, aye, or because that's what the stories say they are. Like ye were gonna do to these here trolls. I wanted ye to see that for yerself. Plenty of situations that don't need swords to get through."

"But they attacked my town."

"Aye they did, but they didn't kill any of ye either and here you come ready to slay some poxy trolls. They did what they thought was right. See lad, everyone's got a reason for doin' what they do. Plenty of fights and wars been started 'cause of people not thinkin' before actin'."

Melick got to his feet and dusted himself off. One of the trolls walked over and handed him his sword. Melick thanked the troll with a small bow. He started to put the swordbelt on then stopped, looking around and then up at the chimera. "I'd feel wrong wearing this here, now. Maybe I should go talk to the chief. Maybe we can come to some kind of trade arrangement. Trolls wear leather goods too, after all." He looked back towards the large hut, where the chieftain had returned after his pronouncement. "I wonder what his name is."

The chimera got to his feet and started towards the chieftain's hut. Melick walked along with him. "Ye never even asked my name."

Melick cringed a little. "I'm sorry, how rude. I didn't know chimeras had names."

The chimera chuffed a laugh and shook his head. "Ye need to find yerself a higher class of bard, lad."

V is for Vagabond

Suzanne van Rooyen

All the words I cannot say stain my skin in inky ribbons. Choking syllables press against my throat and claw their way down my spine. Unspoken apologies gnaw at my ribs, and a murmuration of unuttered *I love yous* writhe upon my belly, twisting in a Möbius dance to the stilted soundtrack of regret.

The furore of the train station sets my heart thrumming. The crowd surges and my elbow connects with a fellow commuter as we rush the closing doors. *Excuse me* blazes across the instep of my right foot, the curling letters burn and itch, catching at the threads of my sock.

Tucked safe in the corner at the back of the carriage, I count the seconds between stations.

At Slussen, the doors open and she wafts into the train, skirts rustling and long plaits swinging. She sees me and inclines her head, her smile shy but spilling into her fathomless eyes. Others shift uncomfortably in her presence, wary of the jangling coins in her paper cup. The train leaves the station and she starts to sing.

Her voice weaves a tapestry of color, sound eddies rippling in neon to splash against the windows. Her music spatters me with red and yellow, a hundred shades of blue I cannot name, dousing my clothes—if only it could douse my skin and extinguish the searing presence of everything left unsaid. She paints her memories through melody, her hopes and dreams for those willing to see.

I see you stitches fire on my cheek, invisible, I hope, beneath a caked layer of stage make-up. *Your music is life itself* flares at my hip. *You are a gift* ignites along my forearm, overlapping yesterday's *If only I knew your name.* The pain in my flesh pricks tears in my eyes, but it's the anguish cinched vise-like around my heart causing them to trail down my cheeks, muddying her vibrant song.

By Gullmarsplan the aria is over, replaced by the tinkling rhythm of kronor in the cup. I give her all I can, crisp bills that draw more than a few raised eyebrows and snide remarks. She thanks me in the broken Swedish she learned on the streets; her smile all the thanks I need.

I love you threads molten lava through my chest, joining three month's worth of declarations littering my skin. She lingers for a moment before stepping through the doors and waves from the platform as the train continues, carrying me away.

I would erase his pain. I would steal his phantoms. I would take his words and make them my own, if only he would give them to me.

My first word was *mamsen.* I would've screamed had I been able as the letters charred to the bone. My mother screamed for both of us and from her atheist tongue fell ancient prayers. She turned to Christ, to Buddha and Allah. She burned candles for Odin and spilled blood for Freya. She sought understanding through her ancestors and enlightenment through the tarot. Still, words seared my skin, a confused babble of fragmented sentences tattooing my toddler hide.

Now, I'm running out of space. Words tangle and entwine, slithering in search of pristine skin.

Abomination scorches my collar-bone. My mother's favorite word, playing on repeat in my mind and silently on my lips. It first made an appearance when I was six, emblazoned between my shoulders. Perhaps the truth lies in my twisted DNA, a convoluted secret held by genes and chromosomes. It's a secret I will never know.

Coward! The word leaves blisters on the back of my hand as it melts into my flesh. A litany to self-loathing trails my body, wrapping serpent syllables around my limbs. If only I could shed my skin. If only I could erase the things I'll never say.

The doors open at Slussen and she drifts into the train, a swirl of magenta and long black hair, unbound today and tumbling viscous across her shoulders. She scans the carriage, her eyes finding mine. There's a darkness in her gaze, something wild and feral.

I want to know you takes me by surprise as it cuts a tingling rill between my legs. *I want you* burns white and hot as lithium in my groin.

Today she sings for no one but me. A rain of greens and pinks, oranges and lilacs splatter my face and hair, her gaze focused with intensity on my face. I lose myself in the music, soaring on sonorous waves as her voice provides respite from strangling syntax.

Her song ends and she sashays through the carriage with her usual cup, her gaze never straying long from mine. This time when I offer the roll of bills she takes them from my hand, our fingers grazing, skin against skin. She sucks in a breath, smile faltering.

I love you. I wish I could give you more. My left shin aches and itches.

With a hurried *tack så mycket* she disappears through the doors. I study my hands, every finger stained with overlapping words. A mother shakes her head at me, keeping her child from getting too close.

Monster. The word is acid in my palm.

I will alleviate his anguish. I will sing the chaos from his skin.

My mother sits huddled in blankets watching the first snows fall on Stockholm from her hospital bed.

"You're not supposed to come." Her words mist maroon, speckled black by the cancer eating at her organs.

It's my birthday, I sign though I know she isn't looking at me. She stopped looking at me when I was fourteen and *why don't you love me?* singed the skin of my forehead.

"I asked them not to let in visitors." She coughs and I rush to her side with her water glass. She grabs my hand, the hand I spent two hours meticulously covering with shades of ocher, tracing realistic skin creases over three decades of silent letters. She tips the water over my hand, soaking her blanket. I try to pull away but her fingers are talons as they rub at my skin, removing the careful layers of concealment.

"Urgh." She throws my hand away when the smudged make-up reveals the twitching ribbons of words below.

I'm sorry, I sign.

"You know what your problem is." My mother holds my gaze. "Even if you could speak, you wouldn't say anything. You're closed off. Shut down. It's why you're all alone." Her eyes fill with tears. "I'm going to die and then you'll truly have no one and it won't be because of what you are." She gestures to all of me. "It'll be because of who you are."

My body is a conflagration of fresh wounds and whole sentences I'll never say.

Soon, I will set him free.

She's thinner as she steps into the train, face gaunt and eyes framed by bruises. Still she smiles.

You're beautiful the words prickle on my tongue and knock against my teeth.

She starts to sing and the colors are pale this time, pastel shades of blue and yellow, a slow drip down the windows leaving bleached puddles at my feet. For weeks, the color in her songs has been fading. Perhaps she's ill. The thought churns in my gut as I imagine her on the unforgiving streets in the creeping winter. Her song ends and as always she makes her way through the carriage, this time teetering as the train jerks, grimacing and massaging her temples before continuing.

She pauses before me when I offer her the roll of bills. This time she takes both my hands in hers and a frisson rattles my bones. She gazes into my eyes, her own limpid despite the bruises. She smells of exhaust fumes and rotting leaves, and I savor her scent.

Through her smile she speaks gentle words in the same dialect as her songs. I don't understand but that hardly matters when she squeezes my hands and dusts a kiss across my knuckles. The doors open and a wave of commuters wash her from the train. I rush after her, too slow, and the doors hiss shut. I search the receding platform for a swish of black hair and bright skirt, but she's gone and I am left alone.

I gave all that I could. I hope he understands.

Winter sinks its fangs into the city and when the train doors open, she isn't there.

Where, where, where? Perhaps the wind has whipped me numb because I cannot feel the words on my skin though they must surely leave a stain. I ride the train to the end of the line, hope diminishing at every stop. I ride the train back into the city, scanning every platform, ready to dash through the doors should she appear.

My love is gone.

My chest is a vacuum.

My days are monochromatic blurs of darkness and snow.

My mother was right.

My love is gone.

On Christmas Eve the city is empty, everyone tucked around tables with family and food, with warmth and holiday cheer I've never known. I ride the trains, switching lines randomly as the hope of finding her withers and scatters like snow in a Baltic gust.

The doors open and she hurries into the train, red hair escaping from her woolen cap. She scans the carriage and chooses a seat precariously close to mine. My heart constricts in a barbed-wire embrace.

Please don't talk to me the words loop in my mind, but I don't feel them on my skin. Ever since my love disappeared, I've felt nothing much of anything.

"Work kept me late. What's your excuse?" She asks with a smile that turns her eyes citrus green.

I consider signing, knowing she'll apologize and shuffle away awkwardly. I consider using my phone and typing a response, which would perhaps have the same result. The words I want to say lie bitter on my tongue, sizzling between my teeth. I open my mouth to take a breath and instead, the words tumble out.

Syllables upon syllables fall from my lips. I try to catch them in my hands, hands littered with black ink fading gray. The words rush from my skin onto my tongue and into the air. Whole sentences pop red and teal, explode magenta and mustard, splashing the woman's white coat and freckled face.

She wipes a swath of purple from her cheek and flicks the color from her fingers with a smile.

W is for Words

Michael Kellar

"Yesterday upon the stair

I met a man who wasn't there

He wasn't there again today

I wish, I wish he'd go away."

— *William Hughes Mearns*

Shannon remembered nothing at all of the wreck.

Her first subsequent memory was of briefly waking up while she was being lifted into the ambulance, and hearing an attendant mumble "I think we're going to lose this one!"

Strangely, her immediate reaction was a question of protocol. She wondered whether emergency technicians were actually permitted to utter such strong proclamations in the presence of a victim. This was immediately substituted with the desire for a second opinion. Then, darkness.

After a number of brief intervals of consciousness over an unknown period of time, she finally came fully awake. A police officer was standing at the foot of her hospital bed, somewhat timidly, with his hat in his hand.

"Miss, I need to ask you some questions about your accident."

He was young and kind of cute. Or perhaps that was just a judgment from the morphine; everyone looked great right now, in a glowing and detached sort of way.

"How much do you remember about the incident?"

His question was rather hesitant. He was obviously uncomfortable, but was this due to being in a hospital or to being in the presence of a good-looking woman?

She knew herself to be quite attractive beneath the bruises.

That thought quickly prompted a frown. Some cops were turned on by exactly that combination.

No, not this one. He oozed a sense of wanting to be doing this interview correctly, to help.

"I was on my way to the beach. It was still early. I was not speeding or in a hurry, but the sunlight caught my eye and I slipped off the side of the highway."

He glanced at his notes.

"This was near the construction site next to the Blossom Motel?"

She nodded.

"Yes. They were opening the exit adjacent to that new parking lot. The shoulder was mushy. When I dropped off the edge, I tried to correct myself with a sharp left turn, but instead of righting itself, my car just flipped."

"Seat belt on?"

Shannon opened the top of her hospital gown enough to reveal a long red welt, which appeared as a diagonal line above the curve of her right breast.

"They told me a witness saw my car flip twice. The first time the seat belt snapped loose and did this to me. The second time I was ejected into the air through the open passenger side window. Fortunately, the car and I did not fall in the same direction."

The kid looked puzzled. Tests had indicated that no drugs were involved. Even though speeding was not a question, and it had been a bright, clear morning, the officer issued a citation noting 'too fast for conditions'. His apologetic tone suggested that he had felt obligated to find *some* offence.

"This won't amount to anything", he commented as he was heading out the door. "I'm sure the judge will dismiss it. Besides, I know you have enough other problems."

That cryptic comment left her wondering what she might not have been told as yet.

As the days passed, Shannon slowly began to sort out fact from drug-induced fiction regarding her recent memories.

She recalled an endless parade of doctors and nurses, all intense and caring and calming and solicitous—probably all real. Remembered forcibly vomiting up the first bit of semi-solid food a nurse had attempted to fed her—definitely real. Then there were frequent visits by an older man she did not know and was not dressed in any kind of uniform. No one else seemed to interact with him. So, probably an illusion. Finally, a couple times a rather formal woman stopped in to discuss some type of legal matters and asked her if she understood the concept of "implied consent". Since the consent forms with her signature on them remained on her bedside table she mentally filed that, too, under 'Real'.

One afternoon, months later Shannon found herself sitting alone on a blanket on a nearly deserted section of the beach. She had remained in Crater Cove, partly due to liking the doctor who had been suggested to her for follow-up care, and partly because she still had no place in particular that she wanted to go.

It was late afternoon and although there was a strong wind blowing in from the ocean, it still seemed unseasonably warm to a displaced Northerner like herself. Her shade stretched nearly to the edge of the incoming tide, and she was playing a game where she had to guess what type of bird was flying overhead by first watching its shadow when a voice spoke to her.

"That group of rocks out there is all that is left of Nikola's Island.

It was named for a medical man. It was his fortune that built the hospital that you stayed in."

Shannon turned and saw an older man standing beside her, staring out into the Atlantic. She was mildly embarrassed that he seemed to know her, but she could not summon up his name.

"We have a rougher patch of land here than in the areas to the north or south. It really was unlikely that so many tourists latched onto it. Did you know that way back in 1682, there was a soldier who suffered a head wound, and his doctors treated him by repairing the damage to his skull with a piece of dog's bone. The operation was successful until the Church heard about the event and who threatened him with excommunication unless the dog bone was removed. Which they did. He died, but still in the Grace of God."

She was about to excuse herself and admit that she did not remember his name when she suddenly placed him. He was the older gentleman who she thought she remembered had visited her from time to time. She turned back to address him, but he was gone.

She didn't think that she had been lost in thought all that long. Then she considered it odd that, unlike the birds she had been observing, his approach had not been preceded by his shadow.

Shortly after the last of the tourists left at the end of the season, Shannon finally decided that it was time to move on. She had not made any friends during her time here—since her accident there seemed to be a difference in the way that felt about or interacted with others. It was as though they were different - or perhaps she was - either way they somehow seemed less real to her now, almost as though she were watching them on a television show.

Two years of high school French had led to a long-held desire to visit Paris, so she did. Of course seeing the Eiffel Tower was first on her agenda, followed by a visit to Notre Dame Cathedral and the Palace of Versailles. She was most surprised to discover, however, that there was a Disneyland in Paris - Euro Disney. She spent the day there and found it a touch surrealistic, although she had to admit that hearing Donald Duck sputtering in French seemed somehow quite appropriate.

Early in the afternoon Shannon found herself feeling vaguely out of sorts. Disneyland may have triggered a bout of homesickness, but it seemed more than that. Lately she had noticed tiring easily, and not having much of an appetite, but now she was also nauseous and was experiencing a pain in her side.

Food poisoning was her next thought, but it was not until she returned to her hotel room and looked into the bathroom mirror that the truth came to her. Her eyes and skin had taken on yellowish jaundiced color and she remembered the warning signs she had been told to watch for upon her exit from the hospital.

Some of these symptoms had been around for much of the past week, but could her liver suddenly be failing that quickly? Her last coherent thought was that she should go to the emergency room, but instead she vomited and fell asleep across her bed.

When she opened her eyes a few hours later, the first thing she noticed was an oddness to the light. Sunlight streamed in through the window, but somehow she had a sense of twilight.

She sat up on the bed, upset at the state of her soiled sundress – which she had not taken off since Disneyland – but relieved to discover that she no longer felt any pain or discomfort.

"I assume that you will have many questions."

This came from a voice to the left of her bed.

"And, no, I am not 'an undigested bit of beef, a blot of mustard, a crumb of cheese, or a fragment of underdone potato'".

Seated in an armchair was the strange half-remembered little old man who had visited her on the beach and had been classified as morphine-induced dreams at the hospital.

"You are not real," she stated uncertainly.

"Oh, I most certainly am real. I merely am no longer alive."

Shannon was surprised that this was not as unnatural an experience as it might have been imagined. But even more disturbing was her growing apprehension concerning the fact she was no longer feeling any pain. Nor anything else, come to think about it.

"Am I…?"

Her visitor nodded.

"But why are you here? Why have you been following me?'

"Because we are two of a kind, my dear."

She looked puzzled and he took that as license to continue.

"Have you ever heard of a chimera?"

This question briefly evoked a picture from a fairy tale book Shannon had owned as a little girl.

"Wasn't that some sort of monster that had a goat's head and a lion's body?"

"Yes, that is the creature from mythology. But in modern genetics it has a different meaning. The term is used to refer to an organism which has tissue or organs inside it that originally belonged to a different species."

She wasn't sure where this was going.

"Some years ago I suffered a massive heart attack and was taken to the same emergency room in Compass Cove that treated you. No viable organs were available, yet I survived."

"But, how…?"

I lived for an additional eight months with the heart of a baboon beating in my chest. Ultimately, however, that noble animal's organ was rejected by my body. The science still has a long way to go."

"But what has that to do with me?"

"Compass Cove is an isolated town, and has a core that the temporary rush of beach visitors never see. Its founder was quite rich and very much was interested in medical experimentation. That legacy continued, although not always openly or even entirely legally. It is a community that very much believes that the end justifies the means. In their defense, they *have* been responsible for many advances which both added to the advancement of science as well as to the wealth of the town."

He paused.

"They were not entirely truthful with you about the source of your liver. In reality it was lab-grown and is composed of a mixture of bovine and human cells."

Shannon was somewhat shocked, but didn't understand how that was relevant to the situation in which she now found herself.

"So what happens next? Do I go on to a better place now like they always told me?"

"That seems to be the issue here. It appears the church was right. Since we are no longer entirely human, we are not fit for heaven, and yet we did nothing to cause our souls – or what remains of them – to be damned. So we appear to just be here. I have no idea what happens next."

Shannon shook her head in disbelief.

"You know, I never really ever believed in ghosts. I never thought they really existed."

"That is the really interesting aspect to all of this. From what I have experienced, there are still only a few others like us.

He sighed and finished.

"Ghosts didn't really used to exist. But thanks to science, they do now."

X is for
Xenotransplantation

Jonathan C. Parrish

They call them cowboys but they are not so much about cows as they are horses. Or bulls. When I look at Trent all I see is bull—muscle and sinew and an imposing presence that refuses to be ignored, like an incessantly quacking duck in a sound-proof booth. Every time he walks past me I can't help inhaling to try and catch his scent. A wake of leather, heated by the sun and his body, rewards me almost every time.

I spend parts of my day moving around so I can watch him surreptitiously, entranced by the shape of his thighs and the way they flex visibly under his jeans as he moves, even when he's just standing. I fixate like that a lot now—just looking at the curve of a single limb, how a lock of hair falls or the way light catches a nose in profile. The images fix in my mind, you know, for later.

I tried talking about what I saw when I looked at the world, once. When I was twelve. Greg told me about his fantasy where he caught a burglar and extracted favours from her in exchange for silence. His story made no sense to me. I told him about a single patch of hair on Steve's arm that caught my eye one day at the town pool, the way the air smelled of chlorine and the water cast un-shadows on the walls.

He didn't hang out with me after that, but he and his new friends would often find me and call me faggot and show me what they thought of the inside of my head.

I didn't talk about what I thought about anymore, kept the pieces of colour and light and shape and texture aside—part of me but fusing in their own space. I couldn't write them down, no mere words could do them justice and there was no real way of expressing that amalgamation of sense. And sure as hell not to the people I shared these streets with.

It's not just people parts. It's horse and goat, cat and chicken. It's grass and flower and root. It's brick and wood and faded paint. That said, it's mostly bull and man. The twisting of parts, the intertwining of sinew and branch, sun halos on the fine fuzz of a rear haunch. Late afternoon heat, and the smell of leather and hay and dung.

I don't have to worry about ever confessing anything inadvertently to Trent, don't have to worry about my stable job because I can't articulate my ideal. It's not him, it's the cow/boy bull/man turning itself inside out that stops me. Stops me where I stand, every time.

Y is for Yahoo

Amanda C. Davis

Part of me is Rabbit (*Sylvilagus floridanus*), an eastern cottontail, a hardy and vigorous species, adaptable, fast-breeding, an important component of many proven and theoretical ecosystems. It's not a very big piece of me. Just a mass inside my torso, nourished by my adolescent Homo *sapiens* body. But it's the piece of me that matters the most. There are many thousands of people on this ship, but I'm the last of Rabbit.

Dr. Ñahui has been checking on Rabbit since I was a baby. Once a month, for the past twelve years, she has slipped the long slim needle through me into the mass that is Rabbit. She tests it against the database to be sure it's still Rabbit, that it hasn't changed or taken on bits of me by mistake. We trust the database, she has told me, but flesh is better. She likes redundancy. Today, for example, she tests Rabbit twice.

Then she sends me to Dr. Rabemananjara.

I've never talked to Dr. Rabemananjara before; he treats humans. Typically humans much older than me, I recall. He doesn't have much to say but becomes very busy with me. When he leaves, I itch behind my ear the way I was told Rabbits do. I taught myself these twitchy mannerisms. They're not innate. They earn me derision. But they feel natural—maybe because I want them to.

When Dr. Rabemananjara returns, Dr. Ñahui is with him.

She says, "Please stay seated."

He says, "Listen closely. You have to make a decision. Soon, before someone else makes it for you."

Dr. Ñahui begins to speak, hesitates, then says, "For both of you."

I am still, but I tremble. I could bolt at any moment.

Dr. Rabemananjara begins talking. Rabbit is fine. But the flesh of me that touches Rabbit has gone wild. Masses. Tumors. They might not be Rabbit's fault. I put a hand on my stomach but I can't feel the cancer. There's quite a bit of it inside, they tell me. Much more of it than there is Rabbit. But the human cancer and Rabbit are too close. To remove it, they must remove Rabbit, and there is nowhere else for Rabbit to go.

My eyes dart between doctors. They are somber pillars of agreement.

I ask, "How long until—" and in words above my education I describe the process of preparing an infant *Homo sapiens* to incubate a mass of Rabbit.

They say six months.

I ask, "How long until—" we will have waited too long and I am sick, terribly sick, too sick to save.

They say three months.

We go silent, counting. I cannot make the numbers come out so that both Rabbit and I survive. I have trouble solving for a value that will save even one of us.

Dr. Rabemananjara tells me my best chance is to act now. Our future requires human beings, he emphasizes. He is willing to perform an emergency surgery and corrupt my records so he can tell everyone he had no idea I contained Rabbit until he extracted it along with the cancer.

I put my other hand on my stomach. My heart flutters the way Rabbit's heart used to flutter when cornered. They talk about that in books. It might even be in the database. But flesh is better.

Dr. Ñahui says she knows of an infant girl of similar genetic makeup to me, older than she would prefer, but someone she could prime to carry Rabbit for me. For us. The infant is so similar to me ("like a sister, that close") that the process might only take five months. Dr. Rabemananjara adds that this sort of thing ("this sort of thing," what he swims among but that I have never seen) is highly variable. Treatment might be possible as late as four months from now.

They are offering me hope from both directions, but their hope cannot stretch far enough to meet.

Dr. Ñahui, who monitors fifty-six other incubators like me, whose purpose on the ship is to deliver the hope of a complete network of life wherever we plant it, whose life's work has been the care of Rabbit, says, softly, "We need human beings."

I get down from the table.

I say, "But we only have one Rabbit."

The halls are full of human beings and I sniff like Rabbit would: cautiously, certainly not to hold back tears. Rabbit is very cautious. Rabbit preserves itself. My bunkroom is full of other kids carrying other little bits of the species we left behind. When I say their names, my mind says their other names: Elephant. Beetle. Dolphin. Hawk. Rat. I've studied the ecosystem charts, the proven and the theoretical. I know we need them all.

I lie on my bunk and wonder how long they'll let me sleep there, until they figure out something is wrong with me.

"Ai, Rabbit," says the boy I know as Worm. "Are you okay?"

I fold my hands over my stomach. It still trembles, but I realize that while Rabbit preserves itself, *Homo sapiens*, unlike all other species, defends. The 99.7% of me that is *Homo sapiens* was strong enough to leave Earth and take almost everything else with it. Rabbit is tricky but vulnerable; I am tough. And Rabbit is surrounded by me.

I close my eyes and imagine I am crouching in a nest of grass taller than my ears. Then I imagine I am the grass, cradling a living, breathing, soft, miraculous Rabbit.

"I'm okay," I say.

And Rabbit will be fine.

Z is for Zoo

Biographies

Alexandra Seidel is a writer, poet, and editor. Her writing has appeared in Strange Horizons, Lackington's, Stone Telling, and elsewhere. If you are so inclined you can follow Alexa on Twitter (@Alexa_Seidel) or read her blog: www.tigerinthematchstickbox.blogspot.com.

KV Taylor is an avid reader and writer of urban fantasy and dark speculative fiction, even though the only degree she holds is in the history of art. (Or, possibly, because the only degree she holds is in the history of art.) In her spare time she enjoys comic books, Himalayan Buddhist art, loud music, her Epiphone, and Black Bush. Her fiction can be found at kvtaylor.com.

Marge Simon lives in Ocala, Florida and is married to Bruce Boston. Her works appear in publications such as DailySF Magazine, Urban Fantasist, Silver Blade. She edits a column for the HWA Newsletter and serves as Chair of the Board of Trustees. She won the Strange Horizons Readers Choice Award, 2010, the SFPA's Dwarf Stars Award, 2012, and the Elgin Award for best poetry collection, 2015. She has won three Bram Stoker Awards ® for Superior Work in Poetry, two first place Rhysling Awards and the Grand Master Award from the SF Poetry Association, 2015. www.margesimon.com, Facebook: Marge Simon (Marge Ballif Boston)

By day, Pete Aldin delivers a program for people with disabilities; by night, he sits at a laptop and writes. His short fiction has appeared in publications including Orson Scott Card's Intergalactic Medicine Show, Andromeda Spaceways Inflight Magazine, and Niteblade. His non-fiction has appeared in parenting and business magazines. He is a big fan of alcoholic ciders, the FIFA franchise on xBox and (being an Australian) Vegemite. He is a member of the Australian Horror Writers Association and the Chelsea Dark Fiction Writers Circle. He don't like pina coladas nor taking walks in the rain.

Michael M. Jones lives in Southwest Virginia, with too many books, just enough cats, a plaster penguin, and a wife who knows where all the bodies are buried. His fiction has appeared in anthologies such as B is for Broken, Clockwork Phoenix 3, and A Chimerical World. He also edited Scheherazade's Facade and the forthcoming Schoolbooks & Sorcery. Visit him at www.michaelmjones.com.

Simon Kewin is the author of over 100 published short and flash stories. His works have appeared in Nature, Daily Science Fiction, Abyss & Apex and many more. He lives in England with his wife and their daughters. The second volume in his Cloven Land fantasy trilogy was recently published. Find him at simonkewin.co.uk.

BD Wilson is a writer from Edmonton, Alberta, Canada whose work has appeared in the anthology Dark Pages from Blade Red press, Liquid Imagination Online, and Niteblade Fantasy and Horror Magazine among others. A firm believer in a virtual existence, BD's home on the Web is located at http://www.bdwilson.ca

Gabrielle Harbowy is a San Francisco-based writer, editor, and anthologist, who rarely thinks in verse. Her debut novel, /Of The Essence/, is available by the time you're reading this. Find her online at gabrielleharbowy.com

Sara Cleto is a PhD candidate at the Ohio State University where she studies folklore, literature, disability, and the places where they intersect. Her poetry and prose can be found or is forthcoming in Goblin Fruit, Cabinet des Fees: Scheherazade's Bequest, Ideomancer, Niteblade, The Golden Key, and others. Her work has been nominated twice for the Pushcart Prize.

Megan Engelhardt is sad that she lives an hour away from the Sasquatch Triangle of Ohio. So close, yet so far away. Wolves and Witches, a fairytale compilation with her sister, Amanda C. Davis, is available from World Weaver Press. Megan blogs at megengelhardt.wordpress.com and Tweets way too much as @MadMerryMeg.

Michael Fosburg is Director of Public Affairs at Secrets of Champions, Ltd, a content media company focused on human performance, leadership, professional development, group synergy, healthy living and quality of life. He does a little writing too. He lives in the Washington, D.C. area with his wife and expanding horde of rescued animals.

Megan Arkenberg lives in Northern California, where she shares her home with the very early stages of a doctoral dissertation on nineteenth-century literature. Her work has recently appeared in Shimmer, The Dark, Lightspeed, and the anthologies B is for Broken

and Daughters of Frankenstein. She procrastinates by editing the
fantasy e-zine Mirror Dance, and she recently edited the nonfiction for
Queers Destroy Horror, a special issue of Nightmare. Find her online
at www.meganarkenberg.com.

Lilah Wild's dark fiction is an ongoing search for hidden cauldrons
within the modern landscape, exploring the contemporary fantastic
and horrific.

Laura VanArendonk Baugh was born at a very early age and never
looked back. She overcame her childhood deficiencies of having been
born without teeth and unable to walk, and by the time she matured
into a recognizable adult she had become a behavior analyst, an
internationally-recognized animal trainer, a costumer/cosplayer, a
chocolate addict, and of course a writer.

Milo James Fowler is a teacher by day and a speculative fictioneer
by night. When he's not grading papers, he's imagining what the world
might be like in a dozen alternate realities. Over the past five years his
short fiction has appeared in more than 100 publications, including
AE SciFi, Cosmos, Daily Science Fiction, Nature, Shimmer, and the
Wastelands 2 anthology. www.milojamesfowler.com

Brittany Warman is a PhD candidate in English and Folklore at
The Ohio State University, where she concentrates on folk narrative
and nineteenth-century British literature (and the ways they intersect.)
Her creative writing can be found or is forthcoming from Mythic
Delirium, Apex Magazine, Cabinet des Fees, Stone Telling, and
others. Her website is brittanywarman.com/

Michael B. Tager is the author of the fiction collection "Always Tomorrow" and "Pop Culture Poems," a poetry chapbook (Mason Jar Press). He is currently writing a book of memoir told through essays about video games. He likes Buffy and the Baltimore Orioles. Find more of his work online at michaelbtager.com.

L.S. Johnson lives in Northern California. Her stories have appeared in Strange Horizons, Long Hidden, Fae, Lackington's, Strange Tales V, and other venues. Currently she's working on a fantasy trilogy set in 18th century Europe. Find her online at http://traversingz.com/.

Beth Cato hails from Hanford, California, but currently writes and bakes cookies in a lair west of Phoenix, Arizona. She shares the household with a hockey-loving husband, a numbers-obsessed son, and a cat the size of a canned ham.

She's the author of THE CLOCKWORK DAGGER (a 2015 Locus Award finalist for First Novel) and THE CLOCKWORK CROWN from Harper Voyager.

Follow her at BethCato.com and on Twitter at @BethCato.

C.S. MacCath is a writer of fiction, non-fiction and poetry whose work has appeared in Strange Horizons, Clockwork Phoenix: Tales of Beauty and Strangeness, Mythic Delirium, A is for Apocalypse, B is for Broken, Murky Depths and other publications. Her poetry has been nominated twice for the Rhysling Award, while her fiction has been nominated twice for the Pushcart Prize and shortlisted for the Washington Science Fiction Association Small Press Award.

Samantha Kymmell-Harvey is thrilled to once again be a part of the Alphabet Anthologies. Her stories can be found in Bete Noire, Flash Fiction Online, and Spark: A Creative Anthology just to name a few. She is also a graduate of the Odyssey Writing Workshop.

Steve Bornstein has been in the military, traveled to distant lands, and held the sorts of jobs you watch shows about on the Discovery Channel. He lives on a big iron island in the Gulf of Mexico. He also lives in Central Texas with his wife and four insane cats. One of these days, he's going to settle down. He blogs infrequently at stevebornstein.com.

Suzanne is a tattooed storyteller from South Africa, and the author of the novels The Other Me, I Heart Robot, and Scardust. She currently lives in Sweden and is busy making friends with the ghosts of her Viking ancestors. Although she has a Master's degree in music, Suzanne prefers conjuring strange worlds and creating quirky characters. When she grows up, she wants to be an elf – until then, she spends her time (when not writing) wall climbing, buying far too many books, and entertaining her shiba inu, Lego.

Michael Kellar is a writer, poet, and occasional online bookseller living in Myrtle Beach, SC.

His anthology appearances include "Side Show 2: Tales of the Big Top and the Bizarre", "Metastasis: An Anthology to Support Cancer Research", "Bones II", "Bones III", "A is for Apocalypse", "B is for Broken", "The Grays", "Zombified: Hazardous Material" and "The Temporal Element II".

He has also had poetry published in "Gothic Blue Book III: The Graveyard Edition", and had fiction appear online as well as in a few magazines.

Jonathan C. Parrish is known by many other names. He goes by Jo because of a poem by A. A. Milne and by Jopa because of an email address he received in 1990 (and a blissful ignorance, at the time, of the Russian language). He spent most of his life in Canada, particularly in Alberta and Nova Scotia and he once made the mistake of taking the train from Halifax to Edmonton and back again.

Amanda C. Davis has an engineering degree and a fondness for baking, gardening, and low-budget horror films. Her work has appeared in Cemetery Dance, Pseudopod, Year's Best Weird Fiction, and others. She tweets enthusiastically as @davisac1. You can find out more about her and read more of her work at http://www.amandacdavis.com.

Like a magpie, Rhonda Parrish is constantly distracted by shiny things. She's the editor of many anthologies and author of plenty of books, stories and poems. She lives with her husband and three cats in Edmonton, Alberta, and she can often be found there playing Dungeons and Dragons, bingeing crime dramas or cheering on the Oilers.

Her website is at http://www.rhondaparrish.com and her Patreon is at https://www.patreon.com/RhondaParrish.

Thank you for reading

C is for Chimera

We would appreciate it a great deal if you would leave an honest review on Goodreads and wherever you purchased this book.

Your stars and a couple sentences mean the world to us!

Truly.

The importance of reviews cannot be overstated—they often make the difference between a book's success or its utter failure.

Always Be The First To Know!

Whether it's a new release, a call for submissions, cover reveal, super sale or I just want to share a new story I've written, you will always be among the first to know if you sign up for my newsletter.

I promise to respect your privacy and your inbox. I will only email you when I have something exciting to share, probably about twice a month.

Subscribe now and you'll receive a free download of my award-winning post-apocalyptic short story, "Starry Night" as a welcome-to-the-newsletter present!

Subscribe to Rhonda's Mailing List!

http://bit.ly/StarryStory

www.ingramcontent.com/pod-product-compliance
Lightning Source LLC
Chambersburg PA
CBHW020419260626
47156CB00007B/2470